Love  and Meatballs

Love and Meatballs

Susan Volland

NEW AMERICAN LIBRARY

NEW AMERICAN LIBRARY
Published by New American Library, a division of
Penguin Group (USA) Inc., 375 Hudson Street, New York, New York 10014, U.S.A.
Penguin Books Ltd, 80 Strand, London WC2R 0RL, England
Penguin Books Australia Ltd, 250 Camberwell Road,
Camberwell, Victoria 3124, Australia
Penguin Books Canada Ltd, 10 Alcorn Avenue,
Toronto, Ontario, Canada M4V 3B2
Penguin Books (NZ), cnr Airborne and Rosedale Roads,
Albany, Auckland 1310, New Zealand

Penguin Books Ltd, Registered Offices: 80 Strand, London WC2R 0RL, England

First published by New American Library, a division of Penguin Group (USA) Inc.

First Printing, August 2004
10   9   8   7   6   5   4   3   2   1

(NAL) REGISTERED TRADEMARK—MARCA REGISTRADA

LIBRARY OF CONGRESS CATALOGING-IN-PUBLICATION DATA:

Volland, Susan.
    Love and meatballs / Susan Volland.
        p.   cm.
    ISBN 0-451-21240-1 (trade pbk.)
    1. Italian American families—Fiction.   2. Triangles (Interpersonal relations)—
Fiction.   3. Family-owned business enterprises—Fiction.   4. Restaurateurs—Fiction.
5. Restaurants—Fiction.   6. Young women—Fiction.   I. Title.
    PS3622.O64L65   2004
    813'.6—dc22   2004004184

Designed by Eve L. Kirch

Printed in the United States of America

BOOKS ARE AVAILABLE AT QUANTITY DISCOUNTS WHEN USED TO PROMOTE PRODUCTS OR SERV-
ICES. FOR INFORMATION PLEASE WRITE TO PREMIUM MARKETING DIVISION, PENGUIN GROUP
(USA) INC., 375 HUDSON STREET, NEW YORK, NEW YORK 10014.

For Karma

ACKNOWLEDGMENTS

Thanks must go first to my delightfully quirky family. How lucky I am to call you friends as well as relatives. Well, at least most of the time.

To all of my dear friends who stayed with me through the early drafts and highs and lows of the publishing process, thank you. Gwen Hayes, Arlene Levins, and Kris Latta were indispensable for their ideas and direction.

To Jim McCarthy, Ellen Edwards, and Serena Jones: Thank you for your support, professional guidance, and kind words.

When I threw my hands up and announced that I was finished with food and needed to try something new, my brilliant husband, Jeff Volland, hardly flinched. Thank you, Jeff, for your patience and wisdom. And for giving me so many years of firsthand experience in true love.

Chapter One

"Hey, Jo! Snap out of it! Go check that order and grab me another bottle of red, will ya?"

I blinked a few times, dropped the meatball in my hand, and came back to the world. A restaurant kitchen isn't exactly what most people consider a meditative environment. The jet-engine drone of industrial range hoods is a bass line for the percussion and melody of clanking pans and cursing line cooks. But for me, the warm, moist air and pungent aroma of this kitchen is as close to returning to the womb as I ever want to get.

My name is Giovanna Cerbone. In this town, that is usually all I have to say to get a knowing nod and an "ahhhh" of recognition. I am the granddaughter of Big Louie Cerbone, the daughter of Little Louie and Isabella, and the fourth of five siblings. I like to think that my name is the least familiar of them all, but I still hear the occasional whisper about the underwear incident or the sardines I "accidentally" left in the difficult-to-reach corners of a cheating boyfriend's Camaro. Most residents of Port Orcas have at least one favorite story about our family. They *all* know about the meatballs at Louie's Restaurant.

I stepped into the hall and signed for the linen delivery. On the way back I went to the storeroom and grabbed a magnum of red wine as my oldest brother, Rocco, had requested. Then, once again, I took my position next to the bowl of carefully blended meatball mix that had ridiculously shaped my family destiny.

I have no memory of actually learning how to perform this simple task. Grandpa Louie had all five kids rolling meatballs practically before we could talk. While this was technically the prep cook's job, I found pleasure in the repeated, familiar motion and the cathartic white noise of the kitchen. And I needed a few minutes of respite before I opened the newest letter from Mindy Monahan's lawyer. Just thinking about her pissed me off. I gave the bowl of meat another aggressive stir.

"You don't have to do that, you know. The prep cook can take care of those," said Rocco, as he uncorked the wine and dumped it into a big pot of sizzling olive oil, onions, and garlic. Rocco never misses an opportunity to explain the obvious. If I ever thought of him as my boss and not just my know-it-all big brother, it would really get on my nerves.

"It's no big deal. I needed to get out of the office for a few minutes," I said.

Rocco just shrugged. He was killing time. He didn't need to make the minestrone any more than I needed to roll meatballs. He was waiting for a new local farmer to stop by with some produce samples, and standing idle in the kitchen is never a consideration. There is always work to be done.

Officially, Rocco is the vice president of the family restaurants. But his primary responsibility is to run the new Louie's across town on Twelfth Street. The place used to be a surf-and-turf joint, but they busted during the cholesterol scares of the nineties. The former owner offered it to Dad for practically nothing. Little Louie bought it with the intention of leasing it out. But Rocco, straight from college, surprised Dad with a workable business plan.

Most locals prefer what they call "the *real* Louie's Restaurant." Twelfth Street is meant to woo a younger, richer clientele, with more regional Italian fare and plenty of fresh seafood. We roped off a small area for a cocktail lounge a few years ago, and the place is really finding its groove. Rocco still fusses and storms around a lot, but that's his nature. He can finally relax a bit these days. Especially since my middle brother, Vince, is back in town. Sometimes I think Rocco stops by here just to push my buttons, stir the pots, and intimidate the newest employees.

I finished my task, cleaned up the station, and decided it was time to face the lawyer's letter. I take care of the paperwork for both Louie's restaurants. It's not like I *have* to work here. We have all, at some point, stormed out and vowed never to darken the door again. But it never lasts. A cook quits or a waiter calls in sick and we run back to fill in. The smells and the memories are too strong and the work is so natural it seems ridiculous to stay away. And besides, what else would I do? The business world isn't exactly in a hiring frenzy for someone with my special skills. I've looked around. I run a search on the big employment Web sites pretty regularly and so far, no *Fortune* 500 companies seem to be in dire need of an economics major with mediocre grades, a solid knowledge of art history, and a knack for cooking spaghetti. And besides, it's not like I hate it here. I set my own hours, eat and drink for free, and can tell my boss to "bite me" whenever I feel the whim.

On the down side, I'm often bored out of my mind. I spend a significant amount of my day in a fixed stare with paper-clipped bundles of adding-machine tape in my hand. When that gets old, I entertain myself by creating fantasy food vacations on-line, helping out in the kitchen, or just doodling.

Now and then, something comes up that requires some actual thought and careful attention. Right now it's this Mindy Monahan fiasco. I spun the unopened letter around on my desk for a while and then made an executive decision about how to handle it. I called Archie McAndrews.

"I got another letter from Mindy's lawyer," I said.

"Just drop it by on your way home and I'll take care of it. It's probably nothing." Those were the magic words I was hoping for.

Archie runs a successful law firm and is a better lawyer than we actually need. But this thing with Mindy was getting on my nerves. I wanted it to disappear. She was a waitress here at the original Louie's. But working for a living just wasn't her thing. Recently she had hired a high-profile attorney to try to convince us that her inactivity still deserved a salary.

Mindy came into town about six years ago and I hated her on sight. She was staying with a friend who knew a prep cook who had worked for us for a while. She was too skinny and was clearly underdressed for the season. Her dark roots were three inches long, and even a putty knife full of cheap concealer didn't cover up the shiner she sported on her left eye. She went on about how she had finally had it with abusive men and was going to make a clean start of things. Louie's needed a daytime dishwasher, and my folks offered her the job. Two weeks after she started she announced that she was pregnant.

On my most sympathetic days, I could forgive her for being attracted to cruel and useless men. My own judgment has been less than stellar in the relationship department. But an unwanted pregnancy? A girl who had been around the block as many times as Mindy surely knew a thing or two about birth control. As for her skinny, twitchy little body, I figured her trembling had more to do with her chemical preferences than the cold weather.

Once Bella found out about the baby, she didn't want Mindy carrying the heavy trays of plates and glasses from the dishwasher to the dining room. She bought her a respectable dress, sent her to get her hair done, and put her to work seating guests and refilling water glasses. But that was the extent of Mindy's prenatal care. She lost the baby five weeks and a couple of cartons of Virginia Slims later. Louie and Bella paid for her medical bills and sent her meals until she was ready to give work another try.

My parents aren't suckers. They knew Mindy was a player. But employees are like extended family, and they felt they had a certain responsibility. When babies are involved my parents' hearts turn to warm chocolate pudding. Bella was determined to at least fill the caverns in her cheeks with buttered bread and pasta before Mindy had her next crisis.

To her credit, Mindy lasted a lot longer that I had expected. I guess she recognized a good thing when she saw it. She kept up a decent pace—changing the table linens and running breadbaskets. Eventually she moved up to server and did a pretty good job when she bothered to write down the orders. But Mindy was a whiner. She was convinced that she wasn't getting her fair share of tips. She showed up late, left early, and always had an excuse why she couldn't do her scheduled side jobs, like folding napkins or cleaning the espresso machine.

I never quite understood why she didn't just get a job as a stripper, because I tell you, she could sure put on a show when the right customers came in. Once she caught sight of silver-haired businessmen drinking name-brand cocktails, she would light up like a Christmas tree. She was all touches, jiggles, and innuendo. Bella finally put a stop to her sitting in laps when she came in one night and saw old man Donavan so worked up he was about to have a coronary.

I'm no Pollyanna. I know the game. It's astounding the

power a pretty face can wield over a table of hungry or drunk customers. I'll even admit to some shameless flirting and touching when I was short on cash. It was almost a game. My brothers could count on an extra ten bucks if they flashed a killer smile and pronounced the specials in fake Italian. Rocco wore tight shirts and flexed his biceps as he ground fresh pepper on ladies' salads. Vince and Tony had a way of fluttering the linen napkins into the laps of mature women that never netted them less than a 20 percent tip. These days I try to stay out of the dining room. I'm not a naturally chatty or perky kind of gal, and it isn't worth the extra few bucks anymore to pretend.

Mindy started acting strange about three months ago. She alternated between shifty nervousness and odd confidence. Most alarming were the bouts of uncharacteristic silence and efficiency. When she called ten minutes before her shift to explain that she wasn't feeling well and needed the day off to see a specialist, I figured everything was back to normal. The next time I saw her, she handed me the first letter from her TV lawyer.

Mindy, like anyone else who owned a TV in the area, had seen the commercials a hundred times. Dane Hagstrom, an attractive guy with graying temples and a nice suit, looks sincerely into the camera and says, "Are you feeling your best? Do you dread going to work each day or return home physically drained and aching? Workplace injuries are more common than you imagine. The United States government has established laws to protect people just like you, and yet few employers inform their workers of their rights.

"Your employer may not care about you. But I do! I assure you that no matter what your condition, you will be granted enough time to recover fully to your preinjury state or receive the compensation and proper disability settlement you are due. My firm has settled more workers' compensation suits than any other law firm in the state. Why not let *me* take care of *you*?" Blah, blah, blah.

I can just picture poor Mindy in her ratty little apartment asking herself, "Do I really feel my best? Am I a victim of unsafe working conditions? Don't I deserve compensation for my aching feet and dry skin?" Then she bit the hook and visited the office of Dane Hagstrom for a free consultation, just like the ad said. By the time she left, she was a victim of environmental air pollution. Her new respiratory specialist confirmed it. The burning candles at Louie's Italian Restaurant had somehow damaged her lungs. And she wanted us to pay.

Chapter Two

Little has changed at Louie's in the past fifty years. Patrons are met with the same rich aromas of fresh garlic, herbs, and slowly simmered sauces. The walls are a patchwork of red velveteen paper, framed reviews, and gaudy oil paintings of ancient Rome. Shelves and gilded sconces hold the same trinkets my grandmother arranged long ago: plump cherub figurines, a pretty clock that has never worked, family photographs, and a couple of Little League trophies.

As a boy in Boston, Grandpa was embarrassed by his traditional Italian family. He wanted to be the Lone Ranger or Wyatt Earp. At sixteen he headed west in search of a loyal stallion and an adoring Indian princess bride. But I guess his life as a cowboy was a bust. (He would send me into girlish screeching when he talked of his love of a fine horse—grilled and served with onions and mustard.) With his youthful enthusiasm and wide, strong shoulders, Big Louie Cerbone quickly found work in the lumber camps. He scrambled around tall cedar and fir trees with an old-fashioned chain saw and chopped off the tops for spar poles. He was lucky to be alive. This was dangerous work and he was easily distracted. A bird's nest, an interesting beetle, and the stunning mountain views all vied for his attention. (At this point in the oft-told tale, we would all holler in unison, "And a distracted lumberjack is a dead lumberjack!")

His life in the kitchen started after an especially long day in the trees. He dragged his big, tired body to the camp stove and the bull cook passed him a plate loaded with dried-up bird parts, some flavorless beans, and a chunk of dusty corn bread. For twenty minutes he berated the cook, explaining how his Italian mother could make meals fit for an emperor with little more than a pig's ear, an onion, and some green stuff plucked off a hillside. The accused accepted this fury with a grin. When Grandpa finally caught his breath and turned back to the table of lumbermen, they had tears in their eyes from holding back their laughter. The rule was, whoever complained about the slop was instantly and officially named camp cook.

The next day Grandpa began his new life at the stove. He never bothered to explain that he himself had prepared little more than buttered toast. He was a Cerbone! And if he wanted to, he could make the best damn camp meals ever served in the high woods. And he did. Maybe it was because the men were so accustomed to truly horrible food. Or maybe he had his mother's natural flair for cooking right from the start. Whatever the reason, this combination of bravado and bull-shit eventually manifested itself into a popular downtown lunch counter. Eventually he convinced his mother to share her precious family recipes, and Louie's Italian Restaurant was born.

In October of 1952, *Gourmet* proclaimed that a little place ninety minutes north of Seattle called Louie's might just serve the best spaghetti and meatballs in the nation. It was a scandal! Established East Coast restaurateurs mailed scathing letters to the editor. One critic suggested that Louie might as well use ketchup instead of real marinara sauce, since a coast full of Scandinavian fishermen wouldn't know the difference. In retaliation, West Coast chefs, writers, and celebrities flocked to Port Orcas by the hundreds. The battle raged on. Reservations at Louie's were booked solid for almost two years. And the Cerbone name was to be forever linked with tiny spheres of ground beef, veal, pork, a splash of good olive oil, and a very carefully protected mixture of fresh herbs and spices.

As with any business, there have been good times and bad. But the bad times were nothing when compared to neighboring businesses. We know how to work hard, think smart, and respect our customers and community. And let's face it: Decent, well-priced Italian food will never go out of style. Grandma and Grandpa may be gone, but Louie's is here to stay.

When I got to work the next morning, I was surprised to see that Mom and Dad were already there. They were in a booth with our attorney. Dad was staring into his coffee cup and Mom was picking invisible lint balls from her slacks.

Mom looked up when I came in and said, "Mindy Monahan is officially suing us."

I couldn't help but sneer as Archie explained, "I set up a meeting for eleven. Why don't you come along? Labor and Industries won't support her claim anymore. The state of Washington doesn't have a system for measuring indoor air pollution accurately, so for extended 'injuries' such as hers they recommend that individuals either drop their claim or seek compensation privately."

In addition to being our attorney, Archie McAndrews is an old family friend. He has looked exactly the same since I was five: bald head ringed with a wreath of curly, pinkish hair, a shy smile, and a manner that immediately puts small children and pets at ease. He likes spaghetti with clam sauce, grows amazing rhododendrons, and if he drinks two glasses of wine he can often be persuaded to recite from a never-ending collection of dirty limericks. I have always adored him.

"So she's suing us?" I said. "I hope this stupid ploy for attention doesn't take up too much of your time, Archie. You probably have clients with real legal concerns." Instead of responding with a quick-witted quip, Archie just fingered the letter in front of him. We looked at him incredulously.

"No judge will take something like this seriously, will he? Do you think Mindy actually has a case?" I asked.

He fidgeted a bit more and then said, "As much as I hate to humor this kind of behavior, it's always best to take these threats seriously. Workers' comp cases are tricky. And Mindy is being represented by the best in the business. Don't discount Dane Hagstrom just because he advertises on TV. That's more narcissism than marketing. And it's true what the ads say. Hagstrom's firm has settled more work and personal-injury lawsuits than anyone in the state. He hires a cheap, eager crew. They start as young, idealistic labor lawyers determined to help "Joe America," and they are bitter, disillusioned hacks before their student loans are paid off. It's like a legal assembly line. They are expected to process artificially inflated cases one after another. And if they don't produce, they are thrown out and replaced with some other poor kid who's dying to get such a famous and successful law firm on his résumé. The man is training a growing pit of legal vipers."

I had never seen Archie so agitated. It convinced me that Mindy's case was worth more attention. But Dad couldn't get his head around the possible risk.

"So, Archie. I don't get it. You shouldn't be wasting time meeting with these jokers. You're a top-notch attorney. Mindy's case is clearly bogus. Your junior partners could eat those punk kids for breakfast."

This was going to be especially hard on Dad. Call him naïve, call him blind, whatever. But Louie Cerbone will never comprehend that cheaters sometimes win. Being a good sport means everything to him. He has distributed a seemingly limitless supply of soccer balls, basketball nets, and free pizza to children's sporting leagues throughout the region. It doesn't make any difference how poor or slow or awkward the kid; they always start the season with a new uniform and end it with a shiny plastic trophy or gaudy ribbon just for taking part. In return, they are expected to learn the rules of the game and to play fair. Needless to say, this attitude is far easier when your team wins. And Little Louie Cerbone never lost at anything.

"Louie, listen to me." Archie looked intently at my father. "For some unimaginable reason, Dane Hagstrom has taken a personal interest in this case." He held up the letter. "This letter isn't just from his firm, but from his actual office. He wants to meet with you personally."

That got Dad's attention. So Archie went on.

"I don't know how he does it, but somehow he's managed to settle multimillion-dollar suits that I'd swear wouldn't even make it to the first hearing. Hagstrom's the one that got that piccolo player at the state symphony a truckful of money for carpal tunnel syndrome. And he never even stepped foot in the courtroom. We need to proceed very, very carefully."

My mother mumbled something about settling the damn thing by giving Mindy a good, old-fashioned spanking. I concurred. Mom and Dad had done everything they could to give Mindy a hand up in life, and she responded like the feral cat that she is, by biting back deep and viciously.

Chapter Three

In the elevator, on our way up to Dane Hagstrom's executive suites, I started daydreaming again. I pretended I had a meeting with the port commission. I glanced at an imaginary wristwatch to check how much time I had. I would knock them dead with my clear grasp of textbook micro- and macroeconomics. But first I would tell my executive assistant to hold my calls and bring me coffee and fancy muffins while I took a few minutes to ponder the merits of an international merger and the current activity of the Nikkei index.

My high-powered business fantasies evaporated the second we stepped from the elevator into the reception area. Dane Hagstrom's law office was my idea of hell. In the upper floors of this slick, glass monstrosity there were some great views of the North Cascades and the San Juan Islands, but they only seemed to make the canned air and fluorescent lighting even more suffocating. As I glanced around the lobby in mock appreciation of my surroundings, I was silently calculating how many days in a row I could wear panty hose before I went completely batty. I wouldn't last a month.

A sour-faced receptionist showed us into a private room. We were early, so we milled about, rubbing our hands on the silky hardwood table and admiring the view. Mostly we waited in tense silence.

Mindy and her respiratory specialist were the first to arrive. They were both wearing small whirring devices around their necks, and their arms were filled with delicate potted ferns. I sat back and watched in amusement as Mindy and her doctor arranged their plants and fiddled with their gizmos. Since I had seen her last, Mindy had affected a little cough. It sounded like she'd swallowed a cat toy.

When she was finally situated, Mindy looked to her guru for approval, then smiled meekly at my folks.

"Hi, Bella. Little Louie," she whispered conspiratorially. "I'm not supposed to talk to you, but I just want to make sure that you understand. This isn't anything personal against you or anything. I just have to watch out for my own well-being. To take care of myself, you know? I hope you understand."

Mom pursed her lips and looked away. Dad took a deep breath and opened his mouth, but before he could respond Archie patted his shoulder and answered for him: "I think maybe you're right, Miss Monahan. Maybe we should wait and talk after your lawyer arrives."

As if he were waiting to be announced, the door flew open, and Dane Hagstrom made his grand entrance. He was quite a sight—a legal action figure in Armani. His shoes probably cost more than my car. His monogrammed attaché case was so slim it wouldn't have held a decent sandwich. Hagstrom reveled for a moment in our appreciation, then smoothed his graying sideburns and flashed a practiced smile.

"Hi, there! Dane Hagstrom. How are you?" He held out a well-manicured hand to each of us. I swear some top-secret laboratory had finally managed to distill money into eau de toilette. This guy had used a bucketful with his morning shower. He worked the room as though we were all there for a cocktail party and not a potentially devastating lawsuit. I think he

might even have grabbed Mindy's ass when he passed behind her. I know he got a good look at my tits before he settled into a chair at the end of the table.

"I'm a busy man, but I like to keep things friendly. I
thought I would introduce myself and we could all chat and
get to know each other before we got down to business. I
hope you got a chance to get reacquainted with Mindy? And
did you meet her doctor, Lionel Love?" We nodded.

"Of course, I won't be handling this case myself," continued Hagstrom, "but once I learned about poor Mindy's condition I couldn't help but take a personal interest." He winked
her way. She giggled and blushed. There was definitely something nasty going on there. "I've put one of my best young
lawyers on the case. Richard Dolfe. He's only been with me
for a few years, but he's a tiger!" He chuckled and looked
over at Archie. "Arch, old buddy! Maybe you should settle
this right now and save yourself the humiliation of facing
Dolfe in the courtroom." He whacked Archie on the shoulder.
"Heh, heh, heh. Just kidding!" Archie was a good sport and
forced out a guffaw. Hagstrom went on.

"Yep, my guy Dolfe's not much to look at, but he's a tiger,
all right."

Dane Hagstrom made me feel like a third grader in the
presence of a sports hero or movie star. I wanted to swing my
feet in the huge chair and ask permission to use the lavatory.
I gave myself a personal pep talk and then made a bold move:
I left my seat and walked over to the window. A few eyebrows lifted, but I didn't get sent to the principal's office.
Everything was good. Standing closer to Hagstrom I noticed
a hint of face powder on the collar of his tailor-made shirt. I
could feel the playing field start to level. We could beat this
pompous son of a bitch for sure!

Then Richard Dolfe walked in, and the room started spinning. It couldn't be true! The skies might have opened and

started raining rubber chickens and I can't imagine things would have seemed much more absurd.

The honorable Richard Dolfe was a boy I knew from grade school. He was in Tony's class, a year ahead of me, but everyone knew him. Back then his name was Richard Gaylord Tines, but everyone called him "Tiny Dick." There's a good chance one of my brothers stuck him with the nickname. It doesn't seem out of character. Dick couldn't shake it. Eventually, even the teachers called him "Tiny."

In most circumstances, victims of childhood ridicule need only to hand out chunks of watermelon-flavored gum or pass around a page ripped from an underwear catalog to make peace. Little things like this will buy a few hours of valuable companionship that eventually lead to friendships, but Tiny Dick seemed to revel in his repulsiveness. He was a skinny, awkward boy with a high voice, a face like a rat, and a sneaky, vindictive personality. His clothes were always rumpled and stained, and he smelled funny. I'm ashamed to admit that we used to entertain ourselves by trying to define his odor. Actually, my little sister, Nina, came up with the best guess ever. Unfortunately, as she loudly proclaimed that Tiny Dick smelled like burning blue cheese in a wet basement, I saw him step from behind the lunchroom door. Instead of laughing with the other kids, I made a show of whacking Nina on the head and reprimanding her for her bad manners. She yowled until she saw Tiny standing there. Then she turned beet red and tried to hide behind her library books.

The only signs that Dick had aged by high school graduation were a few inches in height and a case of acne that was truly alarming to the unprepared. In high school, Tiny Dick would maliciously taunt the jocks and popular kids until they lost their temper and punched him. Then he would get them expelled or thrown off the team for fighting. He was a real weasel. And now here he was. The same puny boy with the shifty eyes and bad attitude had a new name, a thin, pale mustache, and a law degree.

I was rolling through it all in my mind when I realized I had to do something before Dad opened his mouth and said, "Tiny? Dick? Is that you?"

It was too late. I flinched at his words and turned away.

"How the hell are you, son?"

To his credit the little attorney remained calm. He gritted his teeth, focused his eyes on my father, and in the same horrible voice of his youth, he deliberately said, "The name is Dolfe. Richard Dolfe. I took my father's name."

But Dad was never one for subtlety. "Oh, you changed your name? Good for you. Tiny Dick was quite a tag. It must have been extra hard for a little guy like yourself." Mom pinched Dad under the table. Anxiety had dangerously loosened his tongue.

Hagstrom had obviously never heard the moniker. "Tiny? Tiny *Dick*? Heh, heh, heh. Is that your nickname, Dolfe? Tiny Dick?" He snickered.

Dolfe looked at Hagstrom and my father with a pained expression. At each mention of his old name, his body would spasm briefly, as though he were being jolted with an electric current. Dad didn't catch it. He joined Hagstrom in his jesting. I guess he figured that if he could buddy up to the lawyers and talk about old times, he might convince Hagstrom and Dolfe that Mindy was off her rocker—then they would drop the case and everything would be back to normal. Dad's an optimist.

"Can you imagine? Kids can be so cruel! And I thought 'Little Louie' was bad!" Mom pinched Dad again, even harder this time. "Ouch! What?"

Archie jumped in just in time.

"Yes, of course, Mr. Dolfe. You must have gone to school with the Cerbones. Or did you play on one of the sports teams their family sponsored? They are all very well known and respected around here. Surely your paths have crossed."

Dolfe's nervous eyes shot back and forth between my mother and father. His ears were red-hot, and it was hard to tell if his face was pinched in irritation or if it was just his regular look. I shuffled back to my seat and buried my head in my hands. I had been embarrassed by my memories of childhood encounters with the lawyer. I couldn't begin to imagine the flashbacks in Richard Dolfe's head right now. He had entered the room as a respected lawyer, prepared to steadfastly face the father of his former tormentors, and within seconds of his arrival he was being made a fool of in front of the one man he had convinced of his skills and intelligence—his very famous, powerful boss. Dad might just as well have given him a wedgie on arrival. We were doomed.

Archie cleared his throat. "Maybe we should just get down to business. I understand that Miss Monahan seems to think her breathing problems may have something to do with Louie's Italian Restaurant?"

Mindy coughed up another tiny hairball. Her doctor adjusted a plant. Hagstrom looked to Dolfe, who opened a battered brown leather briefcase and pulled out a thick file. To his credit, he had gathered his composure quickly. He cleared his throat and began to read: "'With the aid of expert diagnosis from a regional specialist, it is our contention that Ms. Mindy Louise Monahan has suffered irreparable damage to her lungs, respiratory system, and personal well-being. The cause of her ailment is directly attributable to her workplace, Louie's Italian Restaurant, and her exposure there to dangerous levels of environmental air pollution. The source of the pollution has been determined to be the uninspected, lead-wicked tapers burned at the aforementioned restaurant. We will prove, beyond the shadow of a doubt, that Mindy Louise Monahan's life has been forever marred by this damage, and that her pain and suffering are not limited to the mere disruption of her present career goals. Miss Monahan will never again experience the simple pleasure of a romantic or formally lit meal, a child's birthday cake, or any number of ceremonial events. Her respiratory damage is catastrophic to her spiritual growth. We all know of the importance candles and eternal flames play in most religious studies. . . .'"

I couldn't help but emit a little snort of disgust. I had known Mindy to pray to the porcelain god a few times after a night of heavy metal, cheap beer, and Jägermeister shots, but that was as close to devout as she ever came. The rest of the room didn't share my joke. The entire table sent glares in my direction.

Dolfe continued: "We at the offices of Dane Hagstrom have carefully tallied Mindy's pain and suffering. And since all attorneys are present, we are willing to settle this case today for $4,992,430." This time my snort was accompanied by others.

"Five million bucks?" Dad leaped to his feet and shouted. He looked at Mindy, who was doing her wide-eyed-doe impersonation. "You want five million bucks? Are you nuts? We make meatballs, not gold bricks, for Christ's sake!" Archie pulled Dad down and told him to be quiet. Mom rubbed her forehead as if she had a headache. I just sat with my mouth wide-open. When a bead of drool escaped I snapped it shut.

Archie, as always, handled everything professionally, but with a certain boyish charm. He rapped his knuckles on the table a few times. "Okay then! You have stated your case clearly. Of course, I will recommend that my clients not settle this case. In fact, I'm pretty sure this suit will be thrown out as frivolous by any judge in the state." He looked first to Hagstrom and then the protégé, Dolfe.

"I hear that you are a very good lawyer, Mr. Dolfe, but it will take some kind of genius to overcome the two obvious flaws in your case. First, my client Louie Cerbone has worked around those same candles for an average of sixty hours a week for over fifty years. He and the rest of Louie's loyal staff have no signs of the respiratory distress Ms. Monahan claims to have suffered after a mere six years of part-time exposure. And second, Ms. Monahan is a known smoker. No matter what the tobacco companies claim, that ain't so good for the lungs."

Mindy leaped to her feet.

"I quit! Really! I went on the patch!" She turned to her scowling doctor. "Honest, I quit! Look!" She pushed up her sleeve to show us a sticker on her upper arm. Dolfe silenced her with a look and waved her back down to her seat. Then he spoke.

"Continue as you see fit, Mr. McAndrews. You have an excellent reputation among the local legal community. So I am sure you have informed your clients that the longer they put off settling this case, the more legal charges Ms. Monahan will accrue. And the Cerbones, of course, will be responsible for these fees." He looked over at my parents. "And since I never lose, I assure you that my services are not inexpensive." Hagstrom was noticeably pleased at Dolfe's arrogance. Dolfe puffed up with the approval. "I seem to remember the Cerbone family being especially good at running, jumping, and throwing things. Surely you must have met a team that was just too good to beat. Or will this be a first for your family?" He closed his eyes and savored the moment. When he reopened them the glimmer of joviality was gone. He was all business. "Mr. and Mrs. Cerbone, I seriously suggest you take a look at your insurance policy and find out the extent of your liability coverage. We are always willing to be reasonable. We don't really want to ruin a long-standing local institution such as yours. We are only asking for what is fair."

Dad started to sputter. Archie again managed to remind him of where he was. I inspected Dolfe's face and debated which eye I should scratch out first.

Archie said, "Thank you, Mr. Dolfe, Mr. Hagstrom. I know you are busy men. As fellow barristers, you have sworn to uphold the laws as decreed in the Constitution. You are in the business of protecting the inalienable rights of the American citizenry. It is a valiant task. And I know you would never willfully squander your time and talents by representing a client without a genuine legal concern. We know to take your advice seriously. But it is out of the question to consider settling. We will have to continue this in the courtroom."

I'm pretty sure Archie had just said, "Fuck you" in a way that sounded socially respectable. Archie stood up to go. We followed his lead. By the time we got to the car I realized my teeth were aching. I spent the drive back to Louie's breathing deeply and trying to loosen my jaw.

Of course, Archie insisted that we just forget about the meeting and let him handle everything. He bantered light-heartedly with Dad, but his eyes betrayed a distracted and agitated mind. He kissed me on the cheek, made me promise to stay out of it until I heard from him again, and left.

Chapter Four

Mom called the clan and suggested we gather at Louie's for an early meal, which was actually her secret code for "Get your butts over here. We're having a family meeting." Then she went into hyperdrive, wiping scuff marks off the chair legs and dusting the dining room trinkets. Dad and I shuffled silently into the kitchen. He pointed to a few things in the walk-in refrigerator and grabbed a chunk of pancetta. I automatically knew we were going to make roast chicken and pasta carbonara. Comfort food, Little Louie style.

Dad chopped parsley and grated cheese. I stuffed a couple of chickens with garlic, lemon wedges, and a handful of bruised fresh rosemary. Then I set the birds in a roasting pan, drenched them in olive oil and coarse salt, and loaded them into the hot oven. I would check them in an hour. I topped and tailed some green beans and then helped the line cooks get their prep done for the night. Dad poured himself a tumbler of red wine and sat on an overturned bucket in the back alley. He had stopped smoking when we were kids, but at moments like this, you could practically see the nicotine addiction clawing at his resolve.

Vince and Rocco arrived together and headed out back to

talk with Dad. Rocco made a stool out of a couple of milk crates. Vince leaned against the wall and lit a cigarette. Dad leaned over and deeply inhaled the first few puffs of second-hand smoke.

I scrunched my eyes half-shut and tried to picture them as a stranger might. Would I walk down the alley alone if I didn't know who these guys were? Probably. They weren't scary, just big and confident. Dad suddenly looked old to me. His eyes were tired, and I could tell by his posture that his back ached. The thick black hair of his youth was almost entirely silver now. A few strands, once perpetually combed into perfect submission, dared to stray onto his forehead.

Rocco sat to Dad's left, and I was reminded why Nina and I used to swear that Rocco wasn't a brother at all, but merely a younger, bossier father. In addition to very similar looks, they had the same mannerisms, the same gestures. Rocco often instilled the same feelings of fear and respect in me that Dad did. I desperately wanted their approval, to please them. But with Rocco, I also desperately wanted him to have toilet paper stuck to his shoe when he left the bathroom.

I always thought Rocco would be a real tyrant of a father, but I swear his spine just disappears when he's around his adorable twin daughters. They're only four, and yet they have him completely figured out. A coy smile, a giggle, a pout, and Rocco's heart becomes a squeaky toy in their tiny hands. Rocco's sugary-sweet wife, Emily, has had to step up and act as master and commander of that family. I would never have guessed she had it in her. Emily has always been so quiet and demure, we sometimes forget about her.

My gaze moved on to Vince, and I had to wonder if he was falling prey to the horrible eating habits of many great chefs. I've seen it a million times. Chefs taste everything and pick at the crumbs, but rarely sit down to an actual meal. From what I saw, Vince's diet consisted mainly of black coffee and too many cigarettes. Tonight he looked especially lean and angular next to Rocco's slightly doughy, ex-jock form.

I heard Nina come in through the front door. Nina and I are a team. We're barely a year apart in age, and as kids we were often mistaken for twins, at least until puberty, when Nina got more than her share of curves. I can't imagine anything that would bond two clever little girls together more than three obnoxious big brothers. She said hello and went straight to work, setting the table, slicing bread, and filling glasses.

Good thing I'm not an especially bitter or petty person, or I might find it irritating that the men in my family spend so much time making noise about how the restaurants should be run, but when it comes to getting the job done, they are often off in a corner talking about work while the Cerbone women get busy. Nah, that sort of thing doesn't really bother me too much. It was probably just a coincidence that I suddenly felt the need to drop the saucepan and scouring brush in my hands, pour three glasses of wine, and join Mom and Nina.

Tony finally arrived, all bright eyed and full of fun. When we were all accounted for, it was time to get dinner on the table. I cooked the pasta, then tossed the spaghetti with the crisp Italian bacon, the cheese, a couple of eggs, and probably too much garlic for most palates. I pulled the chickens from the oven, blanched the beans, and broiled a dozen tomato halves sprinkled with bread crumbs. Rocco came in at the last minute to poke at everything and pick at the chicken skin. I bristled.

"Everything up to your standards, m'lord?" I asked.

Rocco said, "I just wanted to make sure you didn't dry out the birds. But I guess they look okay."

He hit a raw nerve. I slapped at his hands and shoved him aside with my hip. "Get your fingers out of my food, you bastard! You couldn't make a chicken I would feed to a stray cat, and you're checking on *my* cooking? You are such a self-righteous, arrogant . . ." He and Vince chuckled. Once again I had fallen prey to brotherly bait.

Vince shook his head in dismay. "I swear, Jo, you're just too easy. It's hardly even sport." I fumed a bit longer and refused to talk to them as we took the platters into the dining room. After we were all situated and our plates were full, Rocco took charge and got straight to the point.

"So what's up? This isn't about Moody Mindy Monahan and her delicate constitution, is it? I heard that Archie stopped by earlier."

Tony nudged Vince and began clearing his throat. Then they both started coughing. "Is that a candle on the table? Put it out! Put it out! I can't breathe!" Tony grabbed his throat and fell to the floor, writhing in dramatic agony. Nina laughed as Rocco started fanning the candle in their direction.

Mom, Dad, and I just stared. Then Mom spoke.

"Mindy Monahan is suing us for five million dollars!"

Everyone froze. Even Tony looked up from the throes of death. There was a moment of silence before everyone broke into hysterics. To hear those words spoken out loud in this environment was just too ridiculous. We all hooted and laughed until our guts hurt and we had to wipe away the tears. Eventually Dad composed himself a bit.

"And that's not the least of it! Tiny Dick is her attorney!" He tried to get the laughter started again, but my brothers just sat in stunned silence.

"Tiny Dick? You mean Tiny Dick from school?" asked Tony in amazement. As if we knew a dozen guys with that nickname.

"Man, what was his real name? He was a piece of work," said Rocco. "He got three of our starters kicked off the team.

Anderson lost his chance at a scholarship because of him!" He twirled some pasta onto his fork. "Tiny Dick just kept after him, telling Anderson that he screwed his little sister Amanda. She was only, what—twelve? But Dick went on and on about how good Amanda was and how much she liked it until one day Anderson just snapped. He whaled on him. I think he broke Tiny Dick's nose. And what was even worse was that Anderson came out of it looking like some kind of monster. Here was this giant, a first-string lineman, bashing in the face of a puny little runt. A few of the cheerleaders even took Dolfe's side for a while. They boycotted our practices and pampered Tiny Dick until he started slipping his hands up their skirts and generally acting like himself again. God! He was such a jerk!"

Mom and Dad gave each other a look of understanding. Dad scratched his head and said, "We should have given that kid a few more breaks. He had a pretty lousy mother. She, uh, did quite a bit of entertaining—"

Mom interrupted. "Good God, Louis, they're all grown-up now. I think they can handle the truth." She looked over at us. "Tiny Dick's mom was what you kids might call a *coke whore*." We all flinched. There are some words you just never want to hear your mother say. "She slept with men for drugs. And, according to the best gossips in the PTSA communication network, she was pretty good at it too. She flew high and fast with the beautiful people, but didn't have two dimes of her own to take care of her apartment or her kid. Little Dick must have had a pretty miserable life."

I pondered what I had learned, but still couldn't generate much pity.

"Tiny Dick is a lawyer! Man, that seems about perfect, doesn't it?" said Vince.

Tony found his voice again. He was obviously disturbed. "That guy must be seriously messed up. He gave me the creeps when he was a kid. I can't imagine what he's like as an adult. I tried to stay as far away from him as I could." He looked over at Vince.

"You remember that thing I told you about in Coach Beckett's gym class?" Vince nodded and blew out a whistle.

"Tiny Dick was in my gym class in eighth grade. Do you remember what an asshole Coach Beckett was? I mean, if you were good at sports he was your best buddy, but Tines was totally uncoordinated, so Beckett really hated him. The guy was a loser, but you could hardly blame him for being crappy at sports.

"I guess since everyone called him Tiny Dick he was especially nervous in the locker room. He usually changed his clothes in the toilet stall and always hid behind a towel in the showers. We razzed him a bit, but for the most part we gave the guy a break. Then one day Beckett walks in and sees Dick in the back corner of the showers with his towel. Coach can't stand it. He yells at him to drop the towel and be a man. 'Take a shower like a man, Dick!' When Dick gets embarrassed and pulls the towel closer, Beckett gets pissed off. 'What are you scared of? You some kind of freak? You got girl parts down there?' He yanked away the towel and demanded that this terrified little boy act like a man. We were all just kids and tried to sneak away. But Beckett wouldn't let it go. He made us all line up in the showers. Then he grabbed Tiny from behind and literally picked him up and held this poor kid's naked body up to each of us to see. God, I swear anyone's family jewels would shrivel up at something like that. Dick was bawling and kicking to get away. It was awful. He kept looking at me and the other guys like we might be able to do something. But what were we supposed to do? We were just kids."

Mom was especially horrified.

"Good Lord, Tony! Why didn't you say anything? Why

didn't you tell me, or your father, or go to the principal? That man was a monster!"

"No kidding!" My brothers nodded in agreement.

Vince defended Tony: "We did tell you about Coach Beckett! We all told you what a bastard he was. But as long as we came home with As in his class, you assumed everything was fine."

"You told us he was hard on some of the kids, but you never told us anything like this!" my father said.

Tony replied, "I would have. I guess I was planning on it, but Beckett crashed his car. I think it was the very next morning—some freak problem with the brakes. We all heard he was sort of a vegetable after the accident. And Tiny Dick seemed to survive the ordeal just fine. He kept horking up nasty snot balls on our lunches and running away. It was hard to pity such an asshole."

We needed to clear our table and get the place ready to serve dinner, so Mom and Dad ran quickly through the details of our meeting with Hagstrom and Dolfe. They explained that Archie would fight the case, but that in the meantime we should take it very seriously. Eventually the talk turned to Mindy and her ferns, and we all started laughing again. It seemed best to laugh when there was a possibility that a dumb blond waitress and a grade-school nerd might send your family into bankruptcy.

Chapter Five

The next day I went back into the office determined to put the entire ordeal with Mindy and Tiny Dick out of my mind. I needed to get the payroll finished and delivered, or I would have still more disgruntled staff to deal with. I gathered up the time cards and tip registers and spent a contented morning mechanically plugging numbers into the computer. When I finished, I had a very disturbing thought. Had I just spent the morning happily inputting FICA information because it offered relief from a stressful situation involving candlewicks? I pushed back from the screen, appalled. I could officially consider myself one of the most boring people on the planet. I needed to get a life! I packed up my stuff and headed to Twelfth Street to deliver the checks.

Vince greeted me by waving a handful of greens in my direction. "Take a look at this arugula, Jo! It's beautiful!" Vince was rarely this animated, so I admired the vegetables.

Vince got into some trouble in his youth. Mom says that things just come too easy for him. She figures that if he were in school today, they would tag him with some kind of syndrome or combination of letters to describe his learning style. He's book-smart, and he always did well on tests, but he can't sit still for long. He cut class a lot and talked back to the teachers in high school. He had a Jack Kerouac spirit and a love of fast motorcycles. His teenage high jinks eventually turned into petty larceny and a drinking problem. He spent a few weekends sobering up behind bars. We were never too surprised when Vince ran off on another bender and disappeared in search of the romance of the road.

Vince has always been the best cook of the bunch, with Grandpa's natural gifts in the kitchen. But being a great cook gives him a freedom that is both a blessing and a curse. He can find work wherever the wind takes him, so he never has to stick it out if he gets bored or when some boss pisses him off. Bella and Louie sent him to Italy a few years back, to study and maybe straighten out. He worked for two years in tough kitchens under some extremely talented and ruthless chefs. They pushed him hard and taught him discipline and a little humility. By the time he came home he had a new passion for food quality and traditional technique. He also had a tendency to postpone shaving and an unlimited capacity for jug wine.

In addition to talent and attitude, God gave Vince the kind of looks that make women stop in the street and stare. You could pave a highway with the hearts he has trampled. Many belong to women he never even met. People say we have the same eyes. They are a vivid blue and tend to catch people by surprise. I hear they flash like neon when we get mad.

Vince's last American adventure ended in a motel in western Oklahoma with a schizophrenic cowgirl, a nasty rash, and more money than he could explain on the bedside table. He came home quietly, sobered up, and it looks like it is going to take this time. Anna helps. She is six feet of pure Slavic goddess. She's a photographer with a passion for death rock, poetry slams, and tantric sex. They met at an AA meeting. Folks in town may look sideways at the couple now and then, but they wouldn't dare say a derisive word. Nobody makes seafood cannelloni like Vince. They want him to stick around.

I handed over the checks and looked into the box of greens. "Nice. Is that rapini?"

"Yes!" Vince seemed overjoyed. "Can you believe it? Organic rapini and it's growing practically in our backyard!"

I couldn't help but get caught up in his enthusiasm.

"Rocco hooked up with this new guy, Tran, who bought a bunch of those alfalfa fields in the foothills out by the old tulip farm, built a couple of hothouses, and now is turning a few acres into organic produce. He even said he'd work to find a source for specialty seeds and plant whatever I want. Do you realize what this means? Do you have any idea how amazing fresh fava beans are?" He flipped through a seed catalog.

"If I could get another case of rapini I could use it in tonight's special. Do you suppose you could run out there and pick it up? It'll be a nice drive. You might even like the guy—he's pretty cool and he's been around. I'll bet he's got some pretty amazing stories."

No surprise there. Many of the small farms in the Northwest are run by displaced Southeast Asians with horrific tales of their war-torn homelands and epic overseas journey to America in tiny, crowded boats. Back home they were doctors, journalists, and engineers. Here they tirelessly work small plots of land and produce impeccable produce and stunning flower bouquets. I am a huge proponent of supporting local farms, and I needed a change of scenery, so I agreed to make the drive. I'd skip on old man Tran's stories. I'd try instead to squeeze in a short hike. Vince made the call and got directions to the farm. I ran home, grabbed my boots and knapsack, and headed to the country.

I stopped at a familiar trailhead and went for a brisk three-mile hike in the foothills. (Yes, I am aware that it is bad form to hike alone. I should have a buddy, in case of emergency. Unfortunately, when I feel the call of the woods, it is often accompanied by a desperate longing to get the hell away from everyone.) The cool air cleared my head and lightened my mood. By the time I arrived at Tran's farm I was singing along with the radio, loudly and horribly. I drove up to what looked like the main production yard and hopped out of my car. A weathered, silver-haired farmer was bent over in a field about a hundred yards away. I headed off to meet him and was immediately intercepted by a short dog with a big bark. I stopped in my tracks and bent down to discuss the matter with the scruffy mutt. She showed me her teeth, so I let her sniff my hand. She wagged her tail a few times (pets usually like the smell of restaurant employees), but when I took another step toward the farm she had a fit.

"Mica! Knock it off!" The dog turned around and dashed toward an old red truck. She danced around a couple of long legs sticking out from beneath the chassis. Eventually an entire body unfolded itself and the dog slurped at it adoringly.

"That's enough! What's your problem?" A greasy man in stained coveralls and a red bandanna finally noticed me and pulled himself upright. He wiped off his hands with a rag, reached into the cab of the truck, and turned down the Latin pop music blaring from the stereo.

"Oh, hey, can I help you?"

"I need to talk to Tran. Is that him out in the field?"

"Nope, I'm Joshua Tran. Who are you?"

I was embarrassed and a bit confused. This guy was my age, and he looked more like a Mexican mechanic than a Vietnamese farmer. But it was hard to tell with the oil smudges on his face. I stopped and stared a minute. Then I offered my hand.

"I'm Jo Cerbone. My brother called about some greens?"

Tran made a face. "You're Joe Cerbone? I was expecting another brother!"

We both shrugged and in unison said, "I get that all the time."

"This is my protector, Mica. I see you two have already met."

"Mica, as in fool's gold? That's what we used to call the shiny flakes we found in topsoil." The short mutt was sniffing my fingers again, and this time let me scratch her ears. Then she flopped over so I could scratch her belly.

"Yep. It seemed like the perfect name. She's a completely worthless mutt that somehow has me believing she's priceless."

I laughed. "I'm no expert, but it looks to me like your dog could use some therapy. Are there vets who specialize in multiple-personality disorders? A minute ago I could have sworn she was an undersized werewolf." Mica was now writhing and drooling with pleasure. But she jumped to attention when Tran started moving. She followed him to the barn for the vegetables. While they were gone I looked around. The air was moist and fragrant. The afternoon sun peeked through the mantle of heavy gray clouds and held just enough warmth to make spring seem like a genuine possibility. A crow called out from the very top of a cedar tree. I scanned the pristine greenhouses, colorful foothills, and budding trees and breathed in the glory.

"It's beautiful up here," I said to Josh as he returned with the box. He stood beside me for a moment to admire the view. I pointed out a red-tailed hawk soaring over a nearby pasture. If this were my place, I would have let out a Tarzan yell of proprietary glee. He just sighed with contentment. "Yep, I'm a lucky man. I can show you around if you'd like."

"Thanks, but I'll take a rain check. Vince wants this for tonight's special, and I already took my time getting up here." I told him about getting sidetracked in the woods.

"Sounds nice." He walked me to my car and put the rapini in the trunk. Then he said, "You know, if you like to hike, I bet you'd like the walk to the old hillside orchard. I'm heading up there tomorrow. Do you want to join me?"

I chewed my lip for a minute and couldn't come up with a good reason to decline. We agreed on a time and I took off to deliver the box of produce. On my way home I kept asking myself if I had, perhaps, made a date with a farmer.

Chapter Six

At home, I found my little sister sprawled on the couch in a nest of miniature candy bar wrappers. She was watching talk shows with her horrible orange cat. We nodded hello, and I left her to stew in glorious misery. Nina is presently in love with a naval submarine officer who just left for two months under some ocean. She can be a bit dramatic at times, and having a submariner lover gives her a chance to perform tearful farewells, brokenhearted misery, and passionate reunions. I'm almost convinced that he's worth it when I see him in his dress uniform.

"Tony wants you to call him. He's got some work for you," hollered Nina.

"Yeah, okay," I answered. I searched for the phone.

Tony is the youngest of the Cerbone boys, barely a year older than me. Until I got old enough for it to embarrass my mother, I'd proudly announce to everyone that I was going to marry Tony. He would be a dinosaur expert and wear a hat like Indiana Jones. I would be a professional cheerleader and discover a cure for cancer in the off-season. We'd live on a beach in Hawaii with our pet monkey and eat fresh pineapple every day.

Tony makes regular appearances at the restaurant. He can fill in anywhere, but we mainly call him when something breaks. He is the only one of us with a "real job." He works at a company that distributes stainless-steel ductwork and HVAC parts to construction sites. He started as a delivery driver and then stayed on forever. The childless couple who owns the business has kind of adopted him. They will let him take over whenever he's ready. We talked for a while about nothing. Then he asked if I had time to sketch out a few spare parts for a flyer.

I have never been comfortable calling myself an "artist." What I do hardly qualifies. I draw mostly clip art—simple line drawings of common things. I'm especially good at forks, saltshakers, and coffee cups. Right now I'm working on a bunch of office supplies: thumbtacks, paper clips, and binders. I have always had an appreciation of common objects. As a kid I would pretend to work on my homework, but instead I'd be doodling the bubbles in my milk glass or the crumpled cigarette butts in my grandmother's ashtray.

My best friend from college opened her own ad agency a few years back. She swiped one of my notepads and used my doodles in a campaign. She's been bugging me for years to put together a professional portfolio, but I can tell she's just being nice. My drawings are pleasant, but hardly something I could consider a career. I feel like I won the lottery every time I get a check.

Tony promised to fax me samples of what he wanted me to draw the next day. We said our good-byes and I went back to the living room.

"Aren't you running a little late?" I asked Nina. She was due at the restaurant shortly and was still wearing her sloppiest sweats. She made a face and ignored me. I instantly got caught up in the personal tragedies of a stranger and stretched out on the couch next to her to watch the talk show. She threw some chocolate at me. At a commercial break she asked, "Got any plans tonight?"

"Yeah. Bob's gonna stop by," I said.

Nina rolled her eyes. "I thought he was lost in Laura Land."

"Her name was Lisa, and that was over weeks ago."

She shrugged. "Whatever." And we both slipped back into a TV trance.

Bob is my boyfriend. Sort of. We have been sleeping together on and off for ten years now. He was a good friend of my brothers and played college ball with Rocco. I think it was mostly Rocco's forbidding us to date that drew us together. We would find ourselves at the same party and our eyes would lock. At first we sincerely tried to ignore it. We would go about our business and check out the crowd. But we could feel each other's presence. We would find ourselves in the center of the dance floor, unable to talk over the sound of the music, afraid to touch for fear of the news reaching Rocco. We would just stand near each other and sway a bit to the music, sipping our beers, staring at each other and imagining what might lie beneath the clothing. Eventually we started stealing kisses and gropes in dark hallways. When we finally had sex it was a bit of a letdown. For me, our hottest moments were back on those dance floors with the sweaty crowds and thumping bass line. Bob makes love like a lot of good-looking jocks. He's not especially creative, he likes to watch himself, and you regularly have to remind him there is no prize for getting to the finish line first. But sometimes it's nice to have another warm body in a big bed, and he gets it right often enough that I keep inviting him back.

Bob regularly falls hard for aerobics instructors and personal trainers at the gym he owns. He'll be gone for months at a time, sometimes a year. But so far he hasn't found the Brittany or Brianna of his dreams. I, in turn, have given my heart to a handful of jerks, a couple of real creeps, and one man who would have been absolutely perfect if he weren't already married. So far I haven't found anyone I like better than my brother Tony. Sadly, I think I have stopped looking.

Bob and I have a pretty good setup. We are never single or lonely for long. We share a bed and hang out together until one of us falls in love again. And there is no denying that Bob is nice to look at. In fact, he's my favorite accessory for a little black dress, but if you want to talk about something more than sports, nutritional supplements, or action movies, he might not be your man.

Eventually Nina pulled her hair into a fashionable tangle and changed into some work clothes. I swear, in five minutes she had made herself look sexier than I had in my lifetime. She waved good-bye and left just as Bob was pulling up to the house. I looked down at my rumpled hiking clothes and unbathed body. Oh, well. Bob loves the smell of a sweaty woman.

"Hey, Josie, how's your pussycat?" That's Bob's favorite opening line. We smooched like an old married couple, and he headed to the kitchen to unload a bag of take-out food. While he plated up the steamed vegetables and spicy tofu, he tried again to convince me to join him on a late-spring ski trip.

"I brought some of the info and a few brochures on Whistler/Blackcomb." He handed me a file folder full of printed Internet pages and glossy flyers.

"Thanks." I tucked the folder under my arm, gave him a more genuine kiss, and took my plate of food.

He talked about the upcoming vacation. He compared ski designs and high-tech bindings through dinner. His buddy David has skied professionally. Bob, never content at being second-best, was always trying to keep up with him—which was the main reason I wasn't going.

I had gone on such tempting trips previously and had learned my lesson. Bob and David race around trying to pack in as many activities as possible, and they make everything a competition. I'm a decent skier, and I love to snowshoe, but I don't feel compelled to hurl myself off a backcountry mountain ledge or break the land-speed record, which to Bob translates as, "Jo doesn't truly understand the sport."

If I pass on their testosterone-fueled challenges, Bob has been known to absently hand me his credit card, pat me on the ass, and send me off "to buy something pretty." He positively glows at the opportunity to treat me like his little lady. I used to throw the card back at him in fury, but I am learning. Last time he did that we were in Vail, Colorado, and I went first to Prada, then Hermes. I did my best to act casual, but I couldn't help but hyperventilate a bit when I read the price tags. I bought a scarf, which I am afraid to wear, and the finest shoes I may ever own; then I finished off the afternoon at a great book/record store and a fancy bath shop, charging everything that caught my eye. Come to think of it, I don't remember Bob offering me his card on any trip since then. Maybe it melted from all the activity.

The evening went as usual. I fell asleep on the couch in the middle of an action movie. Eventually Bob pushed me up the stairs and gave me a peck on the cheek. We slept like logs. And to think Rocco used to try to keep us apart. Sheesh.

I got up at sunrise, made a pot of strong coffee, and headed for the glassed-in breakfast room I call my studio. I do my best work early in the morning. I secured a new sheet of paper, sharpened my pencils, and got out my favorite pens. Then a house finch hopped around on the azalea bush and distracted me.

My family and friends think I am an avid bird-watcher. I get a lot of feeders, full-color field guides, and pocket-sized binoculars as gifts. I have a life list because someone gave me a very nice leather-bound book to write and draw in, but the most interesting entries in it are a couple of Dr. Seuss–style bird cartoons, one hummingbird, and about a dozen crows. I love crows. They are so clever. They may squawk and holler at each other, but a mated pair is never too far apart. They are just like my folks, and no rare or showy bird could entertain me more.

I do like watching birds, but I'm not what you would call a hard-core birder. I'm constantly amazed at the folks in the bird magazines. I wouldn't dream of wading through a snake-filled marsh or hiding for hours behind a frosty blind for a split-second glimpse of something I can see in a field guide or, better yet, at the zoo.

I have purposely misled my friends and family about my hobby. I can't tell them the truth; it would be too hard to explain. I like to watch the common birds outside my window. It seems so utterly amazing that something that can fly, something that has the freedom to go anywhere, has chosen to hop around in my backyard. Watching the finches, jays, and starlings will sometimes soothe the chronic feelings of restlessness I battle. The birds remind me that I live in a desirable location. They are wild and free and enjoy the azaleas and rhododendrons my grandmother planted forty years ago. I need to learn from them.

Nina and I inherited this house from our grandparents. It's a charming two-story place built at the turn of the twentieth century. The street isn't far from the original town center, but the old trees and well-tended gardens make it a green and quiet neighborhood. We did intensive remodeling before we moved in. It would have been way too creepy to be all grown-up and sleep every night in a room where my Nonny used to read to me. Having sex in a room like that would be unthinkable. We spent ages peeling off layers of historic wallpaper, had the wood floors redone, and modernized the kitchen. We stashed Grandma's gaudy junk in the basement and replaced it with our own collection of bric-a-brac. As for furnishings, most of them came from secondhand shops and estate sales, but we splurged on a really nice leather couch and a ridiculously expensive audio system. Neither of us would admit to it, but I think we are strangely compelled to impress our brothers with our great taste in electronics, as if to prove to them that we aren't totally clueless, like the girls they have dated. I have never regretted the purchase.

There are three bedrooms upstairs. Nina uses the spare as a closet and dressing room now that Vince seems less likely to become destitute.

My haven is this breakfast room off the kitchen, which looks out at the trees and bushes of the backyard. I have all of my drawing stuff set up in this room, as well as a big comfy chair for reading and a wide window seat piled with pillows. I love to perch there on rainy days and early spring mornings like this one.

I pulled out a few sheets that I had tucked in a back drawer. Presently I'm in a fairy phase. I have been adding little winged ladies to my old sketches of common objects. I'm sure it's Freudian. Some psychoanalyst would have a heyday with these beautiful, naked women with wild hair, mischievous manners, and strong wings that can take them anywhere. At first the fairies peeked out from behind scissors and spark plugs. But they are getting bolder. Lately they have started splashing around in teacups and luxuriously napping on fuzzy caterpillars and makeup sponges. I can tell they are up to no good.

Bob came downstairs at about seven. He stretched and yawned.

"Mornin', Josie."

"Morning." I didn't bother offering him coffee or breakfast. I knew his routine. After a few yoga poses he drinks two glassfuls of warmish water and then makes himself a high-protein smoothie from the powders he packs along. I tried it a few times, but if I'm going to drink my breakfast, it's going to have to be French roast.

Bob washed up the blender and went upstairs to change. When he came back down he squeezed my shoulders, kissed the top of my head, and left for the gym. I have to give Bob a lot of credit. He truly is a self-made man. His father ran off when he was young, and his mother filled the void with real estate. She was never cruel or purposely neglectful. Motherhood just wasn't her thing. She was too busy taking care of herself to be involved with her kids. Bob and his sister were on their own a lot. As a teenager, Bob hung out at our house. There was always plenty of good food, and he seemed to appreciate how Bella and Louie acted more like traditional parents. Mom was always harping at us to keep our feet off the furniture and drilling us on our homework. She kept on him too, and I think he will always love her for it.

After his college scholarships ran out, Bob went to work at a fancy country club. He milked that place for as much information as he could, and he kissed his share of rich white ass until he had enough money to start his own gym. He still works hard. He is constantly looking into new trends in fitness and health care. He brings in top talent and equipment, and he has built his health club to a level that has been noticed by experts in the field. Lately people from all over the country have been begging for his expert advice. He has made a name for himself in a very competitive field—and has made a good chunk of change too. To think I've known him since his life's goal was to try to recite the alphabet while belching!

After Bob left, my all-purpose printer/scanner/fax machine started ringing and buzzing, and the HVAC parts that Tony had asked me to sketch spit from the fax machine. After a few hours of drawing ducts and registers, I went to the kitchen and made a fresh pot of coffee for Nina. We may live together, but we work opposite schedules and we rarely actually see each other at home. She will stumble down the stairs all squinty-eyed and mussed at about ten. I learned many years ago that to remain unscathed by the Angry Goddess of Morning you must leave generous offerings of caffeine. Or you can just leave the house. I did both.

Chapter Seven

I got to Joshua's farm at eleven and knocked on the door of a small rambler-style farmhouse. Mica did her ferocious-dog impersonation again until Josh greeted me at the door.

"Hey! Glad you could make it!" He looked very different this morning. He was clean. We were similarly dressed in worn jeans, walking boots, and soft flannel shirts. Without the bandanna I could see that his hair was a sun-streaked auburn and quite long. His face, while not chiseled, had a delicate structure beneath the skin that revealed itself in appealing angles. His nose was hawkish and rather large. His eyes were a gentle almond shape that crinkled when he was pleased. It was an intriguing face.

"Can I get you anything? A cup of coffee? Or can we get started on the tour?"

I looked around the messy house and a dozen things caught my eye—wooden carvings, original art, furniture draped with elaborate textiles, and stacks of books and CDs. He saw me eyeing his stuff. "Sorry about the clutter. I didn't think to tidy up before you got here. I don't seem to spend much time inside these days." He directed me to the back door.

"No problem," I answered absently. I glanced around a bit more, trying to take it all in.

Josh grabbed a knapsack and whistled for his dog. "C'mon, Mica. Let's show our guest around."

Within minutes it was clear to me that this wasn't a date. Farmer Tran was just showing off his operation to a customer. He walked me through the greenhouses and explained the humidity controls and watering system. Tomato, eggplant, and pepper starts were thriving, and he had high hopes for the summer crop. Then he pointed out long rows of domed plastic sheeting.

"The plastic may not be pretty, but it keeps the ground warm enough to force the greens you guys like so much."

He introduced me to his head guy, Lester Murakame, the stooped Japanese farmer I had mistaken for the owner when I drove up yesterday.

"Murakame is amazing! I swear he could grow roses at the bottom of the ocean. He had his own farm for years but eventually got squeezed out by developers. I'm sorry he lost his land. But, man, am I glad he's free to work with me."

As we walked through the fields, Josh explained Murikame's plans for various acres of dirt. Eventually we came upon a creek and he pointed out a path up the hillside to the orchard. It was a lovely walk, switching back through patches of native shrubs and glacial rock beds. We walked for a good half mile, and I had to wonder how much of this land was his and what might be county green space or public land. The orchard was a meadow of long grass, wildflowers, and about thirty old, gnarled apple and pear trees on the verge of bursting into full flower. Josh set down his bag and pulled out a couple of bottles of water, some sandwiches, and a blanket. He spread the picnic under a particularly big, beautiful tree with a stunning view of the valley below.

"These big trees fell out of favor when the new miniature varieties got popular," he said. "It takes too much labor to prune and pick from tall trees. I guess the apples are old-fashioned too—they have russet spots and are rarely a uniform shape and size. Wholesalers prefer the pretty hybrids, but Murikame says there is an emerging market for heirloom fruit and graft cuttings. So we are going to try to clean things up a bit and give the orchard some long-needed attention." He patted the tree trunk, then scratched his scraggly dog.

"But we try not to waste too much of our time on the purebred and pedigreed of the world, do we, Mica?" He glanced up at me and suddenly looked aghast.

"Oh, God! I'm sorry! I didn't mean . . . I sure hope you don't pride yourself on your untainted lineage. For all I know you may be a granddaughter of Caesar himself! I'm such an idiot!"

I had to laugh at his embarrassment. "If you ask my dad, he will swear that I am one hundred percent Italian peasant stock, but I happen to know of a couple of Slavs and at least one Irishman penciled into the family Bible. And besides, you have given me the opening to an awkward question I've wanted to ask. Your name sounds Asian, but you have an almost Latin or Native American look. Where are you from?"

His answer sounded well practiced. "I am a spicy serving from the American melting pot. My dad is descended from French-Vietnamese snobs and Western European pioneers. I guess my great-granddad left a pretty nice life in Saigon in search of excitement and ended up in a Chinese laundry on Jackson Street in Seattle. His son fell in love with a big Norwegian blonde, and they disgraced both families by publicly adoring my poor bastard of a father. I look more like my mom. She claims to be the descendant of an Incan priestess, but in reality she was reared in Cleveland on bratwurst and big cars. Her parents were bakers, but she hated their lifestyle.

She's always saying, "There's more to life than playing with dough!" When she was old enough, she ran off to Peru to try to stir up some support for what she called "her people." My folks met in Lima when my mother was leading a political protest and wanted more American involvement. My father is a paper pusher for the state department."

"Oh!" That explained the exotic international furnishings in the farmhouse. "So where did you grow up?" I asked.

"All over the place. I was born in Peru, but we moved around a lot. Mom was eventually offered a diplomatic position as well, once they learned how she could handle herself. She's smart as hell and very convincing when she wants to be. They make a great team."

Josh leaned back on his elbows and looked out over the valley. With a little prompting, he went on to explain that he spent most of his youth in empty diplomatic houses with too many servants and not enough real friends. He chased fruit bats with tennis rackets through long, empty halls in Kenya. He rode an elephant to school in Sri Lanka. His nanny made him an embroidered dressing gown to protect his school uniform from the dust. He dismissively finished his tale with references to boarding school, a business degree, and then some years trapped at a desk for corporate America. His face came alive again when he explained how the Pacific Northwest combined all of the things he loved. He was sick of computers and big business. He wanted dirt and grease under his fingernails, sore muscles from physical labor, and as much fresh air as his lungs could stand. He wanted roots.

My internal radar went to code red. Attractive, intelligent, single men do not stretch out on picnic blankets under blossoming trees and explain that they are ready to settle down. I put myself on guard and vowed to watch him carefully for signs of marriage, homosexuality, or perversion.

He looked blissfully into the distance and then turned to

me. "Jeez! What a bore I must be! I'm not usually a big talker, but today I can't seem to quit. What about you? So far all I know is that you can walk a man into the ground, you have a couple of big, ugly brothers, and you may have the most gorgeous eyes I have ever seen. Anything else I need to know before the wedding?"

I raised an eyebrow at his cockiness and was mortified to feel myself color. It was such an obvious and shallow line. His buttery voice and interesting tales had almost lulled me off my guard. I quipped, "Oh, didn't you notice the electronic ankle bracelet? My parole officer only lets me out on the weekends if I promise to take my medication and leave the hatchet at home. Now . . . about that wedding."

He rolled onto his back and laughed until Mica started barking with concern.

We ate the sandwiches and then some cookies Josh conjured from his backpack. On our way back down the trail Josh pointed out a few notable sights and double-checked the sprinklers. Soon we were at my car.

"If your parole officer agrees, maybe you can come back and I can show you the rest of the place?" asked Josh.

"I don't know; she gets nervous when I'm around heavy equipment."

He grinned and opened my door. "I'm willing to take my chances. Have her call me." .

Chapter Eight

Two days after my trip to the farm, I heard some especially raucous laughs coming from the kitchen. When I went to investigate I was met with a barrage of catcalls and wet kissy sounds. A charming bouquet of flowering herbs and wild-flowers had been delivered with the produce order. It was wrapped in brown paper, tied with twine, and tagged with my name. I shared a few choice kitchen expletives, grabbed the flowers, and headed back to my office followed by wolf whistles and playground taunts. I love cooks.

As I unwrapped the flowers, a thin metal file fell out. There was a note attached: *If you can get free by Friday, maybe we can have dinner?—Josh.* How could I say no to that? I called, and we set a date.

As soon as I hung up, I got a much less appealing phone call from Dane Hagstrom. "Hi, there. Dane Hagstrom here. How are you today?" Ugh! I took a breath and managed a sickly sweet phone voice.

"Fine, thank you, Mr. Hagstrom. What can I do for you? Are you interested in making reservations?"

"Ha, ha! Reservations! Ha!" He seemed genuinely enter-tained. "No, I don't think we can make dinner tonight, but it

sure is nice of you to ask. Actually, I'm calling to help get this
mess with Ms. Monahan all straightened out nice and easy."

"How kind of you to think of us, Mr. Hagstrom. Of course,
I don't think it's appropriate for me to discuss this over the
phone with you. Perhaps you should contact our lawyer. Let
me get you Archie McAndrews's phone number."

"That's just why I'm calling. You know I love Arch. He's
a peach, but when we met the other day I got the impression
that you hadn't even discussed the possibility of settling. And
that made me wonder if Archie is slipping a bit. Maybe he
hasn't explained the situation clearly to you. I'm in the business of taking care of people, not ruining local businesses. I
couldn't sleep at night if I thought one of my clients might
damage a community treasure like Louie's Restaurant. You
know that, right?"

I was puzzled. I remained silent, so Hagstrom continued.
"Ms. Cerbone. That's why you have liability insurance."

I couldn't quite form words, so I just stuttered into the
phone. Hagstrom went on, "I never would have pegged ol'
Archie as a gold digger. Does he bill you for the whole team
over long lunches and a lot of overtime? I swear he's the kind
of guy who gives lawyers a bad name. He should have explained all this weeks ago. All you need to do to clear this up
is to sign a few papers with your insurance company. I've
looked into the paperwork personally. You're well covered.
In fact, we might be able to arrange it so your family doesn't
have to pay a dime. How does that sound? Your premiums
will go up a bit, but that's why you really have to be careful
when it comes to the safety and well-being of your staff."

"Hmm." I gritted my teeth, but remained quiet. I wanted
to hear him out.

"Why don't I transfer you over to the front desk so you
can make an appointment? If we take care of this in the next
few days, I'll even talk to your old chum Dick Dolfe and see

if he'll sweeten the pot a bit. Maybe he can find you a way to help cover the added insurance expense. We have a few friends in the biz, and can hook you up with some special coverage quick as can be. Everyone wins!" I heard a few pages flicking. "I've got an early tee time tomorrow, so how about if we schedule something for later in the day?"

I gave Hagstrom a few suggestions as to where he might store his putter and slammed down the phone.

Chapter Nine

Rocco called me at home the next morning.

"Hey, Jo. You mind coming to Twelfth Street for a while this morning? We got ourselves kind of a situation over here, and I'm not quite sure what to do about it." I agreed to come, and thanked him for calling without even bothering to ask what was going on. Rocco has some great managerial skills. He's amazing when it comes to team building, and he can somehow get people inspired about even the most mind-numbing of chores, but when he gets frustrated, he tends to solve problems by shouting. I'm always thrilled when he's willing to delegate the more delicate situations.

To my infinite surprise, there were about twenty protesters in front of the restaurant when I arrived. They waved banners and chanted through megaphones. BABY KILLERS! read one sign held by a particularly large, hairy woman. I grimaced and tried to remember if I still had a pro-family/pro-choice bumper sticker on my car. I drove around back and parked my car in the loading dock to avoid a confrontation. Rocco had called Vince too. They met me in the kitchen.

"I guess someone called and got the animal-rights people

all worked up about the veal on our menu. As if we're keeping it some kind of a secret," Vince said.

"So what do you think? Should we call Archie? Mom's
gonna flip when she sees some of those signs!" Rocco said.

I shook my head no, then headed into the dining room to
make some phone calls. I was on my way out the front door
to talk to the protesters just in time to see Mom's car screech
to a halt at the curb. Someone had obviously called her and
reported the activities and slogans. She jumped out and lunged
at the woman carrying the BABY KILLERS sign. They grappled
as Mom shouted, "How dare you step on my property and
make such a claim?" She was furious. "I have five children! I
have grandchildren!" A few strands of her hair worked loose
as she pulled at the sign in the large woman's hands. The
woman held on tight while shouting, "Meat is murder! Meat
is murder!"

Mom screamed at the crowd, "I volunteer each month at
Children's Hospital! I've cuddled crack babies! How dare you!"

I called for Rocco and Vince. They gathered up Mom and
dragged her into the restaurant while she spit and hollered.
"If they want to see murder, I'll show them a murder! Rocco,
let go of me. I'm gonna kill that fat one with the plastic shoes."

Once Mom was safely locked inside, I asked to speak
with the rally organizer. An angry woman stormed up to me
looking for a fight. I flinched as soon as I saw her. She was the
worst kind of vegan/health nut—the kind of person who ex-
tols the virtues of a healthy diet while looking as robust as a
prisoner of war. Her skin was a transparent blue tone more
commonly seen on the bellies of deepwater fish. As she yelled
at me, she nervously twisted at her scraggly hair and pulled
out tiny tufts. I wanted to offer her some soup. Instead, I admitted that Louie's did serve veal. In fact, we served quite a lot
of veal—in the form of succulent osso bucco, buttery scallopini,

and crisp veal Parmesan. I explained that there was even veal in our famous meatballs. The crowd gasped in horror and again screamed angry epithets my way. I didn't get the chance to continue.

Good thing I had taken the time to call the local paper and news channels to explain that Louie's had stopped using lily-white milk-fed veal in the seventies, when the horrors of veal factories were first revealed. We bought ours from a local organic dairy that raised their stock in pastures, not pens, and until Americans are willing to give up milk and cheese, bull calves would be a disposable by-product of the dairy industry. We paid a lot more than we had to to make sure that our ingredients were humane and wholesome. Louie's just wasn't the place to protest this kind of thing.

I tried once again to explain our stand to the protesters. I applauded their dedication. I explained the growing techniques and quality of our products, and I reminded them of the many vegetarian items on our menu. But they were too riled up to listen. I didn't sweat it. When the truth came out, we would end up getting some great press out of this. Hopefully Rocco and Vince were inside explaining that to Mom right now.

I leaned against the door and watched the demonstration for a while. When I saw a late-model silver Lincoln with smoked windows creep along the road out front, I figured the driver was just appreciating the show. My skin crawled when Tiny Dick Dolfe stepped out of the huge car. I immediately knew he was behind this. It was just his style.

Dick scampered over to join me and gestured to the protesters. "Tsk, tsk. That can't be good for business."

I set my jaw and attempted a nonchalant look, which was pretty much impossible. Then I recited the *Schoolhouse Rock* version of the preamble to the Constitution in my head. It was a trick I had learned back when keeping my cool drove my brothers crazy. I needed to keep myself focused for a few more seconds or I would explode. Dolfe stepped close. He wore too much cologne, perhaps in a misguided effort to mask any residual aromas from childhood.

"I was with Mr. Hagstrom when he so kindly called and explained how we are trying to help you, not ruin you. While I am not a big fan of golfing myself—we have that in common— I'm afraid your suggestions were uncalled-for. He is a very busy, very important man." He became agitated. "No one hangs up on Dane Hagstrom. Don't you understand that?" He looked away and gathered his composure again.

"I remember you as a polite girl, Giovanna." He ran his eyes slowly up and down my body. I wanted to run away screaming and spray myself down with Lysol. "You weren't like the rest of them. You had manners." He looked into my eyes and his voice dropped to a whisper. "I only wonder what you might remember of me."

I shuddered and stepped back a bit.

"You know, it's amazing how little I remember from those days. I'm getting old, I guess!" I exclaimed. I needed to be careful about what I said when dealing with this freak, or things were going to get ugly fast. I reverted to the safety of restaurant babble. "Since you know that I can't discuss the lawsuit without my attorney, you must be here for dinner. Oh, I mean, lunch." It was barely 9:30 A.M. "Uh, you want to make reservations? Let me get the book. Will you be dining with Mr. Hagstrom or someone else? It's always nice to have new customers."

He sent me an irritated glare. "See, there you go with the manners again. I knew you were a nice girl, Giovanna, and I remember you being a smart girl too. That's why I am so surprised that you haven't convinced your family to accept our very generous offer. You really must see that the best thing you can do is sign the papers and settle this case."

I sucked in my lips and shook my head. "No way."

His tone changed to a coarse growl, and the tiny hairs on my neck all stood on end. "You don't seem to understand, Giovanna. Your family is going to lose this time. I'm the better player in this particular game. So go grunt and snort, or do whatever it is that you do to communicate to your gorilla-brained father and brothers. Tell them that I've given you a chance to save your silly little spaghetti restaurants. But this time you'll have to play by my rules, or you'll lose everything." He was angry and intense for a moment, but then his face relaxed and he started making the most horrible sound. From his pleased look and smug smile, I could only assume it was a giggle. It sounded like a small animal whining in pain. Some of the protesters actually looked around in concern.

"I can only imagine the wonderful things the great Louie Cerbone will make with canned meat and real government cheese! It makes me hungry just thinking about it! Perhaps I *will* make dinner reservations." He laughed all the way to his expensive phallus of a car.

My forced smile turned into a sneer, and I muttered to whoever was close enough to hear, "He can't win. I've got to stop him."

I went back inside and sat in stunned silence for a few minutes. Then, to be on the safe side, I called our insurance company and asked a few carefully worded questions about our liability policy. As usual, our overly friendly agent reminded me that we could never be too careful and tried to sell me additional coverage. This time I surprised him and agreed to everything. I was never a big fan of fixing problems by throwing money at them, but in this case it seemed like a good plan. I didn't mention anything about the lawsuit. I figured if they found out, they would drop us like bruised fruit. Then we would really be screwed.

I called Archie, and he agreed to meet with me. I paced

around his office and ranted about Dolfe. "It's just like school again. He's out to get us, and we've got to do something."

"No, Jo. That's where you're wrong. You've got to do nothing." Archie sat on his desk. "He's just playing with you. I want you to forget you know anything about Tiny Dick. Put him out of your mind."

I answered with a dumb stare, followed by an eye roll.

He tried another tack. "Okay, then just try to look at it unemotionally. I know I told you to take this seriously but c'mon—a big-name law firm is actually representing Mindy Monahan and suing your family for five million dollars because you burn candles at dinner. Don't you see how ridiculous that is?" It did sound silly when broken down like that.

"This isn't a threat—it's a joke! You just need to steer clear of him. Ignore him. Don't even listen to his demands to settle. I'll call and remind the meat haters that they are on private property, but once they find out that the press is on your side, they'll probably go home. Call the cops if they start getting violent or cause your customers any grief. In a few more weeks, my firm will have plenty of ammo for your defense, and we will get this case thrown out before it ever hits the courts. Trust me!"

On my way back to the restaurant, I started to feel better. Archie had said all the right things, and I did trust him. Dolfe was just an unscrupulous lawyer. We needed to keep a low profile and try to keep out of his crosshairs until he found some other, bigger case to try. It was time to stop thinking of this as if it were a game or sport. It wasn't about winning or losing. It was about professional behavior, maturity, and self-control. So why did I desperately want to whack him with a gym bag full of bricks?

I watched the protesters for a while. Someone had brought a stuffed cow toy, and they were amusing themselves by cramming the thing into a hamster cage. Then they would pass

the cage around to shout and weep about the poor calf's condition until someone would liberate the plush toy to be
hugged and pranced about on the scraggly patch of weeds
near the parking strip. As if the world would be a better place
if Holsteins could frolic in the woodland hills with bunnies
and deer. I must admit I felt much better after watching the
sanctimonious show. It was oddly comforting to see these
profoundly determined individuals fight for the rights of the
helpless, even if this particular battle was misdirected.

I filled everyone in on what Archie had to say and headed
back to my tiny office at the original Louie's. I forced myself
to do some filing and shuffle some papers around my desk.
Archie had eased my mind, but the threats from Tiny Dick
Dolfe were still looming. I wanted to do something useful. I
drummed my fingers on the desk and looked over at the computer. What would it hurt to do a little on-line investigating?
I punched in a few keys and logged on.

To my surprise, there really were some valid concerns regarding candles. Pet birds had died when exposed to certain
strongly scented candles, and for many years lead fumes did
indeed accompany many a romantic evening. I panicked. What
if Mindy's lawsuit was for real? What if she *was* the canary in
our coal mine? Were we all destined to end our lives dragging
around personal oxygen tanks and wheezing? I wrote up a
memo to the staff suggesting that they each schedule a complete physical examination. I was so used to Mindy's whining,
it had never occurred to me that she might actually be sick.

I did some more digging and started to relax again.
Louie's had never used scented candles, and while I couldn't
make any guarantees that we never had a lead-wicked candle
in the place during my grandfather's day, I was confident
that while Mindy was employed, her breathing space was
safe. Eventually I surfed my way to the Web site of Dane
Hagstrom, attorney-at-law. It was a very professional, expen-

sive site full of American flags and smiling folks with crutches and splints. There were lots of photos of Hagstrom looking concerned and busy with a team of young, perfectly groomed juniors. I cursed myself for not spending more time with hackers in college. I wanted to black out a few of his teeth or send the firm a particularly nasty virus.

I searched public records, court reports, and electronic bulletin boards for information on Hagstrom or Dolfe. Hours later I hadn't dug up much dirt, but I did have a pretty decent list of companies that they had sued or represented. Near the top of my list of those they had sued was a place called Suzy's Children's Boutique. That seemed tame enough. I envisioned a seasonal window display of colorful umbrellas and cuddly stuffed ducks. I could practically hear the well-used cassettes of happy sing-along songs playing in the background. What could it hurt to call them? I dialed the number. A sweet-voiced woman answered the phone.

"Hello. May I please speak to Suzy?"

"Oh, dear, no. Suzy was the name of my baby girl and she's all grown-up now. This is Maureen. Can I help you?"

"Well, yes. I certainly hope so, Maureen. It seems we have a mutual . . . umm . . . acquaintance. And I thought maybe we could compare stories."

"How lovely! Who do we both know?"

I told her, and her response actually made me blush. I thought I was conditioned to bad language after spending a lifetime with cooks. But, whoa! This little old lady could have given classes at the longshoreman's union hall. I made eleven more phone calls. Six of the numbers had been disconnected, two responded like Maureen (albeit with slightly better language), and the remaining three said almost nothing. They clammed up at the mere mention of the law firm. This phone thing was obviously not working for me, so I decided to make a personal appearance at the next name on the list, Best

Deal Appliance Warehouse. The address was on the outskirts of town, close to Tony's work, so I called him first, and we arranged to meet for a late lunch.

We went to a teriyaki joint. They sprout like mushrooms around Northwest industrial parks. Tony has befriended the Korean family who owns the place. While the folks around us shoveled in their sweet meat and sticky rice, we savored large bowls of chewy noodles scattered with vegetables and assorted seafood in a fiery broth. I told Tony about the veal protesters, my temporary fear of candles, and then the investigation into Hagstrom and Dolfe and some of the responses I had gotten.

"Phew! Remind me never to buy the girls anything from Suzy's House of Hate!" He fished around with his chopsticks until he found a piece of squid. "Did Archie say it was okay for you to do all this digging? I *know* Dad and Rocco would never approve of it."

I shrugged and slurped a long noodle.

"Jo!"

"What? You want me to just sit around? These people might be able to help us! The company I'm going to next is Best Deal Appliance Warehouse. Hagstrom totally nailed them for a personal-injury claim and yet they're still profitable enough to pay for those tacky newspaper flyers every Sunday. I want to talk to them and find out how they managed it."

Tony agreed that it couldn't hurt to talk to them. "I know a guy who had an industrial insulation company. He got reamed when some loser fell off a ladder during a job. Maybe I'll call him and see if he has any advice."

I agreed to swing by on my way home to tell him about the meeting.

I spent a few minutes at Best Deal Appliance Warehouse wandering around the dishwashers and trash compactors to get a feel for the business. According to the flags, arrows, and huge signs, this was clearly the place for DEALS! DEALS! DEALS! Half a dozen sales associates with overextended smiles and bone-cracking handshakes introduced themselves. Each of them reminded me that there was no pressure at Best Deal. They would give me all the time and space I needed to browse; then they hovered a few feet away as they pretended to adjust a sticker or dust a panel. Finally I mustered up the courage to ask one of the young salesmen if the owner was available. He looked nervous, like I was going to bust him for not informing me that the stovetops were all available in almond.

"You're looking for Jerry Montgomery. Let me introduce you."

I had expected the owner to be a hard, determined man. He had clearly fought for what he had. But life had been good to Jerry Montgomery. He wore a short-sleeved dress shirt that pulled a bit around his belly, a cheap, wrinkled tie, and roses in his cheeks. He seemed like a perfectly happy, normal guy. He introduced himself with a polished version of the same smile and handshake his crew used.

"What can I do for you, Ms . . . ?"

"Monahan. Mindy Monahan." I don't know what inspired the lie. The name just popped out of my mouth. I fluffed my hair, widened my eyes, and prepped myself for my new role. "I'm working with some people that you know, and I just thought maybe we could talk for a minute."

"That's super!" Having mutual acquaintances seemed to give him permission to caress my hands. "Tell me about your friends!"

"Well, actually they're my lawyers. Dane Hagstrom and Richard Dolfe?" His smile remained, but the shine in his eyes lost that neighborly gleam. His look sharpened and his posture stiffened like a cat spotting a wounded mouse. He dismissed the salesman at my left.

"Of course! How are those fellas? It might take us a few minutes to catch up, so how about if we go into my office?" He looked around to see who was watching and did that embarrassing thing some men do, making a gun out of his thumb and forefinger and clicking a few imaginary "buddy bullets" to the guys nearby. Then he winked at everyone and guided me into his soundproof office. He dropped the best-friend act once we got into the room.

"Okay, sugar, what's your story?"

"Excuse me?" I asked.

"What's your angle? You must know a thing or two or you wouldn't be here, would you?"

He caught me by surprise. I tried a few scenarios in my mind but decided to stick close to the truth. I have never been a good liar. "I work at a restaurant and I haven't been feeling my best. Hagstrom has agreed to represent me. I heard that someone working for you did the same thing, so I thought I would talk to you and maybe get some advice." I expected to be thrown out immediately. The appliance king just nodded and looked at me with suspicion. So I lied a little more.

"They said that you're the man to talk to. That you're the best." Unspecific flattery is a very powerful tool.

"He said that? It's good to see that they appreciate quality work." He settled back into his chair and puffed out his chest. "I got where I am through hard work and street smarts, ya know?" He tapped a fat finger to his skull. "You don't learn this kind of stuff in business school, that's for sure! I've often thought about offering my services to the local community college. Someone needs to get these naïve kids up to speed on what goes on in the real world."

I spoon-fed him some more sugar. "And it sounds like you're just the man to do it."

"Maybe I am. Maybe I am at that." He pondered for a moment. "So, princess, what can I do you for today?"

"I guess I just wanted a little of your best advice. I'm not really sure what to do." I looked dumb and confused. It came easy.

"Let's start from the top. What injury are you claiming? Ah, never mind. It doesn't really matter. As long as you don't get Labor and Industries involved. They can be hard-assed and hire investigators and everything. I learned that the first time."

I was shocked. "You've been sued more than once?"

He sat back in his chair. "Hell, yeah! And I hope I am again. Who would've thought getting sued would be so profitable?" He winked conspiratorially and leaned back in his chair. When he spoke again it was with a professorial tone, as though I were his favorite pupil there for a private lesson. "That's why it's so important for you to work with your employers. I know some people who weren't able to get it together and they really got hit hard. It's good that you're doing your homework. What are you asking for?"

I wasn't sure what he meant.

"How much? What are you asking for?"

"Oh, they said five million dollars."

He whistled. "Well, aren't you a lucky little lady? You got some kind of neck or stomach thing? Something that can't be seen but could give you a lot of trouble the rest of your life?"

I coughed a little for effect. "It's my lungs. Indoor air pollution."

He threw up his hands in celebration. I guess I got extra credit for having such a good answer. "Brilliant! That's genius! And with five mill at stake, you should be able to take home, what . . . maybe even a million yourself! What are you going to do with all that money? You interested in some appliances? I'll take good care of you!"

"One million?" I asked. "But the lawsuit is for five. I'm not sure I understand."

"Sweetheart, don't get greedy! You've played it perfectly

right up to now. But I guess that's why you're here, huh?" He explained the whole scam to me slowly and simply.

"You have a workplace injury—asbestosis, black lung, TB, whatever. And Hagstrom has one of his quacks backing it up, right? They go to your boss and tell him that you need compensation for your suffering, they talk a bit behind closed doors, a few numbers are tossed around, and a deal is made. Then everyone goes to the insurance company. Your people must be covered pretty deep or our friends wouldn't be asking for so much."

I nodded.

"Now, if your bosses settle for the first number thrown out there, the insurance company will get curious. Don't forget that they're footing the bill for this little party of yours! You've got to let them fight it for a while. Let them talk you down to three, three and a half million. That way the investigators and insurance lawyers feel like they made a decent deal and saved the company a big box of money and everybody wins!" He started tapping numbers into an adding machine.

"Of course, Hagstrom will take his share. Forty percent seems like a lot, I know, but I've shopped around and his kids are better at closing these deals than anyone around. And if you and Hagstrom have something going, it's money in the bank! Get that pretty boy in the right light and all he has to do is smile and the opposing counsel starts writing checks!" Montgomery started scratching some figures on a pad. "Don't skimp on your payments to the restaurant. They're gonna want at least fifteen, twenty percent. It's only fair. They have to pay their own lawyers, and the increased liability insurance—that's a doozy! If any of your fellow employees get wind of the deal, they can be pricey too. You might be able to walk away with a mill and a quarter. But don't count on much more than that or you'll be asking for trouble."

I nodded and thanked him for his time. Then I stroked his

ego a few more times in genuine appreciation for his understanding of the scam, but he wasn't about to let me go just
yet. He walked me into the showroom, threw his arm around
me, and gave me a tour of the newest in computerized refrig-
erators and European washer/dryer sets. I agreed that they
would be perfect and that I would write him a fat check the
next time I visited. The slime bag even managed to cop a
good feel as he hugged me good-bye. It felt a little like waiting tables again, but this time I felt the tip was well worth the
fake smile and a cheap grope.

I was eager to see Tony and fill him in, but when I got to
his office he wasn't alone. Manuel Gonzales, the industrial in-
sulator who had been sued, was with him. I learned quickly
that Jerry Montgomery had gotten one thing right: These
dirty deals worked best when all sides teamed up and took
on the insurers. Manny Gonzales had lost everything trying
to fight a bogus lawsuit involving Hagstrom's firm. He
looked exhausted, but seemed glad to talk about it.

"Construction isn't exactly a nine-to-five career. The work
is scattered and never consistent, so the workers have to be
flexible. I've found that the best guys in the business are fish-
ing fanatics—they have to work hard to make their boat payments, but they don't bitch when they have a week off." Tony
and Manny nodded and laughed.

"There's also a whole other breed who are nomadic. They
go where the work is. Sometimes you've got to hire a new
crew fast, and you don't have time to really get to know them.
That's how I ended up with Marvin. He knew how to wrap
pipes, but he was a drunk. He fell off his ladder while he was
redoing the hot-water lines at St. Theresa's hospital. Luckily
he was only a few steps up, so he just knocked his head and
loosened a bone spur in his foot when he fell. Since he was in
a hospital they gave him the royal treatment. They put him in
a wheelchair and got him to the emergency room quick. That

bastard didn't even need stitches. They just taped up his head, handed him an ice pack and a couple of Tylenol, and sent him home. They could tell he had been drinking and they took a blood test to confirm it.

"Of course, I fired him. I guess it's kind of funny when you think about it. I fired the guy 'cause I was afraid that he would screw something up, and I'd get sued. Instead, he's the one that sues me. While he was recovering on his couch and administering his own form of anesthesia, he saw those damn commercials for Hagstrom's law firm. Next thing I know, these punk lawyers are telling me that I *let* him drink on the job and was therefore responsible for his accident. I guess a small-business owner is now expected to check the pee of his employees regularly. Who knew? I always thought my job was to insulate pipes and take care of my wife and kids!" He was still furious. I couldn't blame him.

"This nasty little legal bastard that looked like a rat kept coming around, trying to convince me to settle. He kept telling me it was no big deal. That my insurance would pay for it. But I ran a clean shop. Once you do one dirty deal and it gets around . . . I just didn't want to step in that mess. And I wasn't about to let Marvin win. I mean, the asshole got drunk on the job and fell off his damn ladder! Why should I pay for his stupidity?" He looked over at me and apologized for his language. I assured him it wasn't a problem.

"I hired a lawyer and we fought it. But everything went to hell anyway. It was one thing after another. My truck kept breaking down. It was the damnedest thing, just freaky little things started snapping or falling apart. Then an entire shipment of insulation was stolen. Somehow word spread that my workers were dangerous and lawsuit-happy. I guess I was so busy with that stupid case that I didn't spend enough time bidding on jobs. The work just disappeared. My best guys went to the competition. My lawyer finally convinced me to settle, and that loser Marvin got two hundred and fifty grand from my insurance company. They tripled my monthly premiums. The lawsuit was over, but I was left with no work and a stack of stupid bills. I had to sell my shop and all my gear just to break even.

"Now I work for the competition too." He tried to put a positive spin on it. "I guess it could be worse. It's nice not to have all the pressures of having my own place, but I forgot how much that damn fiberglass dust itches." He shifted in his seat in a way that made me want to scratch all over. "My wife isn't taking it too well. She wants to go to some counselor— says she never sees me anymore, but what am I supposed to do? My youngest is gonna need braces soon, and my daughter has her hopes set on Whitman College. I'm gonna have to sell a kidney to get her there." He beamed with paternal pride. "They're growing up so fast. Jeez, Tony! Why am I hanging around here telling you my problems when I should be back at work? You put me in one of these comfy chairs and I start acting like the boss again. I'm getting lazy!"

"Manny, you don't know the meaning of the word *lazy*. You worked like a dog even when you were the boss." Tony slugged him on the arm and they pretended to spar.

I said, "Thanks for talking to us. I guess we know a little more about what to expect."

Manny said, "If you're looking for advice, I think you're talking to the wrong guy. I keep trying to figure out how I could have done it differently. Maybe I should have hired better lawyers, but that would have just cost more. I guess technically I didn't really lose the lawsuit, but I did lose my business. Now I just want to hold on to my family."

After he left, Tony and I sat in silence for a while, trying to make sense of what we had learned. "So, sis, now what do we do?"

I told him what I had learned from the appliance king.

"I'm hoping that Archie is getting better news. Right now it feels like the only way to get out of this thing unscarred is to play along, but I just can't stand the idea of Tiny Dick and Mindy getting money from our insurance company. We could report it as insurance fraud. I imagine that's the right thing to do, but I suppose as long as Mindy has that quack swearing she's sick, they might actually have a valid case. And quite honestly I'm not quite ready to piss off Tiny Dick. He scares me."

Then Tony put into words what was already in my mind: "Maybe we're going to lose."

I thought about it for a minute. Then Tony smiled and said, "But if we do, I have no doubt that you will do your damnedest to take those bastards down with us." I gave him my most innocent look, but I knew he was right.

Chapter Ten

By Friday afternoon I had spent far more time than I care to admit worrying about what to wear for my date with Josh. He had seen me in my hiking gear and seemed to like the all-natural look. At least, he liked it enough to send flowers and ask me out. But, as the child of international diplomats, he might have something dressy planned. Surely he knew a thing or two about which fork to use with the fish course. I dug deeper into my closet in search of a "What, this old thing?" outfit that might make his eyes pop out. Then I had a long talk with the cat and explained to him that it didn't really matter what I wore. I wasn't actually interested in Josh. This was business, nothing more. The cat stuck a hind leg in the air and licked himself in the crotch a few times in response.

"No, it's not like that!" But in the back of my mind, I had to wonder. In the end I went with my favorite black skirt and a soft sweater with a flattering neckline; then I sneaked into Nina's bathroom to use a few of her fancy hair products and to steal a lipstick. What are sisters for?

I poured myself a glass of wine and cranked up a Billie Holliday CD to remind me of what can happen when you let men mess with your life. I peeked out the front window in search of Josh's old truck, but I was distracted by an adorable red convertible. Then my jaw dropped. I was out the door gawking before Josh even turned the engine off. So much for my rehearsed "alluring but not over enthusiastic" greeting.

"Oh, my God! This is an Austin Healy! This is a *red* Austin Healy! This is perhaps the coolest car in the universe!" I said.

"You like it?" He grinned like a proud kid.

"It's amazing!" I circled it in admiration. Our old neighbors owned a scrap yard and raced cars on the weekends. They had an Austin Healy parked in front of their house for a couple of months when I was about twelve, and I have included it in my imaginary lottery jackpot ever since. It was my version of the Barbie Corvette.

"You don't grow up with a bunch of brothers without learning a thing or two about cars. This is, what, a 'fifty-five? I didn't see this at your farm."

"I told you that you should come back for the other part of the tour. I have some neat stuff tucked away on all that property," explained Josh. "You look great, by the way."

Actually, so did he. He wore a supple brown leather jacket and a beautifully cut blue shirt. The colors set off his skin tone and angular face. His wavy hair was rumpled by the wind, and his eyes crinkled and glistened with the pleasure of pulling off a successful surprise. He smelled of soap and fresh air.

"So where are we going?" I did a flirty little thing with my eyes as I asked him; then I caught myself. Damn it! I am *not* the kind of girl who is drawn to a man just because he drives a cool car. Am I?

"Well, I've been told that the best place for a first date is an Italian joint called Louie's on Twelfth," said Josh.

I grimaced.

"Yeah, that's what I figured," he went on. "If you don't have anything in mind, maybe you can suggest a place that makes a killer cheeseburger and serves good beer?"

I was pleasantly surprised. People can kind of freak out when it comes to eating with a cook. They either get all flustered and try to impress you with how much they know, or they constantly apologize for things not being up to your supposed standards. I love burgers and beer, and I knew exactly where to get them. I ran back inside for my jacket and handbag and gave myself a quick check in the mirror. I *was* looking pretty good! I locked up, eagerly jumped into the passenger seat, and directed Josh to the Longhorn Bar and Grill.

We settled into a booth, asked to try the seasonal ale, and placed our orders. Then I drilled him on what seemed to be an obvious contradiction.

"It's a little odd to me that you are an organic vegetable farmer and you just ordered a double bacon cheeseburger. What's the deal?"

He just shrugged. So I continued.

"I know times have changed, but I still envision organic farmers as tree-hugging hippies. You're supposed to be wearing a lot of hemp clothing, bathing in rainwater, and baking loaves of sprouted wheat bread for your hairy-armpitted wife and naked children. I kind of figured the folks who care enough to grow organic are willing to embrace poverty in exchange for a clean conscience. What they *don't* do is drive convertibles and eat unnamed cows."

Josh smiled in a charming, kind of lopsided way and explained, "I eat a lot of vegetables, and I'm a big fan of clean air and water. Don't forget my grandparents were bakers, so I've made a few loaves of bread in my day. I might be categorized by a few of your blatant stereotypes. But in truth, I just love a good burger. I guess growing up abroad left me a few hundred cheeseburgers low on the American quota. I'm making up for lost time." He sipped his beer and continued: "As for your romantic visions of politically correct farmers, I did my research before I bought the land. This region doesn't need another big alfalfa producer or cornfield. Certified organic vegetables can be very profitable in the right marketplace. Once you start crunching the numbers and look closely at the price of hybrid seed and high-tech pesticides, and then environmental impact, it just plain makes financial sense to grow organic. Besides, my farm is beautiful and I want to keep it that way."

I could hardly argue with that. Our food arrived, and for a while it took all our concentration to manipulate the messy burgers. When we were done mopping up our sticky fingers, we fell back into our chairs and groaned with contentment. He asked a few questions and, feeling chatty, I told him about my family and about my drawings. He acted as if I were some kind of real artist. Appreciative of an attentive audience, I found myself telling him about Mindy and the lawsuit, and how the lawyers had offered us a kickback if we settled quickly. It felt good to talk things out with someone who wasn't so closely involved. He listened, he laughed, and he was outraged at all the right spots. As the night drew to a close, he became the man of my dreams: He let me drive home.

Josh walked me to the front door and I automatically braced myself. At this point in a date, I usually expect the guy to turn up the heat and start sweet-talking his way into my bedroom. But Josh was a perfect gentleman. He just brushed the windblown hair gently from my face and looked into my eyes. My stomach fluttered.

"I had a great time, Jo. I hope we can do this again." He kissed me sweetly on the cheek, then left.

"Mmmm," was all I could manage in return. I watched that marvelous car drive off into the night, and then I floated up the stairs.

Chapter Eleven

I spent the next day in my studio, but my drawings were dreadful. The more I demanded of them, the worse they got. I knew better than to force my pencils and pens into submission. I went to the gym and took my frustration out on the treadmill. It did the trick. My mind cleared enough to ink some clean lines and draw decent curves. I was pondering what to make for dinner when Rocco called.

"Jo! Mike just cut his hand and it looks like it's gonna need stitches. Can you help us out tonight? I'd do it, but I promised I'd take Emily and the girls to some princess-on-ice thing. They'll kill me if I bail."

I had no problem with that. "Yeah, sure, I'll come in. Give me ten minutes. And tell Mike he'd better be gone by the time I get there, or I'm going to call an ambulance." Mike Coccio has been our lead chef at Louie's for almost seven years. He's fast, and he's reliable, and like a lot of really devoted cooks, he is almost physically bonded to the stove. He could be bleeding from his eyes and still swear he was okay to finish his shift. I have seen cooks like this get third-degree burns and just shake it off as another day at the office. It's insane, especially for the money they make.

I ran upstairs, changed into my favorite chef pants, packed up my knife kit, and drove downtown. Of course, Mike was still there when I arrived. He had his hand wrapped in a bloody towel and was rattling off a list of detailed instructions to the remaining line cooks.

"God, I'm sorry about this, Jo. It's just so stupid! I swear I'll be back to close."

"Go to the emergency room, Mike. If you are even considering seeing a doctor, I'm guessing it's pretty bad."

"Well, yeah. I think I did a pretty good job this time." He unwrapped the towel to take a look. I peeked at the deep gash on his hand, got dizzy, and looked away.

"If you don't leave right now, I'll call the cops and tell them I stabbed you. You think I don't know how to run your station?" Finally he let Rocco guide him out the door.

"And I don't want to see you tomorrow either!" I shouted after them.

This was why we paid L&I insurance. Real accidents happen to hardworking, honest people. I would never begrudge someone like Mike his due. I buttoned up my white coat, tied an apron around my waist, and took a look at the station. Vince called. His sous chef had the night off and was willing to come in to run the line. Mike had everything set and ready to go, so I passed on the offer. I was ready to do some cooking. Besides, we had a new pantry chef on board and I wanted to see what she was made of.

I'm glad I don't work in the kitchen every night. It's hard physical and mental labor, best suited for the young or fanatical, but I love to step up to the stove now and then. There is a sense of teamwork and artistry that I have not found anywhere else. When you are busy, you can easily slip into a place where you are no longer aware of your surroundings, but you're focused completely on your body and the acts that need to be accomplished.

I poked around Mike's station and double-checked all of the ingredients for freshness and quality. I tasted the soup and sauces for seasoning. It looked like Mike had planned to use fresh mussels and scallops for a special. So I ran with the idea. I would sear the shellfish in olive oil with plenty of aromatics, splash in some white wine, some good fish stock, and a ladleful of bright tomato sauce. This simple pan sauce would be tossed with a tangle of hot linguine and sprinkled with nothing more than chopped fresh parsley. Our customers liked their food simple but well flavored. This ought to keep them happy.

The call had gone out that there was trouble at Louie's, and the family responded quickly. Nina came in early. Tony called to see if he could help. Bella and Louie arrived soon after. When they saw the emergency had been handled, they decided to sit, have some wine, and share a plate of pasta. Mom and Dad have worked hard all their lives. I love to see them finally slow down and enjoy the spoils.

Bob gave them each a complimentary membership to his health club. Dad goes almost every day. It's mainly a social thing for him. His knees and ankles are shot after spending so many years on his feet, so he just sits in the juice bar and holds court, talking sports and doling out business advice. Between the restaurant and all of the Little League teams he has sponsored over the years, everyone in town has something to say to Little Louie. He has a standing appointment for a weekly massage and loves the sauna and steam room. I am a little worried that my dad may be turning into one of those old guys who just stews in the whirlpool and checks out the new bathing suits, and I'm not sure Bob has the guts to call him on it. Mom loves to refer to her health club membership in conversation, but mostly she just goes to the salon to get her hair and nails done.

A few years ago we finally talked Mom and Dad into going on vacation. They went on a cruise with some old friends and had a ball. The lush life of a cruise is about perfect for them. They eat, shop, and get to talk about all of the exotic places they have visited without ever getting their loungewear mussed. Mom and Dad were like giggly newlyweds for weeks after they returned. They couldn't keep their hands off each other. Maybe that's why I've had such lousy luck in relationships: I still believe in true love. I see it practically every day.

I was lost in thought, mincing shallots, when Nina stormed into the kitchen, followed by Bella. Nina's eyes were scary and she was waving her arms as she raved. "Those arrogant sons of bitches! I can't believe they have the balls to show their faces around here, let alone expect us to feed them. Jo, do you have any rancid butter or rank seafood stashed anywhere? I'm going to need a special order. Tiny Dick is at table twenty-four and he's with that smarmy TV lawyer boss of his." She peered in the trash, perhaps looking for something particularly awful to serve.

"That's enough, Nina," Bella said in her MOM voice, all capital letters. It is the sound of the law for us. "Go kick the trash cans if you have to. Break a plate. Throw bottles in the alley. I don't care what you do. But when you step back in that dining room, you will treat each of our customers with the same graciousness and respect. If you can't behave professionally, then go home right now."

Nina and I performed our famous tandem eye roll.

"Your father is out there right now, shaking their hands, maybe talking about baseball. Who knows? It is our *job* to welcome them into our restaurant." She glared at Nina. "We will feed them our best food." She shot a look to me. "It is our *responsibility* to show these men what decent behavior looks like. They must see that even in the face of selfishness and greed a Cerbone will react with kindness and dignity."

She smoothed her hair, straightened her spine, and turned to face her foes. "What these two men need more than anything is a good meal. Maybe it will warm their cold hearts." According to Mom, the world's ills can *all* be solved with a decent meal.

I peeked out the swinging door to get a look. Nina joined me and scoffed, "Give me a few weeks without waxing, and I could grow a better mustache than that rat bastard!"

Dolfe's small, dark eyes shot around the room looking for potential danger. He didn't speak much, but when he did, his voice carried in that oddly high-pitched and raspy tone. I could hear him all the way back in the kitchen as he requested that the candle be removed from their table. There were drips on the wine bottle that held it, so it was obviously cheap and smoky. He was sure it was an uninspected import, the wick full of lead. Nina graciously removed the light. A minute later she walked through the kitchen to the delivery door. I heard her violently kicking and ripping apart a cardboard box. She was rosy cheeked and mussed, but looked a little calmer when she returned.

Rita Caldwell waited on the duo. Rita is a wiry old bird who has been with us forever and has seen it all. She has survived a mastectomy, a child with Down syndrome, and a third husband who lost their car on a bad tip at the track. Nothing can ruffle her. She brought me the order.

"It looks like the handsome guy is a health nut," she said. "His body is a temple, don't you know. He reminded the whole restaurant in his movie-star voice about how saturated fat seizes up in your veins like bacon grease in a cold can. Then he listed the items on our menu that include sausage and cheese and proclaimed them to be pure poison. Apparently he is not a big fan of pasta either. He went on and on about triglycer-somethings and blood sugar and said he might as well just weave the spaghetti into a noose and kill himself right there.

"He wants a plate of sliced tomatoes, a cup of the broth from the minestrone with some whitefish cooked in it, and a double-size green salad with no dressing. The rat-faced one wants the antipasto plate, the baked penne with extra sausage, and a side of garlic cheese bread."

Special orders are a hassle, but they aren't unusual. We do what we can to accommodate everybody. A few more orders came in, so I was forced to actually cook instead of gossip. I was plating up two specials and an eggplant Parm when I heard a crash and shouts coming from the dining room. I ran to the door to see what was happening.

The Doblowski family was celebrating a family birthday at the table next to our special guests. They had been coming to Louie's for over fifty years, so we knew them well. As usual, Doris Doblowski went to freshen up after her meal. She slowly rose onto her swollen ankles and grabbed her huge, ever-present vinyl handbag. But tonight, as she swung the bag onto her shoulder, she somehow managed to connect with the tray of hot soup Rita was carrying. The whole ensemble landed in Dolfe's lap. Chaos ensued.

He leaped up and hollered, "Jesus Christ!" Hagstrom, worried a spot might get onto his own suit, jumped up as well and proceeded to knock the wineglasses and most of the tableware onto his dining partner. Mrs. Doblowski shifted into nursemaid mode. She reached for the lawyer's crotch with a napkin. Dolfe, with a lap full of hot soup and Chianti, ripped the napkin from the old lady's hand and screamed at her.

"Leave me alone, you clumsy old bitch! Get away from me!" Mrs. Doblowski ignored him. She saw a small man with hot soup on his pants and did what she knew would ease his suffering. She grabbed his belt and dropped his drawers. Right there in the dining room. Dolfe shrieked like a young girl and tried to cover himself with the soiled tablecloth. His squirmy attempts to redress himself with one hand garnered him even more attention. There were whispers and giggles at nearby tables and talk of leather and straps. Everyone's eyes were focused on the lawyers' table when Rita picked up the soup-stained tube sock that had fallen to the floor, held it up for inspection, and then asked, "What's this? I think it fell out of your pants!"

Dane Hagstrom was the first to break the silence. He let go with a big, booming laugh. He kept repeating, "I think this fell out of your pants, Dick! I think this fell out of your pants!" Other diners joined in the laughter. My family and I stood in openmouthed horror.

Mrs. Doblowski kept muttering pathetic attempts at an apology, but I caught the theatrical wink she sent to Nina. Mom shuffled her off toward the relative safety of the ladies' room. If spontaneous human combustion were possible, it would have happened right here in Louie's restaurant. Tiny Dick shrunk into a small, dense cosmic mass of rage and hatred. He was nitroglycerine.

Dad bravely threw himself at this live grenade. He offered a change of clothes and made many references to medical attention, free dry cleaning, and anything else that came to his mind. He started to call the paramedics, but Dolfe wasn't about to stick around and have his crotch inspected. The angry little man threw cash on the table and walked through the restaurant with as much dignity as he could muster. Hagstrom, the brute, continued to guffaw until he caught his reflection in a wall mirror. Then he became mesmerized by his own good looks, forgot about his associate, and began grooming himself.

My father chased Dolfe to the door with a handful of bills. "No, no, Mr. Dolfe. I will pay for your meal! Of course we will pay for your dinner!"

It would seem impossible for such tiny black eyes to
shrink any more, but they did. Dolfe turned and directed his
quiet fury at the restaurant patrons, then my father. He said
nothing, but the room went silent.

Even my powerful and optimistic father was stilled by
this display of pure hatred. Hagstrom's mirror fixation broke
and he looked curiously at his protégé. Then he solemnly followed Dolfe out of the restaurant. Dad chased them out the
door, trying to soothe them all the way to their car.

Bella sent the Doblowski family a complimentary
chocolate-chip ricotta cake and a round of espresso to help
celebrate the birthday.

The rest of the night was miserable. I was stuck on the
line with rowdy cooks who were wired from the activity and
excitement. They relived every moment of the evening, and
at each retelling of the tale I was tempted to flee the line. I
wanted to fix it, but in reality there was nothing to fix. Scald-
ing liquids and tender anatomy should never meet. That is
one of the cardinal rules of the restaurant business. Dolfe had
a real case now, and a couple dozen witnesses.

I bought the kitchen crew a round of beer and sent them
home. I would close up myself. Nina did the same thing in
the dining room. When she finished up, she came back to
check on me.

"You want a hand with anything? I'm all done up here."

"Naw, I'm done too. I just need to put the mats back down
and sweep out the walk-in. I'll be finished in five minutes."

"I'm stopping at the store on my way home. What flavor
do you want?"

I didn't need to ask what she was stopping for. The Cerbone sisters needed ice cream and plenty of it. "Anything involving chunks, swirls, and lots of chocolate. But get more
than one pint, because I don't feel like sharing."

"Are you kidding? I figure I'll have the first pint polished off before I make it out of the parking lot! If God is really watching out for us, He surely will grant us twenty-four hours of free calorie intake after a night like tonight." I nodded in agreement. Cerbones tend to become closer to God whenever ice cream is involved.

The night was clearly cursed. Just as I was aligning the fatigue mats, I managed to knock a two-quart container of garlic-infused olive oil onto the floor. I had to start the entire process of cleaning the floor all over again. Nina was asleep on the couch when I got in. By then, even large quantities of ice cream weren't going to soothe my mood. I just went to bed.

I couldn't sleep. I kept thinking about Mindy. It was her fault that Tiny Dick was back in our life, that we might lose everything. At about four in the morning, just as I was finally dozing off, the phone rang. It was Mom. Louie's was on fire.

Chapter Twelve

The firefighters reacted quickly, and most of the flames were extinguished by the time Nina and I arrived. They said it probably started in the kitchen and was most likely a gas leak, but the investigators had to have a look to be sure. Louie's is an old restaurant. The kitchen still had a lot of painted wood and wallboard rather than the modern sheets of brushed stainless steel found in newer establishments. The back half of the restaurant had exploded. The dining room was still standing, but everything was ruined by the smoke and water. We all huddled together in the early-morning drizzle and watched in stunned silence as the sun began to rise and police secured the smoldering remains.

Mom was the first to rally. "All right, I think we have done enough standing around in this freezing cold. I want everyone home for breakfast and a family meeting."

Mom and Dad still live in the house we grew up in. It isn't huge, but the seven of us had managed to live there without killing each other. One doorjamb is still covered in scratches and initials comparing our childhood heights. There are a few obvious spackle jobs from the years we watched a lot of pro wrestling, and the woodwork is forever saturated with the

aromas of holiday meals and good times. The fridge is still
plastered with drawings and craft projects, and there are piles
of toys and books lying about, but that is the work of precious
grandchildren.

Dad set to work as soon as we got home, handing out
towels and dry clothes. Mom made gallons of strong black
coffee. She must have said something to Vince back at the
restaurant, because he and Anna arrived a little later with
their arms full of groceries. The cooks got busy. We peeled potatoes, chopped onions, and sliced thick slabs of dense bread.
The familiar actions and crowded space comforted me. I might
be completely helpless when it comes to fixing the ruined
family business, but I could make these red peppers, fresh
tomatoes, and herbs obey my every whim. I sliced and diced
with intensity. Tony and Nina kept us entertained by aping
along to an old album of opera classics. We had seen their shtick
a dozen times before, but it never failed to make us laugh.
Our restaurant might be ruined, but our family was safe, and
that was all that mattered right now.

After we ate and drank our fill, we started making plans.
It wasn't just our family that was affected; we had a staff to
take care of too. It was decided that longtime staff members
were due at least a week of vacation; then they could join the
others in filing for unemployment or picking up whatever
shifts we could arrange at Twelfth Street. Nina and Vince would
step back and give up their hours to those in need. Vince had
always wanted to try making fresh mozzarella and curing his
own pancetta and salami. Now he finally had the time to experiment. He would also schedule training sessions to teach
the staff some of the techniques he had learned in Italy. Nina
would focus on marketing. We needed to make sure that the
longtime fans of Louie's were not forgotten. She and Bella were
already writing up flyers and ad copy. Louie's might be closed
for a while, but that was no reason to deny our customers

their regular meatball fix. Louie's on Twelfth would serve all
of the classic Louie's preparations at the regular price. Die-hard
traditionalists would just have to close their eyes to the con-
temporary art and furniture for a while.

Tony was already on his cell phone, hooking us up with a
good contractor and a source for wholesale materials. As usual,
Rocco would oversee the whole operation. I, of course, would
take care of the paperwork, filing claims, arranging for permits,
and managing the books.

All work stopped the moment Rocco's wife, Emily, arrived with their adorable twin daughters. Everyone fidgeted
a bit while Rocco greeted his family, and then the living room
erupted into a three-ring circus. Tony juggled and sang silly
songs. Vince and Anna pulled out a stack of coloring books and
games. I could hear Dad's knees pop and crackle from across
the room as he got down on all fours to play horsey. Mom ran
from one girl to another, cooing sweet nothings and reaching
out to touch and tickle them adoringly. The kids were used to
such fawning, and there was never a shortage of foolishness
when the four-year-olds were around, but this morning there
was a desperate air to the play. It was as if the innocence of
these children could somehow erase the evils of the morning.

Emily, Nina, and I stood at the kitchen doorway and
watched the show. Dad's knees didn't last long, so he had to
resort to a backup plan. He sat up and sang out, "Who wants
candy?" The girls ran to him. The abandoned adults were
forced to come up with new, exciting second acts.

Emily slapped her forehead, then looked over at Nina
and me. In a pleading voice she asked, "So how are you two
doing in the relationship department? Any new hopefuls?"
We pretended like we didn't hear, but both pointed her in the
right direction when she mumbled, "Where does Bella keep
the aspirin?"

Tony and Rocco each had a giggling girl sitting on his left

foot, clinging desperately to their pant legs. Anna was about to shoot off a cap gun to start a race.

Nina whispered to me, "Don't you think it's a little pathetic the way these guys humiliate themselves around the girls?"

"Yeah. It's kind of ridiculous," I said. We watched the screaming horseplay in the other room and cheered them on. Nina wasn't exactly above reproach. "At least they don't try to buy their love."

Nina scowled at me. "What do you mean by that?"

I offered an innocent shrug in response. She knew exactly what I meant and spit out her reply.

"Unlike *some* people, I have to look professional and well-groomed at work, and sometimes when I'm shopping, I run across a few things I think the girls would like! Is that a crime?"

I remained quiet.

"Okay, I'll admit the fairy-tale princess gowns and spar-kly shoes were a little extravagant, and Rocco doesn't want them to get their ears pierced yet, so the earrings were premature, but those red raincoats and adorable ladybug boots were just too cute to pass up. And they were on sale!"

I reluctantly nodded in agreement. The girls just loved their new stormy-weather gear. And I would have bought the same ensemble if I had spotted it first. Instead, I had whisked the well-dressed pair outside for an afternoon of puddle stomping and mud pies. It wasn't as if I was immune to the girls' charms. I just wasn't willing to fight for their attention this morning. I wasn't in a playful mood.

As usual, the fun came to an end rather quickly. One of the girls bumped her head on the coffee table, then kicked her sister to even out the discomfort. They both started crying. Emily managed to pull them away from my parents before they found more candy. The party started breaking up. Nina made gestures as if to leave with the others, but I said, "I'll grab a ride with Dad later. We still have some insurance details to work out." Actually, we hadn't even started on the insurance details, and, quite honestly, I wanted a nap before we stepped in that hornets' nest. I wanted to stay because there was one conversation yet to have.

After everyone was gone, Louie and Bella sat on the couch. Dad looked blankly at his shoes and Mom wiped away some nonexistent dust from the end table. They knew what I was going to say and clearly wanted to avoid it.

"So?" I asked.

"I'm sure it's just a coincidence," said Mom. Dad just rubbed his chin.

"You think it's a coincidence that a restaurant that has stood for fifty years in the same spot blows up a few hours after a known villain is publicly humiliated on the premises?"

"They said it might have been a gas leak."

"Mom, I worked last night! There was no gas leak."

"It's an old restaurant, and besides, Tiny Dick is all grown-up. Sure, he was embarrassed, but he's probably laughing about it now. No one really saw anything."

"*Everyone* saw something, Mom! I was all the way back in the kitchen and *I* even saw Rita hold up the sock!"

Mom covered her face with her hands. Eventually she couldn't hold back her laughter. "Oh, Lord! That pathetic little man! A tube sock, for Pete's sake! With all his money you would think he would be able to buy some fancy prosthetic."

Dad looked ashamed at his own laughter, but added, "Maybe that's why he's suing us. He needs one more big case to buy the johnson of his dreams." He snorted a few times. "I've heard there are some interesting things available online."

Mom said, "Maybe we can find him something heat-proof. Jo, honey, why don't you go look up fake penises on your fancy computer, and we'll have one sent to poor Tiny

Dick with our condolences. It's the least we can do." They fell into each other's arms in hysterics.

This was *definitely* not the conversation I had had in mind. I sat in stunned silence and watched as my parents held their sides and tried to control their giggling. They sobered up when they saw my face. Dad got up, wrapped a huge arm around my shoulders, and mussed my hair like old times. Mom gave me one of *those* looks. You know, the loving, cocker-spaniel Mom eyes. The kind you got as a kid when you got stuck in the toilet or did a face plant on your bike because you were showing off. She was desperately trying to look concerned instead of entertained.

"We're sorry, Jo. We know what you're trying to say, and we shouldn't be making jokes," Mom said.

Dad added, "I never thought I would see the day, but I guess I'm just so used to leaving the business of the restaurants to you and Rocco that I may not be taking this situation as seriously as I should. You've done such a great job of running things that I just figure you'll be able to take care of this too."

Mom nodded. "I haven't let the reality of the fire sink in yet, but at this moment I just can't seem to get too upset. My kids are all safe and we can still sing and laugh and eat like old times. My granddaughters are healthy and happy, and that's much more important to me than any smelly old restaurant."

Dad nodded. "It's a mess. But it could be worse. We'll live through it."

I had planned to fill them in on the details I had learned earlier in the week. To inform them of the threat I genuinely believed Dolfe to be and to suggest we file a police report, but now I couldn't bear to diminish their confidence. I just nodded and kept my opinions to myself.

Dad and I drove back to the restaurant to check out the damage in the daylight. We met up with the fire and insurance investigators, and they agreed to let us walk through with hard hats as soon as the photographer was finished. At first it wasn't as traumatic or emotional as I had feared. This burned wreck of a building wasn't our family restaurant. The floor was ankle-deep in water, and scattered with broken china and glassware. Everything in the dining room was sooty and drenched. Most unusual of all was the bright natural light illuminating what used to be a dark, moody room. The back door had blown off and most of the roof was missing. This was some kind of a movie set, not the restaurant that my grandfather had built. It couldn't be. Luckily the office was off to the side and the heavy door was closed. It had survived relatively unscathed. I gathered up some crucial files and phone numbers and packed up the computer.

Dad was in the dining room collecting old photos and picking up broken pieces of sentimental knickknacks. Now and then he would stop to look at the scorched walls or run his fingers over the upholstery. It broke my heart. I set down my load of stuff and gave him a hug like I hadn't done in years.

"Grandma's favorite putto is broken," he said, showing me the pieces of the chubby little Italian cherub. "You know, I never liked this thing. I always thought it had a nasty, smug look on its face, like it was watching me and knew my secrets. I couldn't bear to throw it out. I felt like as long as this thing was around, my mother could check up on me. He was her little ceramic spy." He just stared down at the figure in his hands for a moment. Then he carefully placed the pieces in a box with his other treasures. His armor finally cracked and he wiped away a tear. I thought I might just die right there on the spot. Dad pulled himself together quickly. He spun his remorse into promises.

"You know, our customers are so sentimental about this

joint, I swear we couldn't even clean the carpet or buy new chairs without them screaming for months. Now they can't complain about a remodel, can they? All this light sure makes this place look a lot different. Maybe we should put a few more windows in when we rebuild?"

I nodded and picked up my box of paperwork. The lump in my throat made it impossible to speak. We took one last look around and kicked some debris, and then we left the old Louie's Italian Restaurant for good.

Chapter Thirteen

I guess the rest of the family wasn't ready to be apart. They were all at Twelfth Street when we got there, just hanging out. Rocco had made an executive decision. No one was ready, emotionally or physically, to serve dinner, so he called the scheduled crew and gave them the night off.

I was touched by the many cards, flowers, and messages already delivered by well-wishers. It gave me the strength I needed to call Archie, the bank, and then the insurance company. Then I contacted the utility companies and our purveyors to explain the necessary interruption in service. I saved Josh's farm for last.

"Josh? It's Jo Cerbone."

"Hey, Jo! I've been trying to reach you all day but I couldn't get through. You guys need anything else for tomorrow's delivery?"

I told him about the fire, and he was properly stunned. He insisted on driving into town, and I didn't really feel like turning him down. In fact, I looked forward to seeing him again.

Of course the family flocked around his car when he pulled up—the guys to admire the machine, and Nina and

Mom in appreciation of the sheer quantity of flower bouquets and baskets of greens he had packed into the tiny car. I had explained that we wouldn't need an order for a few days, but Josh wanted to give us something for our tragedy and generously distributed the gifts. Mom looked smitten. There was plenty of backslapping and joke cracking with my brothers. It didn't take long before they had the hood open and their talk shifted to horsepower and the availability of parts. Nina slipped into the driver's seat and vamped a bit.

Just like this morning, I played it cool. I didn't feel like competing with my family for someone's attention. I went back inside and added a few dozen more entries to my to-do list. Gradually everyone returned to the dining room. There was more reminiscing about beloved cars and motorcycles. Mom kept offering Josh food. I sensed that Nina had powered up her flirt factor. Her giggling had that predatory tone. She can't really help herself—when she sees a desirable man she exudes sex appeal from her pores—but I vowed to keep a close eye on her.

I was pretty much sick of the whole scene and had decided to walk the four miles home when Josh finally sidled up to my chair and smiled. "Hi."

I responded by leaning into him and pleading, "Get me out of here!" I grabbed my coat, signaled to my mother that we were leaving, and headed out back to his car. I think we managed to slip out the back door relatively unnoticed. I directed Josh to my favorite Mexican dive, a shabby former tavern east of town. The margaritas there are all about tequila. Blenders, plastic mermaids, and sissy paper umbrellas aren't even a consideration with this crowd. Josh ran into a couple of guys he knew from a nearby farm. He joked around with them in perfect Spanish while I vacuumed up my first drink. I don't speak Spanish, but there was no need to translate the messages the sexy bartender, Inez, was sending Josh's way. In all my years of visiting this place, I had never noticed how large her breasts were. Tonight Inez was practically falling out of her blouse as she shamelessly leaned over the bar to touch Josh playfully and bat her huge chocolate-brown eyes.

I sat and drummed my fingers on the table until he got the hint. He brought me another drink and a basket of warm, paper-thin chips with a scoop of chunky guacamole.

"What are you drinking?" I asked. It looked like milk on ice. Gross.

"*Horchata*. I like to think of it as a low-fat milk shake. Basically, it's just rice milk, sugar, and a little cinnamon. I kind of figured I would be the designated driver tonight."

— "That deserves a toast!" I raised my glass and threw back half of my new drink. He looked amused. I didn't bother to explain myself or to justify my drunken behavior. It may sound pathetic to crave a veneer of alcoholic ambivalence, but that was my goal. I desperately wanted some kind of padding to protect myself from the sharp rocks and pointy things flying around my life. More likely, I was craving a little bitterness to offset the overwhelming sweetness and goodwill of my damn family. Whatever the reason, I wanted to dull my overtaxed nervous system just a tiny bit, and whacking myself in the head with a hammer seemed extreme. Tequila with a golden-skinned farmer seemed to be just the ticket.

I admired him for a while as I pretended to look at the menu. Josh was complicated. He seemed solid, self-assured, and capable, but there were a lot of men in my life who fit that description. I took another sip of my drink. I needed to watch myself or I might convince myself, once again, that I had met the man of my dreams. He was an organic farmer with more class than anyone I had ever met. He was a rock. A big rock. I, however, was a shipwreck. I needed to be careful.

By the time I finished my second drink I had deemed myself quite charming and very clever. I told interesting stories and made funny wisecracks. I tossed my hair around a bit. Another drink and I became morose. I rambled on about the restaurant and how my grandfather had started it and how watching my dad touch the ruined furnishings was about the saddest thing I had ever seen. Josh ate his tamales and quietly paid attention. He nodded and asked a few questions. Halfway through my dinner I realized I had lost count of my margaritas and I was feeling no pain at all. I pushed away my plate and looked at Josh through a light haze.

"You know, you are very sweet. Here I am, drinking and talking like some kind of sorority girl, and you're just sitting there, looking adorable and listening to me!" Suddenly he was the most wonderful, kindest, handsomest man I had ever known. He called for the bill. I giggled.

I watched the twinkling streetlights as he drove me home. Again he walked me to the door. He looked at my glossy eyes and smiled a sideways grin. I blinked slowly and played with a few strands of my hair as I debated the best way to invite him in without being too forward. Then I decided, the hell with how it looked. I wanted to see this man naked! I reached for his collar, pulled him close, and gave him a kiss with meaning. He didn't seem too offended.

"You want to come in for a nightcap or something?" I asked in a sultry tone. "I don't think I actually have anything to drink in the house, so you may have to settle for the second option."

He put his arm around my waist and pulled me close. He let me down gently. "Maybe another night. I think maybe you should get some sleep."

I wasn't interested in his excuses. I ran my fingers through his hair, pressed my hips against his, and gave him my most alluring, smoldering look. "I think you're chicken. You're afraid of my brothers, aren't you?" It was a tired old line, but it always worked for me.

Josh responded to the taunt just like I wanted him to, by pressing me into the door and showing me with his hips and mouth and hands just how terrified he was. I had almost lured him inside when my sister pulled up and spoiled the mood. At the sound of her footsteps, he let go of me, stood tall, and blew out a deep breath. Then he took a step back, looked at me as if I had just been beamed here from Mars, and practically ran to his car, shaking his head. Having a man run scared isn't my favorite way to end a date, but it's not as if it's never happened before. Usually they bolt after we have sex, not before. I must be losing my touch.

I thought hard for a minute. Had I absently murmured something inappropriate about love or fresh-baked muffins in the morning? I don't think so, but I had had quite a bit to drink. I scowled at Nina as she pranced through the front door. At least I could blame part of my romantic failure on Nina's bad timing. We went into the house, turned off the lights, and watched Josh from the darkened window.

He was just sitting in his car, staring at the front door with a confused look on his face. It was as though he were slowly awakening from some kind of witchcraft. (I *am* a hell of a kisser!) I knew it wouldn't take him long to get his head around the events of the night. A drunk, miserable woman had attacked him and tried to tempt him with her devilish charm. Luckily he had managed to slip away without harming her delicate virtue. Congratulations to Josh! Three cheers for the Prince Fucking Charmings of the world and their high and mighty code of honor. Never mind that what a lady in distress might just need is a night of uninhibited, sweaty sex! I pounded on the windowsill and shouted, "To hell with the white knights! Bring on the goddamn dragons!"

Nina looked over at me. "Huh?"

I shushed myself with my index finger and waved her off. Then we watched as Josh illuminated the street with his big, gorgeous, smug smile. He drove off into the night, laughing. Nina turned the lights back on and voiced my thoughts exactly. "Phew! That man is *smokin'* hot!" I don't remember anything else.

Chapter Fourteen

I'm not the kind of person who can party all night and not pay for it the next day. I tried to relieve my poisoned system with buckets of water and a handful of vitamins, Advil, and Tums, but I knew that I was just going to have to suffer through the hangover. I brushed my teeth twice to try to get rid of that taste of old dog bed. My pasty face looked as if it needed a belt sander rather than mere exfoliant.

I thought I looked pretty good when I got to Twelfth Street, but when you work with your brothers, "pretty good" is fair game.

"You need some sunglasses or something?" Rocco asked as I winced at the bright kitchen lighting. He gave me a closer look. "Jeez! You look like hell! Why is your face all pink and shiny like that?"

I said nothing, just dropped my bag and poured a cup of coffee. I had eyed the espresso machine but decided it would be too loud. My brothers circled me like wolves to a wounded caribou.

"Hmmmm. Squinty eyes, excessive but carefully applied cosmetics, soft fabrics."

"She's balancing her head on her neck like it might roll to the floor and shatter."

"Yep."

"I think our little girl had a bit too much to drink last night! What do you think, Vince?"

"I'm gonna bet she feels like she's been thrown off a wild horse and dragged through crushed glass. Ah, the good old days."

I didn't actually growl in response, but I considered it. I guess they were feeling beneficent this morning. They left me to suffer in silence after a few feeble taunts. I didn't deserve such charity.

For the next couple of hours I worked on setting up a temporary office. I didn't want to squeeze the staff out of their precious changing room, so I moved some things around in the back storeroom and shoved boxes of files in alongside the olive oil and onions. It wasn't comfortable, but it would do. The physical work cleansed my system a bit. I was considering some breakfast when Rocco hollered for me from out front. Bob was on the phone.

"Josie, honey! My God! I heard about the fire. Is everyone all right? Is there anything I can do?" asked Bob.

"I think we're all fine. We're a little freaked out, but we're fine."

"How did it start? What happened?"

"We can't figure that out. It's weird. They claim it must have been a gas leak, because there was clearly an explosion in the kitchen. But I worked that night and the burners and pilot lights were all working fine. There was no gas smell or whine like there can be when the jets are clogged. I talked with the utility company, and they told me that gas fires are really rare. I guess the gas is lighter than air, so it rises and dissipates really quickly. There is a narrow window of temperatures where it becomes combustible."

"So are they blaming the equipment, or claiming that it was negligence on your part?"

"Oh, no. The gas company is actually being sweet as pie. They double-billed us last month, and I gave them hell for it. Now our restaurant blows up and the fire marshal is pointing his finger in their direction. I swear, they would bring me warm cookies before bedtime if I asked them. They don't want a bunch of bad publicity."

We chatted a bit more about the plans my family had made and how everyone was dealing with the accident. Then he said, "Do you think you can get away by three? I've got something special planned for you at the club. Then maybe we can grab a bite."

I agreed, then hung up the phone. I was figuring out how to run an extension into the storeroom when Archie and my parents appeared. They looked very serious. Dad spoke first. "Can we talk to you for a minute? We've got a bit of news about the fire."

"Sure! What's up?"

Dad said, "Let's sit down in the bar and get comfortable. This isn't anything to discuss standing around in the storage room."

Eek. That didn't sound good. I poured out a round of coffee and ice water and met them at a window table. Archie began.

"I don't suppose it will surprise you to hear that the fire marshal thinks it was arson. There were signs of a propellant other than natural gas in the kitchen."

I was almost relieved. "I bet if they really look close they can find something to connect Tiny Dick to this. I know he isn't stupid enough to leave a business card on the ground or anything. But we can always hope, huh? God, I hope we nail him!"

They all exchanged glances. Then Mom patted my hands. "Honey, it's not that simple. Actually, it's all just really, really messy right now." Her eyes filled with tears. Dad fidgeted in his seat and looked out the window. Archie got to the point.

"Jo, they think you started the fire."

"What?"

"The fire was clearly arson. There was no sign of forced entry, and you were cooking that night," said Archie.

"You must be joking!"

"Did you recently make any changes in your insurance policy?"

I was stunned. "Well, yeah. I did just a few days ago. I figured with all the craziness around here it wouldn't hurt to be extra careful."

"The insurance company doesn't like it. You asked your agent a lot of suspicious questions but wouldn't answer his queries. You spontaneously doubled your policies after years of refusing extra coverage. You volunteered to work that night even though there was a line cook willing to fill in. You were the last to leave. The office computer and vital records were virtually untouched by the fire, and it looks as though the arsonist entered the premises with a key. The insurance company really, really doesn't like this. They are not ready to press charges, but they are refusing to pay Louie's a dime until a thorough investigation is done."

I was too astonished to speak. Dad got up and started storming around. "This is just so much bullshit!"

When Dad is angry enough to swear it's a good idea to duck and cover. "We've been paying those damn agents a fortune for years, and when we finally need their help, they accuse my daughter of burning the place down. Goddammit!" He looked around for something to break or throw, but I guess it occurred to him that enough damage had been done recently. He gathered his composure.

"You were right, Jo. It's that asshole Tiny Dick. I knew we would have to pay for what happened the other night, but this . . . this is just too much." Dad looked broken.

I tried to lighten things up a little. "Well, I just hope I get a blue jumpsuit in prison. Horizontal stripes always make me look hippy." I was the only one laughing.

"You will not go to prison, Jo," declared Mom. "I swear on my dead mother's grave that my beautiful, intelligent child will *not* go to jail for a crime she did not commit. That restaurant belongs to us, not the insurers. And they will never see another penny from me, or anyone who ever ate at Louie's Italian Restaurant, if I have anything to say about it. I will pave that land over myself before I let them entertain such a ridiculous idea all for a stupid check. I'll go on *60 Minutes* or *Dateline*! By God, those insurers will rue the day they took on a Cerbone. I'll gather every spaghetti-lovin' mother in this damn state. No, in the whole damn country! That's what I'll do." When Bella got that look on her face, she meant business. She'd have Dan Rather or Diane Sawyer on the phone within the hour.

Dad nodded vigorously in agreement. "She's right! I'll start talking to folks right now and tell them to change their insurance policies to another company. I'll call the papers. This is ridiculous!"

"No, no. Hold on a minute," said Archie. "Let's not blow this thing out of proportion. They haven't made any formal charges. Jo isn't going to jail just yet."

I agreed. "Hey! Don't make this into a big deal. You've got enough to worry about right now. You don't need to start a national campaign on my behalf. I shouldn't have been so spontaneous about increasing the policies. When I think of the conversation our agent and I had, I have to admit it did sound kind of strange. It sucks that this is going to delay any rebuilding. But I didn't do it! You know that, and the insurance company will figure it out soon enough." I sounded good, but the more I thought about it, the more I realized how bad things must have looked.

Archie nodded. "I'll talk to the company again and try to

set them straight. And I'll fill them in on the activities of the night before. But if they're hell-bent on proving this was arson, and Jo doesn't mind the slander, let's let them dig around for a while. They might turn up some useful information."

Mom looked skeptical. "I don't want people thinking that Jo is some kind of criminal."

Dad added what he meant as a bit of comfort: "Let's face it. Anyone who knows Jo would never believe this. She's the levelheaded, responsible one. Sure, she's got a temper, but she could never do something like this. It's not in her nature." Mom and Archie nodded in agreement. I was sort of disappointed. I kind of liked being thought of as an outlaw. Our meeting broke up with lots of hugs and caring smiles.

I just sat and pondered my life for a moment. It was ugly. I felt like a kitchen towel at the end of a long shift—limp, stinking, and overused. Every metaphorical thread of my being was saturated with the day's shit.

Last night talking to Josh made me feel better, so I thought I would try it again. I dialed his number, half expecting to get the answering machine, and was surprised when a young woman answered.

I stammered, "Hi. Uh, I'm looking for Josh."

"Josh?" She yawned. "Oh, he's outside somewhere. Do you want me to go get him?" She mumbled something about having to comb her hair and find her shoes. I didn't like the sound of this.

"Just tell him . . . No, never mind. I guess I'll call him later." I slammed down the phone. That son of a bitch—abandoning me on my doorstep to hook up with some chickie closer to home.

The walls started closing in on me. I needed some fresh air. I needed to walk. I told my brothers I'd be gone for the rest of the day and I drove to the mountains. I laced up my boots and started up my favorite trail. I hiked fast, with my attention focused on the mechanics of each step. There were still patches of frost in the shady spots, and the spring air was brisk so there weren't a lot of hikers today. I made it to my favorite rock overlooking a tiny alpine lake in record time, just under two hours.

At the top I took a few minutes to catch my breath, drink some water, and appreciate the view. I looked purposefully at each and every tree. I listened to the birds and watched the squirrels. Then I focused my attention inside. I listened to my pounding heart, felt the blood running through my veins and the oxygen scouring my system clean. I watched as my sweat turned to steam in the cool air.

A personal problem becomes smoke and dust when it is held up and viewed in the sunlight and grandeur of the natural world. The human body, *my* body, is a miracle of cells and synapses. That's real. That's what really matters. The bastards of the world can plague my thoughts and complicate my life, but they can't get inside and mess with the bits that really matter. I climbed to the rocky peak and swung my arms up into the air. Then I let loose a primal scream that rippled the water in its intensity. The world made sense again.

I jogged back to the car and made it to Bob's gym just before three. I had to sit in his office for twenty minutes while he finished up some calls. Then he held out his arms.

"C'mere, sweetie. Let me give you a hug." He wrapped me in his arms, squashed my face into his chest, and started rocking me from side to side. "I'm so sorry about the fire, babe. You must be a wreck. I know how much that restaurant meant to you. All that history, burned to the ground. It's a crying shame." We rocked in silence for a few seconds.

"If there is anything I can do, anything at all, you just let me know. You need some money, a shoulder to cry on, anything, you just come to me. I'm always here for you, Pussycat. You know that, right?" He held my face in his hands and helped me nod up and down, then tenderly kissed me on the forehead.

It was all the sweetness I could stand. I backed up a step. "I'm sorry, there must be some mistake. I came here to see Bob. He's not exactly what you would call a sensitive guy, but he's handsome as hell and great in the sack. Have you seen him anywhere?" Bob pretended to be hurt, but I didn't fall for it. A few minutes of tender sentimentality were all he could usually manage, and that was in a good year. He threw his arm around my neck and stuck his tongue in my ear. That was my Bob!

"Your dad came by earlier. He looked kind of tired but he sounded okay. You should have seen the crowd that gathered around him at the juice bar." Dad must have loved that.

"I made sure he had an extra-long session with Randy. He came out of the massage room looking like a jellyfish."

"So do I get a massage too? Is that my surprise?"

"Not exactly." He led me toward the therapy pool. "I've been looking into this new Watsu water treatment. And you get to be the first to try it out."

I frowned. I didn't want to be an experiment. I immediately pictured myself in some kind of tank being pummeled by water jets or sprayed down with a fire hose by a masochistic fräulein from Baden-Baden.

"Do I have to do anything? I kind of wanted to turn off my brain and just disappear from the world for a while."

Bob chucked me lightly on the chin. "You'll like this, sweetie, I promise." He sent me off to the locker room to meet with Ty, my Watsu therapist.

Ty was petite but obviously strong. She handed me a nose plug. I didn't like the look of this. When she explained that Watsu was formed by combining water and ancient shiatsu massage, I perked up a bit. She led me into the private therapy pool, dimmed the lights slightly, and turned on some very calming, tinkling music. Okay, so far, so good. We got into the shallow end of the pool together and she became my new best friend. She tipped me onto my back and told me to close my eyes. She carefully supported my head and body. I was instantly weightless and carefree and could only hear the sound of my own breathing and the caress of the water. As I floated on my back she stretched and manipulated my arms, spine, and hips. I was barely aware of her touch as she swooshed me around the warm pool until she would pinpoint a tight spot and release the stress with a gentle motion. Ty made my body feel as fluid as the water I was floating in. I was no longer a land mammal. I belonged in the sea. After an hour of this bliss I opened my eyes and saw Bob standing on the edge of the pool watching me adoringly.

"I'm sorry, Bob. We have to break up. I am hopelessly in love with Ty, and I am never stepping on dry land again. Can you arrange to have my computer and meals sent here?"

"I thought you might like this, but I'm afraid Ty is already married. And you can only stay in the pool if you are willing explain to Mrs. Connors why her Seniors Active Aquatics group can't have their scheduled class in fifteen minutes."

I groaned.

Bob made a sympathetic noise. "Cassie has an opening. Why don't you dry off and visit her for a few minutes while I finish up. Then we can go have some dinner."

I turned to Ty and thanked her for changing my life forever.

"You know, if it doesn't work out between you and your husband, I'm a great cook." She humored me, but I had the distinct feeling that most of her clients swore their everlasting devotion to her. She must average one or two proposals a day. Maybe I should seriously think about changing careers.

I didn't bother to put on any clothes. I wore my robe and padded barefoot into the salon. I plopped down in Cassie's chair. She berated me for not wearing a swim cap, then remembered the fire and rewarded my bad behavior by running warm conditioner through my hair and giving me a thorough scalp massage. Then she wrapped my head in plastic, handed me the newest *Cosmo* sex quiz, and arranged me under a dryer. When my follicles were thoroughly conditioned, Cassie trimmed a few scraggly ends and made my hair do pretty wavy things that I could never manage at home. Cyndi, the cosmetologist, insisted on doing my makeup. She promised to keep it looking really natural, so I gave in. When they were finished with me I looked fabulous. I was clean, relaxed, and positively glowing when Bob came to get me.

"Wow!" he exclaimed. "I think we'll have to cancel our dinner plans! I just want to walk around the gym with you on my arm and show everyone what a truly beautiful girlfriend I have."

"No way, buddy! I'm starving, and unless you've started serving something with a good amount of grease in that juice bar of yours, we are going out."

He shook his head in mock frustration, and we left for dinner. We went to a sweet French bistro, then finished the night sipping herbal tea and watching the view from his waterfront condo. He agreed that in order to fully release the day's tension I might need some very special attention in bed. He got everything right that night, and I slept like the dead, curled up beside Bob in his big, comfy bed.

Chapter Fifteen

The rest of the week was boring. I sat in my tiny corner of the storage room, filled out forms, made calls, and spent a lot of time on the Internet constructing fantasy vacations. I had just created a trip to the beaches of Madagascar in search of fresh cloves and nutmeg when Vince came in with another sample. The day after the fire he had started cooking like some kind of mad scientist. He was never seen without an oil-spotted notebook and a pencil tucked behind his ear. He mumbled and muttered over his concoctions, dishes, and scales.

The first few batches of mozzarella were rubbery and flavorless or a grainy ooze, but then he found a new source for the cheese culture and some good fresh cream. The subsequent batches were divine. He bought fresh pork bellies and trimmed, seasoned, and salted them; then he rolled them to make long logs of pancetta to hang from the vents in the walk-in to cure. He tested spice mixtures for fresh Italian sausage and would run in with assorted fried crumbles for me to compare. He was determined to create a unique, natural bread starter, so there were sticky bowls of goo tucked in warm corners. He had stirred organic raisins into a slurry of hard wheat flour in the hopes that any residual wild yeast would feel right at home and begin bubbling and brewing. I sincerely hoped the health inspectors would understand if they chose to stop by this week, but I'm a worrier. It was all perfectly safe, just not especially attractive.

Nina came into the storeroom with a serious look on her face and asked, "Have you tried some of the stuff that Vince is making?"

"Yeah, it's great!"

"It's amazing, but how are we going to serve it?"

"What do you mean? We'll just do what we always do. He'll add a few items to the menu and maybe make up some great new specials."

"But that will never work. Moving things over here is already sending the regulars into a tizzy, and the Twelfth Street menu has some pretty loyal fans too. Who's going to order marinated octopus salad when they have their hearts set on seafood cannelloni?"

It was a good question. Louie's was popular because we were consistent. A successful restaurant needs repeat business, and that only happens when people can come back to enjoy their favorites. Some might get a little crazy and try an interesting special now and then, but Louie's pasta is comfort food, and people expect it to taste just like they remember each time. Consistency seems simple enough, but it is actually one of the hardest achievements for a small restaurant. In fact it is virtually impossible. Products change, cooks change, tastes change. If you dumb things down and follow exacting formulas and procedures, you wind up with a bored kitchen crew, and quality inevitably suffers. If you give the staff too much freedom you can end up with horrors such as "Tuscan Tacos" offered as the nightly special, and purveyors who deliver jars of "beef-flavored bouillon paste" instead of ingredients for fresh soup stock. It's a fine line.

The battles between Big and Little Louie about the menu

are infamous. Big Louie wanted everything to taste like his mother's good cooking. He was never willing to fudge on quality, and he had a very exacting palate. Little Louie will always admit that he was more interested in finances than the food. He had a taste for money and knew it came easy if you bought cheap goods. Mom says that the fights wouldn't end until Grandpa threw saucepans at his son to chase him out of the kitchen. The end result of these battles was that Little Louie became a genius at manipulating prices. He's a master at gauging exactly how much our customers are willing to pay. Big Louie finally drilled into him the idea that skimping on quality is no way to succeed in the restaurant world.

"So what should we do? Tell Vince to stop making such great food?" I asked.

"There's only one thing I think we can do," Nina replied. "We have to open another restaurant. We have to open Vince's Italian Delicatessen."

We just looked at each other. I think Nina was a little stunned by her stroke of genius. I know I was. I had been focused on avoiding bankruptcy and staying out of jail. Nina was looking at this crisis as the perfect opportunity to expand.

"It doesn't have to be a big space, but we'll need some special equipment for curing the meats and making cheese," she went on. "If we could get a good oven, we could start making our own rustic breads. One good deli case could hold salads and marinated vegetables. We'll need a few tables for people to have sandwiches and espresso. It will give us a chance to finally expand the dessert menu. The bakers can make those killer semolina cookies, and the Delmonicos and Steins won't have to special-order the cannoli anymore."

It made a lot of sense. "Have you talked to Vince about it?" I asked.

"Not yet. I thought I'd run it by you first, in case you thought it was a stupid idea."

"Well, I think you're brilliant! Go get Vince, and let's see what he thinks."

Vince was elated. He too had been trying to figure out how to incorporate his new recipes without upsetting the balance of the restaurant. The deli idea was perfect. Vince and Nina started bouncing ideas off each other at light speed. I directed Nina to some Web sites that clearly described how to write a proper business plan. She needed to get some of these ideas down on paper.

Chapter Sixteen

Josh called. He had left a message earlier in the week explaining that he was leaving town for a few days and would call when he returned, but I figured he was just avoiding me. I had invented all sorts of scenarios to explain the barefooted temptress I spoke to on the phone the other day, and decided that the only possible explanation was that she was a tramp—a late-night booty call.

There was no way she was his cleaning lady. Or, if she was, she was terrible at her work. I had seen the state of his house. If she were a farm employee, why would she have to comb her hair and put on shoes before finding Josh? If she were professional office help, wouldn't she have a more polished phone manner?

The only answer was that I had made a fool of myself on our date the other night. I got him all worked up and he had found some easy way to release his pent-up sexual energy. I had three horny brothers; I knew how men thought!

Maybe he was right to put some distance between himself and the drunk floozy. It was probably best for me to just forget him.

Imagine my surprise when I picked up the phone and

heard Josh ask, "You feel like going on a road trip this week-end, Jo? I've got to pick up a few things east of the mountains, and I thought maybe you might like the trip. Whaddaya think?"

I couldn't think of anything I would enjoy more, but I wasn't exactly sure of his intentions. I managed to sound non-committal, saying, "The whole weekend? Or just a day trip?"

"Oh! Just for the day. This is delicate cargo and I need to get it home quickly. You want to meet me here Saturday morning?"

I was definitely interested in getting out of town for a day, especially if there was even the smallest possibility of driving his car on the open road.

"I'll be there. And I'll bring lunch."

Saturday morning was beautiful, and since I figured that it was pointless to look sexy, I wore a comfy Earth Mother dress. I pulled my hair back and pinned a cute straw hat in place so I wouldn't look like Roseanne Roseannadanna after a ride in the convertible. As promised, I had packed a picnic lunch. I snagged a few of Vince's better experiments and added a loaf of crunchy bread.

When I pulled up to the farm, Mica yipped with excite-ment and Joshua looked almost as thrilled. He was clearly ex-cited about the trip. I tried to hide my disappointment when I discovered that we were taking a shiny new truck instead of the Austin Healy, but there was a horse trailer hooked onto the back, and that piqued my curiosity.

"We're picking up a horse?" I asked.

Josh just smiled. "I think I'll leave you in suspense."

"How about twenty questions? Clearly your precious cargo is not vegetable or mineral, so it must be animal. A cow? Goats! You're getting dairy goats so Vince can start making chèvre!"

"Nope. And I'm not playing along. You are just going to

have to wait and see." I tried my utterly adorable pouty face on him. It always worked on Grandpa, and sometimes Dad, but Josh just laughed and opened the truck door for me.

The dog jumped in before me and gave me a very dirty look. Josh hollered at her, but she wouldn't budge. I asked him to step aside and give me a crack at the mutt. I scratched her nose and we talked it out girl to girl. "It's okay, Mica. I know the rules. You're the dominant female around here. I'm just here for the ride." Her ears relaxed and she cocked her eyebrows. "But do you suppose you could skooch over a bit so I could at least have the window? Or are you expecting me to ride in the back?" The wiry pooch was a sucker for an ear rub, so she relented. An hour and a half into the drive Mica had fallen asleep with her head in my lap. I had won her affections.

Josh and I were pretty quiet during most of the drive. It was a comfortable silence. We were both hypnotized by the spring colors and the grandeur of the North Cascades. After a couple of hours, he handed me a crumpled yellow sheet of paper and I did my best to decipher his hastily scratched-out rural route codes and arrows. Finally we pulled up to the Cozy Corner Camelid Farm and were greeted by about a dozen curious llamas.

"A llama? You're buying a llama?" I asked incredulously. Llamas never made a lot of sense to me. I know they are great pack animals, but I prefer to carry my own pack and not worry about regular water stops and piles of poop on the trail. And to be truthful, llamas never look quite right to me. The first time I had ever seen one was in the Rex Harrison version of *Dr. Doolittle.* From then on I always wanted them to look more like the mystical Pushmepullyou. They never seemed complete without a head on either end.

The friendly owners, David and Gloria Houk, led us to a charming barn where Josh introduced me to his new pets. They were not llamas but alpacas, and any bias I once held against the animals melted instantly away. It took only one look at the young alpacas to fall in love. They were like cartoon sheepdogs with stretched-out necks and teddy-bear noses.

Joshua's eyes were huge and his smile radiant. "Aren't they great? I've been waiting for these little guys to get old enough to travel, but then I figured, if they're so dependent on their mamas, I'll buy the mamas too!"

These silly little shaggy creatures were all big brown eyes, huge lashes, and ridiculously gangly appendages. The alpacas were smaller and cuter than the llamas. Little Hester was almost pure white. The other, Pino, was a warm caramel tone. The mothers were similar but looked Rastafarian—they were covered in long, narrow dreadlocks.

"I always swore that when I had enough room I would raise alpacas," Josh said. "I loved to watch the grazing herds in Peru. We would go camping in the mountains and run into them. I was really little, but I remember lying in the tent, watching the rolling fog and listening to the whistling and humming sounds they would make. There are still lots of herdsmen in the mountaintops of the Andes. Some of them claim to be descendants of the Incan alpaca breeders. And alpacas were domesticated before the pyramids were built, so we're talking about five thousand years of tradition."

I had no idea.

"I would love to have a vicuña, but the Spanish conquistadors ravaged the mountain herds for meat. Vicuñas are still endangered. Besides, there is a more practical side to raising alpacas. They are cheap to take care of and you can get top dollar for their wool if it's of a superior grade. My mother has become a bit of a knitting fanatic. I can't wait to send her the fleece from my own herd." His enthusiasm was contagious.

The little caramel-colored alpaca got cocky and nuzzled my hand. Then he jumped around the pen, spinning and kicking like a clown.

"Pino is a handful!" said the owner. "He's got spunk. Hester, the white one, is shy at first, but she's a real sweetie. I tell ya, we've got us plenty of young ones around here, but my daughter is gonna miss her the most. If I had any idea how perfect her wool was going to be, I would never have sold her to you for the price I did. People are going to be knocking down your door to buy fleece that color and texture."

Joshua smiled and stroked the grown alpacas on their long necks. Eventually we were able to tear our eyes from the animals and set up the horse trailer so they would be comfortable for the long drive home. Mica sniffed and nipped at the legs of a mother, but a quick kick taught her some manners. Josh wanted the animals to get used to the feel of the trailer before he started driving, so we invited the Houk family to join us in a picnic. They refused until we agreed to let them contribute. They added some fresh asparagus, a dozen deviled eggs, and a pitcher of lemonade.

Three kids came running at the ringing of an old school bell. We gathered and ate at a charming wooden table under a huge oak tree. There was talk of alpaca care and fleece markets. Josh told stories of the Andes and the elaborate fabrics and costumes llamas wore at festivals. He cracked the young boys up with an imitation of an old animal he once knew that would spit at a cranky groundskeeper. After lunch, we checked that the alpacas had settled into their stalls and decided it was time to head home. The Houks' daughter, a small girl with straight blond hair and very sad eyes, handed Josh a piece of paper. It was a card for Hester with a big heart drawn on the front and a little stick-figure girl with a frown on the inside saying, "Good-bye, from Ashley." Josh looked carefully at the words and the drawings. Then he knelt down to speak to little Ashley.

"Ashley, I know Hester is going to miss you. And I think this card will really help her. I have a big farm, just like you do, with lots of grass and trees and a beautiful view of the mountains. I bought the land because it kind of reminds me of the mountains of Peru, where I grew up and first saw alpacas, but I could really use your help. Can you tell me a few things about Hester? Maybe some of her favorite things?"

The little girl was quiet. And then she mumbled incoherently into her sweatshirt.

"What was that?" asked Josh.

She looked up and repeated: "She likes to eat her hay just a few pieces at a time. She's not a pig like Pino. She likes it if you hold just a couple pieces for her." Josh nodded enthusiastically. "And she doesn't much like it if you touch her face. But she likes it okay if you scratch right here, on her chin."

"Okay! If I give you my address, do you suppose you could draw another one of these cards and send it to her, maybe in the next few days? And then as often as you feel like she might need one? So she knows that you're still thinking of her?"

Ashley nodded so hard I thought her neck would snap. Josh wrote down his address and gave it to the little girl. She was finally smiling. She chased the truck down the driveway, waving and blowing kisses.

The rest of the day was entirely focused on the comfort and safety of the livestock. We stopped about a dozen times to check on how they were traveling. Josh had read that alpacas like clean water, so we freshened their trough twice during the ride. When we got back to the farm we carefully led them into their new pasture. They were nervous on the leads, but calmed down pretty quickly. Josh had set up a couple of divided acres of lush grass. There was a lean-to to protect them from wind and rain, and a breezy paddock near the stream for fresh air and shade in the summer. If it came with plumbing and a coffee machine, I might have moved in myself. We stood by the fence watching them with silly grins on our faces until we finally realized it was too dark to see them clearly.

"Yikes! Where did the day go? I'd better get going," I said, after realizing what time it was.

"Really? Do you want some dinner or something?" He was kind to ask, but it was clear that we were both exhausted.

"I'm still stuffed from lunch. I gotta go, but you'd better call and give me regular updates on their progress!"

"Well, of course! And they will expect you to come visit. You are officially Auntie Jo now."

I gasped. "Such responsibility! Does that mean I have to carry alpaca cookies in my pockets forevermore? Good God, where do I find alpaca cookies?"

"Well, we don't want them too spoiled—maybe just a handful of grain now and then." He put his arm around me and gently rubbed my shoulder. My whole body buzzed with electricity. He walked me to my car.

"I'm glad you came. It was fun to share this with someone."

When we reached my car I gave him a friendly peck on the cheek and rather abruptly turned to leave. I wanted to maintain at least a little self-control after the boozy and emotional makeout scene I had initiated before. Josh didn't let me go so easily. He stepped close, blocking my exit. I looked at his face. His eyes had gone all warm and yummy. We kissed, tenderly at first, then hungrily. He leaned into me. One arm slid around my waist to warm my lower back; his other hand caressed my neck. I was on fire.

I ran my hands over his strong chest, gradually exploring his rock-hard belly and waist. Then I tucked my hands in the back pockets of his jeans. He was lean and strong from working in the outdoors. I inspected the laugh lines at his eyes and the angles of his jaw. I brushed back his hair. He had perfect ears. I wanted to nibble them.

He punctuated his talk with tiny kisses. "My alpacas will need lots of visits. Maybe even overnight care at times."

"Well, I've always been an animal lover. I'll do whatever it takes to make sure those babies are comfortable."

He slowly ran his hands up and down my sides. I could feel the strength of his fingers through the flimsy fabric of my sundress. I involuntarily shivered with excitement. He nuzzled my hair, ear, cheek. We were making out in the driveway like teenagers, but there was no mistaking that he was all man. It was time to move this party indoors or stop it altogether.

I wanted desperately to get all hot and sweaty with this guy, but I knew from experience that hormones affected my sensibilities like alcohol or pot. In the throes of passion I tend to vow my eternal love to a penis I might use and abuse, with little regard for the man connected to it. I'm trying to kick that habit. And I hadn't completely forgotten how he ran off the other night into the arms of a sweet young answering service.

My brain told me to back off. All this bucolic charm was a fantasy. My life presently involved multiple lawsuits and accusations of firebombing the family business. I didn't need to complicate things. A night of great sex in an old farmhouse with an incredibly hot and intriguing man couldn't be real. This must be some kind of mirage for my deranged and desperate soul. With my luck, I would wake up the next morning and be faced with his distraught wife and bevy of wailing kids. A couple of times today he looked as though he wanted to say something, but he held back. Maybe Josh was a South American drug lord! He traveled a lot, he delegated most of the farm duties to Murakame, and he didn't seem worried about money. DEA agents were probably watching our every move right now! I pulled away and searched the underbrush for nightscopes as I said, "I thought this was going to be a day trip. I didn't bring my overnight gear."

He looked into my eyes. "It can be whatever you want it to be."

My insides started melting. This man made me crazy! I wrapped my arms around his neck, kissed him one last time, then tore myself away to drive home. I almost turned around twice. I even pulled over at one point and walked in circles around my car. I didn't need to complicate my life any more right now. If he was as perfect as I imagined, there was no need to hurry. I would save the fun for a night when I had a little more energy and didn't smell like a barnyard.

Chapter Seventeen

I didn't get much sleep that night no matter how many alpacas I counted. Before dawn I gave up all hope of rest and
went into the studio to draw. I finished drawing the last of the
HVAC parts for Tony; then I doodled a few lusty nymphs
frolicking in fireweed and clover. It was Sunday, but I was
still tempted to go into the restaurant. I had never really considered myself a workaholic, but I couldn't seem to stay away
these days. I wanted everything perfectly organized so we
could effortlessly get to Mindy's records and whatever we
might need for the interrogation by the insurance company.
Dolfe still hadn't contacted us about what he planned to do
about the hot soup incident, but I was convinced he wasn't
through with us. The fire was merely a tantrum or warning.
As I was creating a mental list of jobs to be done, the phone
rang. It was Vince.

"I can't believe our luck! Did you see the paper? I'm on
my way over right now!" And then he hung up.

I stared at the phone receiver for a minute. Then I went to
the front porch and picked up the thick paper. I didn't see
anything out of the ordinary. There were big headlines of yesterday's news and a lot of glossy flyers. As a rule I just read

the comics and the Lifestyle section on Sundays. Sometimes, when I feel really smart or have too much coffee, I'll attempt the crossword puzzle. I scanned the doom-laden headlines again. *Standoff in the Middle East, Congress Battles over Budget Talks, Victim of Dog Mauling Mourned, Child Seats Recalled.* My eye caught a piece about the new insurance commissioner on page five, and I was reading it for clues when Vince roared up on his motorcycle.

"Can you believe it? Anna knows the guy who shot those photos. She says we can probably get the whole roll! She's on the phone with him right now."

I looked down at the article. There was a head shot of the new insurance boss, but that couldn't be what he was talking about. Vince could tell by my confusion that I wasn't keeping up. He grabbed the paper from my hands, turned to the front page, and pointed.

"There, right there! Just behind the kid in the stupid hat. That's Mindy!"

I inspected the grainy photo. It *did* look like Mindy. She was in a cluster of scraggly youths wearing black armbands and looking miserable. I still didn't really understand.

"Didn't you hear about Porkchop? He was killed a couple of days ago. There's been a huge candlelight vigil at the Seattle Center the last few days. Mindy went to pay her respects and ended up in the newspaper. There's no way she can sue us now," said Vince. He filled me in on the details.

Porkchop was the lead singer of Bite the Dog, Mindy's all-time favorite metal band. According to the newspapers, the "accident" happened while the band was working on their newest album cover. *Bite This!* was due to be released in a few months. The band posed in an expensive California studio that was set up to look like a dogfight pit. They were wearing complicated leather restraints and baring their teeth.

The early shots went well. At lunchtime the band and

crew guzzled and snorted a lot of their meal. They started brainstorming on how to spice up the photo. Some phone calls were made and the photographer's assistant added some filters and tweaked the lighting for more drama. Nobody seemed to notice when Porkchop disappeared. Eventually he showed up in position with a chain of fresh sausages around his neck. Everyone had a good laugh. A few minutes later two young men from a nearby grocery walked in pushing wheelbarrows. They dumped globs of flesh-covered bones and chunks of bloody meat into the pit. The band went wild, rolling in the stuff and grabbing for the best pieces to pose with. The photographer was intently shooting to catch the carnage.

It was simply a case of bad timing that this was the particular moment when the dog handler arrived. As a rule, the pit bulls and the mastiff were very sweet and well behaved, but there is only so much a dog can take. Stoned, growling rock stars covered in meat were just too much. The handler was knocked unconscious and Porkchop was dead within minutes. The drummer and bassist would be hospitalized for weeks. If the Rock and Roll Hall of Fame didn't document this act for posterity, it would always be remembered in the Darwin Awards. Personally, my emotions waffled back and forth from horror to hysterics.

What mattered to us was the vigil. Hundreds of distraught heavy-metal fans gathered at the Seattle Center International Fountain to console each other and mourn the passing of their idol. They wore dog collars, leashes, sometimes fangs. They brought photos and CDs. They lit candles . . . thousands and thousands of candles. And in the center of it all, near the hastily prepared altar to Porkchop, sat Mindy Monahan weeping with her brethren. Her misery was so genuine it caught the eye of a photographer. And there she was on the front page, nestled in a sea of candle flames nearly three months after she claimed to be unable to breathe anywhere near a lit wick.

We tried to get hold of Archie, but he was unavailable. We knew we should wait, but we couldn't contain our excitement. Vince called Mindy and asked her if she was feeling well enough for some company. Having Vince make the call was a dirty little trick. Mindy would eat soap if Vince asked her to.

We swung by a convenience store and picked up a couple of extra papers. Mindy wasn't much for the news. When we arrived at the scratched and dirty door of her apartment, we were giddy. Vince and I couldn't look at each other. We had to step back and take deep breaths and pinch each other to prevent new outbreaks of inappropriate giggling. Mindy answered right away. She was wearing high heels and her hair was all done up. The air around her rippled as the first layer of her sweet, sickly perfume evaporated. Just another Sunday morning at home for Mindy, I guess. The little electric gadget around her neck to purify her breathing space was blinking and humming loudly. The room was full of houseplants, all in various stages of wilted agony. They were doing their best to try to clean the air, but the place still reeked of burned coffee and cat pee.

She licked her lips. "Vince! I'm so glad you called. I hope this medical condition of mine doesn't mean we can't be friends. I've missed you!"

Oh, barf.

She finally noticed I was there and was forced to acknowledge me. "Oh, hey, Jo. I wasn't really expecting you too." She choked out a few coughs and did up another button on her blouse. She invited us in. "I heard about the fire. That really sucks, huh? But at least you get some time off! What's up?"

"We came to check on your health, Mindy. How are you feeling?" Vince asked.

She directed him to her best chair, then perched on the

arm and began mauling a leaf on a nearby philodendron. Vince just sat and grinned stupidly my way. I shoved aside piles of laundry and old magazines and then sank into the grubby leather couch. It felt like the cushions had been stuffed with dryer lint and Cheerios.

Mindy cooed, "You are just the sweetest thing, Vince! I have to tell you, it hasn't been easy. Thank goodness I found Dr. Love. He's a miracle worker! He has taught me how to breathe again." She stopped talking for a moment and demonstrated, using her hands to illustrate her new skills at inhaling and exhaling. "I go to breathing classes three times a week now. You should join me, Vince. You just don't know how bad things are until someone shows you."

Vince had a look that I recognized. I could tell he was going to mercilessly toy with her like a cat with a string. So I spoke up. "We heard about the mauling."

Vince bowed his head and lowered his voice. "It's so sad about Porkchop."

Mindy gasped a bit, then covered her mouth and started sniffling.

"Oh, God! I still can't believe he's dead! I don't know what I'm going to do."

"You go to the vigil?" I asked.

"Of course I did! I loved him! I couldn't let Porkchop be buried without saying good-bye."

I held the newspaper up and she snatched it from me. She was thrilled. There she was, on the front page, proving to everyone that she was indeed Porkchop's biggest fan. Her lips moved as she worked on the text.

"Did you take any candles?" I asked.

"Of course! Everyone had . . ." She looked up from the paper in alarm. She had finally realized her dilemma. "Uh, no. You know I can't . . . Oh, shit!" She looked again at the photo and then burst into tears.

Vince was in a tough spot. His first instinct was to jump up and do an end-zone victory dance, but even he isn't so heartless as to laugh uncontrollably in the face of tears. He reached up and wrapped a long arm around her shoulder and gave her a pat. Mindy immediately slid into his lap and clamped onto him like a starving squid. She whined through gulping sobs.

"Porkchop is dead! I loved him. I had to do something to honor his life." Vince patted her back. She wiped her nose on his shirt. "And I would do it again! Some things are just more important than money, you know?"

We mumbled a bit in agreement. She was just so pathetic. She looked into Vince's beautiful eyes.

"I knew you would understand. Those stupid lawyers were all wrong about you guys. I mean, Jo, you can be a real bitch, but you really do care about me, don't you?" She grabbed Vince's head and pressed his face against her chest. He squirmed and tried to pull himself free.

I was entertained by his discomfort, so I tried to think of a few more reasons for Mindy to thank Vince. "Of course we care, Mindy! That's why Vince insisted we come. To find out if you're really okay." He glared at me and tried to peel her off, limb by limb, so he might stand up. I had my own challenge, wrestling my way up and out of the carnivorous couch. Mindy just kept talking.

"You know, I only went to see those guys because of their ads. They say you can have a free consultation to find out if you qualify for Labor and Industries or see if the government owes you any money. I had a crappy week in tips and I've been wanting to get a new TV, so I thought I'd check it out. And Dane Hagstrom is so hot! He reminds me of that doctor on *The Loving Life*. You know, the one with the tumor? Anyways, so I go into the office and there he is! The TV lawyer! He is just as gorgeous in real life as on TV. So I turn on the charm, like at the restaurant, you know? And I'm wearing that cute little green dress—the one with the little straps that Bella won't let me wear at work. So Dane and I just start talking. He's not anything like what I thought he would be. I mean, the guy likes to party! Can you believe it?

"It turns out I couldn't get an appointment that day. They were too busy. But Dane makes special arrangements to meet me over drinks that night. We go to this swank club and he buys me real champagne with a cork and he just talks and talks. We did a few lines, and I guess I got a little wasted, 'cause one thing led to another and we ended up getting busy right there on that couch."

Eeew! Yet another reason to hate her furniture.

"Can you imagine? Now when I see him on TV, I think, 'I fucked that guy right here in my own place. Mindy Monahan, you're really going places!' Anyways. Dane calls a couple of days later and tells me I have an appointment with Dr. Love. They send this big car and the next thing you know, they say I could make a million dollars! All because I'm allergic to candles! Who would have guessed? I mean, I used to burn a lot of those scented candles in the jar around here all the time. I love that one that smells just like chocolate-mint ice cream! But I don't do that anymore.

"I promise, I told them I didn't really want to sue you guys, that I only wanted the money I was due from the government. Bella and Louie have always been so nice to me. And you too, Vince." She pressed Vince's hand to her face, then her chest, and ignored his attempts to pull away. "Dane explained how they're really good at this lawsuit stuff. He said that you wouldn't actually have to pay anything. The insurance company would take care of everything. And that's what insurance is for, isn't it?" Vince finally got free, wiped his hands on his jeans, and started for the door. Mindy blocked his way.

"I've been so good too! Dane and Dr. Love both told me to stay away from candles. Even birthday candles, they said, and I couldn't go out 'cause they didn't want me in smoky bars. I've been such a total coach potato lately. To be honest, I'm pretty glad this whole thing's over. The smoke-free bars in this town are *so* lame!" She put her finger in her mouth, as if to gag. Then she got introspective.

"You know, I may have blown my shot at a million bucks by going to Porkchop's memorial, but I was true to myself. You can't say that I don't know what is really important in this world. I mean, it's all about love and loyalty, right, Vince? And I proved to everyone that my love for Porkchop was more important even than money. Besides, now I can go party again!" She did a little bump and grind against Vince's hip.

He pushed her away. "Easy come, easy go, huh, Mindy?" asked Vince. She was clueless as to how her little escapade had troubled our entire family and threatened our business. I think she finally picked up a vibe from Vince that he was irritated.

"I *told* you it wasn't personal. It was just a little scam. Everyone does it! No hard feelings? I mean, I *understand* if you don't want to give me my job back or anything." She looked at me as if it were a possibility. I can't imagine what my expression was, but it seemed to make my opinion clear.

"No, I guess not. That's okay. I met a girl at the vigil who serves cocktails at Sugar's. She doesn't even have to go topless and she brings in loads of tips. I bet she could get me an interview." She shimmied a bit. I managed to get through the front door without attacking her. She was still pawing at Vince, trying to convince him to stay, when something occurred to me.

"Mindy, do you still have the key to Louie's? It won't do much good anymore, since the fire, but I'd kind of like it back."

She shook her head. "I don't have it anymore. I lost my

whole set of keys. It was the wackiest thing! Richard Dolfe called me one night, I think it was even the night of the fire, to go over a few details. I tell you, those guys never stop working! They're really the best! Anyways, we met for a few late drinks and I lost my keys at the bar. I swear, they just disappeared. We must have looked for an hour. He had to hot-wire my car so I could get home. He was good at it too. It's amazing what lawyers learn from their customers. Luckily the apartment manager keeps a spare or I might have had to move in with his boss, Dane Hagstrom, the TV star!"

I took a step toward Mindy. I wanted to shake her until her teeth fell out. Vince sensed trouble and shoved me toward the parking lot.

Chapter Eighteen

I think I called Archie's home number every five minutes until he answered. He had been at a seminar on exotic flowering shrubs and didn't get home until the late afternoon. When he found out about the photographs, he was elated. He drilled me for information and promised to get to work immediately. Meanwhile, Vince's girlfriend, Anna, had contacted the *Seattle Times* photographer. He agreed to overnight a complete set of duplicates to Archie's law firm. In addition to the image in the paper, he was pretty sure he had gotten a few close-ups of Mindy. He remembered her being especially dramatic.

Because I am maybe a little bit of a control freak, I went to the office and parked myself in front of the computer. I outlined all of the details regarding Mindy's case. I tried to remember dates, times, and exact conversations. I found that everything having to do with Mindy Monahan was inextricably tied to Hagstrom and Dolfe, so I included notes on my encounters with the lawyers. I wasn't exactly sure what I was going to do with this information. But I figured it was safer to have a backup in the hard drive rather than depend solely on my muddled mind.

Archie called at about ten that night.

"Jo, can you meet me tomorrow at three? Come to my office. I should have some good news."

Vince and I had agreed to keep quiet. We didn't want to get everyone's hopes up until we had the photos in our hands and a professional assessment from Archie. I stayed away from the restaurant on Monday because I knew I would let something slip. I was completely unable to concentrate on my drawing, so I performed the ideal task for numbing the brain: I cleaned the house. I scrubbed, dusted, polished, vacuumed, ironed, and swept. The house was gleaming and I was exhausted by the time it was time to leave for Archie's office.

Mom and Dad were in the reception area talking to Archie's kind wife. She was sharing her condolences about the fire and asking about plans to rebuild. My parents looked frayed around the edges and seemed relieved to see me.

"Oh, good, you're here. Archie says he has some new information on the lawsuit."

I played it cool.

Archie burst out of a conference room right at three o'clock. He confidently directed his team of associates into action and they scattered with their arms full of manila files and legal pads. His face was flushed with excitement. When he saw us, he did a little jig.

"Hello, hello, Cerbones! Come into my office. I have some great news!" He grabbed me and gave me a spin and kissed my mother on the cheek. His joy was contagious. We followed his dancing form into the warm office like kids chasing a parade. I beamed with pleasure.

He twirled his big leather chair. "Isn't life grand?"

Mom and Dad just looked stunned. "What is it, Archie?"

He looked at me and then at my parents. "Jo! I can't believe you didn't tell them!" He tossed over a file and explained. "Your very clever kids turned me on to some rather damning information this weekend." He winked at me. "I called an emergency meeting with Hagstom and Dolfe. They have agreed that in light of the photographs published in yesterday's newspaper, it would be best not to pursue Mindy Monahan's personal-injury lawsuit." He showed them the newspaper and a full sheet of proofs the photographer had sent. There were at least five clear shots of Mindy meditating over a big gothic candle spewing dark smoke. It was better than I had ever imagined. Archie and I explained about the mauling and the public memorial to Porkchop. Mom was speechless. Dad howled.

"I explained to little Dick and his big pretty friend that Mindy spent nearly twenty-four hours at this event. We have photos taken by a professional photojournalist proving that she was often holding a candle of her own as well as being situated very close to a flaming altar. And there is no shortage of witnesses. We could certainly track down some of the kids in the picture. Surely they would remember if Mindy displayed signs of severe respiratory trouble. Did you note the absence of her personal air purifier or a single fern? I explained that unless they were willing to come up with a way to disprove our findings, we would consider this matter closed.

"Dolfe wouldn't give up. He's convinced that he can beat it. He claims Mindy's tears and misery were due to the candles, but Hagstrom overruled him and hastily dropped everything."

We shouted, "Hooray!" and leaped to our feet to try Archie's little victory dance, but he shushed us.

"No, no, don't start dancing quite yet. I'm not finished. While I was there, I decided to take a moment and discuss the delicate matter of hot soup meeting Mr. Dolfe's tiny . . . oh, I mean *tender* anatomy." We were instantly silenced.

"I know we haven't talked much about this, but I have been doing a little investigating. I figured it would be best to start thinking about a defense even though a suit has not yet been filed." We nodded in agreement. He could do whatever he wanted to at this point.

"Did you know that Doris Doblowski goes to our church? She makes a very nice apple pound cake. It's got a splash of whiskey in it to keep it moist." He looked lost in his recollection.

Dad couldn't take it anymore. "Cut the crap, Archie. What's this all about?"

Archie didn't even flinch. "She might use a little nutmeg too."

My feet tap-danced eagerly under my chair.

"I asked Doris for a few details about the other night, and she told me some very interesting things. Funny, I don't remember you mentioning anything about his undergarments."

"What's your point?" barked Dad.

"During our meeting today, I asked Mr. Dolfe if he had seen a doctor in regard to any burns he might have incurred. I explained that I would need the name of his doctor for our records, photographs of the damage in and around his genitalia, as well as full disclosure of his clothing that evening. Special attention should be given to any . . . um, accoutrements he was wearing that may have offered special protection from the hot liquid."

We were wide-eyed.

"Then I informed him that there were quite a few people willing to testify that they had seen a bit of extra protection in his pants. Of course, nothing could be proven until we went to court, but for his records seven patrons swear they saw . . . let's see." Archie put on his reading glasses and read from the file. "'One pair of very realistic-looking leopard-skin underwear of the thong variety, perhaps with leather or leather-simulated straps. And one boy's tube sock with blue striping, rolled into a sausage shape.'"

"Dick threw me out of his office before I could proceed

with the less substantiated claims. That's where things get really wild. I don't know how people come up with this stuff. One guy swears he saw a hamster jump from a garter belt!" Archie leaned back in his chair with a smug grin on his face. "I can't imagine any man who would be willing to stand up in front of a jury and voluntarily explain why he had so much gear in his trousers. Especially not a rich lawyer who used to be known to his peers as Tiny Dick. I think we can safely say that case will be dropped as well."

Mom jumped up on the coffee table, pulled up her skirt and did a goofy little folk dance while Dad clapped and hooted. Then we tackled Archie and pulled him into our victory scrum. Now, if I could just shake the firebug rap, our troubles would be over.

Chapter Nineteen

I suddenly found myself with too much time on my hands. Rocco and Dad were working with designers and contractors as if there were no delays in the insurance settlement. Bob left for his ski trip. Josh was out of town again, and Nina was buried in her plans for the deli. There was only one thing left for me to do. I packed a bag, told my family I was taking the week off, and left a note for my sister that said it all: *Gone bird-watching.*

As I mentioned before, my fascination with birds is mostly myth. It's a cover for a dark and very selfish secret—I like to run away. It all started one weekend in college. My former roommate's family has this rustic place on a tiny island in the San Juans. It's very remote, accessible only by private boat. There is no phone, no TV. It is a wonderful getaway where you can just kick back, dig clams, and watch the otters, seals, and sea birds. A group of us would go there for long weekends to drink wine, play cribbage, and get some well-deserved rest after exams. But one year I just didn't feel up to it. I wanted to be alone, so I lied. I told my roommate I was going home, and I told my family I was going to watch the birds on the island. Then I just drove away. I spent forty-eight hours with no itinerary, no destination. And for the first time in my life, absolutely no one knew where I was. It was intoxicating.

I will never deny that a close family is a blessing. I was smothered with more love and attention within the first weeks of my birth than some poor souls get in a lifetime. But at times I resent being an involuntary member of a team. I don't always want to be an important link in the Cerbone chain. I want to be selfish, independent, and irresponsible. I want to just be me, not somebody's daughter, not somebody else's sister or girlfriend.

So, once or twice each year, I run away from home. I usually drive, but sometimes I get on a plane or a bus. I rarely know where I'm going. I tell my friends and family that I am headed to that cabin in the islands for some peace and quiet. I tell them I am going bird-watching, and then I am free. Once, I spent an entire week in the art museums of Chicago. At night I read romance novels and ate room-service french fries. I have wandered barefoot on hidden beaches in California, gone on horseback trail rides through the autumn splendor of the Smoky Mountains. Once I just drove around western Montana. I bought some cheap camping gear and lived on minimart corn dogs and powdered sugar doughnuts. I didn't speak to another soul for an entire week. I listened to the swaying trees, boastful chipmunks, and lonesome frogs. I smelled the sap of the trees and clean river water. I walked, I sat, I breathed.

I can't tell anyone because they wouldn't understand. An intelligent, attractive woman just isn't supposed to wander the country alone. What if my car broke down? What if I ran into a homicidal rapist? What if something happened at home and they needed to reach me? If I told them the truth, they would argue with me. If I told them the truth, it would hurt them. And the reality is, I simply don't care.

I'm smart and careful. It's not as if I get drunk at roadside bars and announce that I am a single woman with a wild streak. I keep a low profile. Sometimes I will have a drink or two. Sometimes I get a little chatty and talk to friendly strangers. Once—well, actually twice—I had anonymous (but safe!) sex with a gorgeous cowboy trucker from Texas. Being a morning person, I appreciate a good pancake house more than a hot nightclub. I'm aware of the risks, but sometimes it seems more dangerous for me to stay home.

This time I just headed southeast. I had the whole country in front of me. Once I got onto the freeway I cranked up the music and drove for hours. I could feel the stress melting off me with every mile. I didn't need to worry about stupid waitresses, arsonist attorneys, or out-of-work chefs. I spent the night in Winnemucca, Nevada, and decided I was going to Vegas for sunshine, slot machines, and a smidge of ostentatious hedonism.

I charged a Jacuzzi room at the Monte Carlo, flopped onto the king-size bed, and pondered what to do first. I felt the sun calling to me, so I tied on a bikini and headed for the pool. I found an open lounge chair, ordered a piña colada, and read the newest *People* magazine cover to cover while I broiled. Then I got cleaned up and spent the day shopping. I tried on a lot of jewelry I could never afford, had a pedicure, and ate ice cream for lunch. Then I took a long nap. Do I know how to live or what?

That night I fluffed up my hair, put on a pair of new strappy shoes, and settled in at a five-dollar blackjack table. Jerry and DeeDee, the dealers, took pretty good care of me. He shooed the boozy frat boys off his table when they started getting crude, and she distracted the old, horny conventioneers when they would paw and snort like bulls. I smoked three cigarettes I bummed off a Japanese businessman, and I lost sixty bucks. Not too bad for a couple of hours of great entertainment. I finished my night with a long, bubbly wallow in the tub and an old Cary Grant movie on TV.

The next morning I bought a map. Vegas is fun, but I wasn't about to spend all week there. I was feeling a little too reckless for Vegas. It would be hard on my bank account. I caught myself perusing the high-limit slots looking for one that might pay off the restaurant remodel, and I knew it was time to leave. California didn't draw me, so I just followed the signs in the opposite direction. For a while I thought I had taken a wrong turn and was on the surface of the moon. Eventually I ended up in Page, Arizona. I spent the next few days exploring Lake Powell. Julie, the friendly owner of a cute espresso shop called Sit 'n' Bull, directed me to a fly-fishing outfitter, a great swimming hole, and a barbecue joint full of European backpackers and some old-time fiddlers. They made great pie.

The lake was amazing. It was warm and clear and the smooth rocks and colors made it feel like you were swimming through the Grand Canyon. I found two arrowheads and a turquoise bead on one of my walks. By Thursday I was rested and rejuvenated and it was time to head home.

In Provo, Utah, my purse was stolen. It was a stupid mistake. I was at a gas station. I filled the tank and then ran inside for a diet Coke. I thought my purse was safe. It wasn't even really a purse at all, just a few measly flaps of leather. I had it sort of hidden in the debris of the passenger-seat floor. I was in Utah, for God's sake! This was the home of well-scrubbed Mormons and Brigham Young University. They didn't smoke or drink here, so who would guess they would steal? But my cards, money, and ID were gone along with all of my CDs. I was screwed.

I dug through the seat cushions and found enough change for a cup of bad coffee. I sat in a café and stewed for a while. Then I sucked air and called Tony collect.

"Where the hell are you?" he asked.

"I told you. I'm in Utah. Let me give you the number for this pay phone and you can call me back." I read the numbers slowly to him and hung up. He called back instantly.

His words were harsher than I had expected. "Everybody's been looking for you since yesterday. Mom found the number for your old college friend, and she said she hadn't heard from you in months. Her brother's using the cabin this week. Mom and Nina are convinced you're dead. Dad and Rocco are just stomping around in an undirected storm of testosterone. They keep yelling at each other about nothing. What the hell are you doing in Utah? We all thought you went bird-watching. Are you really okay?" He sounded panicked.

"Fuck!" I banged my head with the receiver. I knew this would happen someday, but why now? "Tony, I'll explain it all to you when I get home, I promise. I'm safe, but I'm kind of stuck. Someone stole my purse and I'm never going to make it home on a single tank of gas. I need some money." I gave him the name and number of a check-cashing chain from the phone book.

"And Tony? Just tell everyone I found a bed-and-breakfast on the islands once I found out the cabin was booked. Please, please?" I pleaded. "I'll drive straight home. Don't breathe a word about this until we talk, okay?"

"Whatever. It doesn't even matter where you are. You just need to get home, *now*. Bob's in the hospital. He might be paralyzed."

Chapter Twenty

Bob was heavily sedated when I got to the hospital, so I had a chance to wash my face, drink yet another cup of coffee, and talk to the doctors. My brain was fuzzy from too many hours of driving, but I got the gist of things. Evidently Bob didn't think skiing a sheer and rocky ledge was exciting enough, so he decided to try snowboarding. Like always, he took to the sport quickly, but his confidence exceeded his ability. He concluded his extreme adventure by attempting a flip, landing on his head, and breaking his neck. I sat by the bed, held his limp hand, and tried to hold back both the fury and the tears.

The doctors were cautiously optimistic. Bob hadn't been able to move his arms or legs since the accident, but he claimed to have some sensation when they pricked his fingers and toes. The MRI had them suspecting a cervical spinal contusion. Best-case scenario, he would be up and moving around, slowly, in a few days. He had a metal "halo" bolted to his skull and shoulders and a complicated container around his neck and torso like a plastic body cast. I wouldn't even let myself consider what life would be like for Bob if he didn't get better. He woke up while I was wiping my eyes.

"Is that you, Pussycat?" he mumbled. He couldn't move his neck to see me, so his eyes looked strained. I stood up and moved to the foot of the bed so he could relax. "Where have you been? I thought maybe you had abandoned me." He moaned.

"Well, now that I have seen you, maybe I will. That thing on your head makes you look like Frankenstein wearing a lamp shade." He smiled weakly.

"God, I'm glad you're here. Everyone has been tiptoeing around me with these sweet, caring smiles glued on their faces. I can't stand the pity. I was an idiot pretending like I was sixteen again, and no one is willing to admit it but me."

"I'll admit it. You're an arrogant asshole and a damn fool. But you are a lucky fool. I'll give you that. The doctors think you'll get better."

He squeezed his eyes shut. I wandered back to his side and rubbed his hand. I felt a flicker and twitch in response. I whooped and called the doctor. It was a great sign and they whisked him away for more tests. It was a couple of hours before we were alone again. "Can I get you anything? You want a drink of water or the TV on?" I asked.

"No, Josie. Thanks. How about if you just keep sitting there? That's all I need."

I spent almost every minute at the hospital over the next few days. Bob seemed to genuinely appreciate my company. I read to him from *Sports Illustrated* and *Men's Health*. We watched a lot of TV. He had been secretly addicted to *The Young and the Restless* for years, and he talked me through the complicated story lines. I kicked his butt in *Wheel of Fortune*.

After a few days Bob could lift his arms a little, and his toes curled when the doctors ran a key along the sole of his foot. When he was able to take careful, stiff steps they sent him home, but the metal frame and plastic torso would stay on for at least another six weeks.

The staff at the gym threw a surprise party to welcome him home. Friends and family filled his modern condo with balloons, banners, and a gaudy low-fat layer cake. They blasted dance music on his stereo, drank bottles of imported beer, and promised him he would be back on the ski slopes in no time. When he started to fade, I quietly shooed the crowd home and tucked him into his big bed. It felt good to take care of someone else. My own problems became insignificant. I cleaned up some of the mess, changed into one of his T-shirts, and then crawled under the blankets next to him.

"I love you, Josie. I don't know what I would do without you."

I maneuvered through the metal cage and kissed him. "You'd better stop taking so much pain medication. You're talking crazy. Go to sleep."

Bob's mother and I set up a schedule of people to look in on him. He had dated a lot of massage therapists and sports-medicine majors over the years, so there were plenty of reliable and eager caretakers. It was time for me to stop playing Sweet Mother Mary and face my own life.

I sneaked into the restaurant to look at the stack of mail that had piled up on my temporary desk. My family had kindly avoided any kind of direct confrontation about my disappearance while Bob was in the hospital, and they left me in peace for my first few hours back, but there was no mistaking the formal tones and furrowed brows. Nina tried a couple of times to talk, but I managed to shut her down quickly by making a sad face, mentioning Bob, and dashing out the door. Vince was the only one who didn't seem too bothered by my going AWOL. He looked at me a little differently at times, and once he just threw his head back and laughed. At least I entertained him.

When I tried to quietly slip out of the office that afternoon, Mom, Dad, Rocco, and Nina were guarding the doors. I was busted. Dad spoke first.

"Not so fast, young lady. I think it's time we had a talk." When I am fifty my father will still be calling me "young lady" when he is pissed off.

"Sure, Dad, what's up?" He grabbed my arm and walked me into the dining room like I was ten. The jury had gathered and it was time for my trial.

I swore that the story Tony told was true. I had gone to the cabin and when I found out it was booked for the week, I just changed my plans. No big deal. I had found a bed-and-breakfast and did a lot of beachcombing. I saw the most adorable baby buffleheads and mergansers. When they started drilling me about the name of the B-and-B and the town I stayed in, I acted offended. Why didn't they trust me? Why would I lie to my family?

Nina gave me a poisonous glare. Rocco rubbed his fore-head. His daughters had better not grow up to be so much trouble.

"We're sorry, Giovanna. It's been a difficult few weeks," explained my mother. "The lawsuit, the fire, and then Bob's accident. We just couldn't bear to think that something had happened to you too. I've never liked you staying on the is-land by yourself. It's just too dangerous. We were worried."

"I know, Mom." I made myself look properly repri-manded and gave them each a dutiful kiss. Then I was al-lowed to leave. I could tell by the look in Nina's eyes that she didn't buy any of it, but I would deal with her later. Right now I had to face Tony.

Chapter Twenty-one

Tony has a cheap condo on a fancy bluff that overlooks the city. It's one of those generic places that were built in the eighties. From the outside it looks like a neglected dollhouse, but the inside of his place is surprisingly cozy for a bachelor pad.

I rapped on his door and presented my peace offerings— a bottle of Glenrothes scotch and a plate of warm oatmeal-raisin cookies. I know how to buy Tony's allegiance, at least for an hour or two. He met me at the door.

"Well, if it isn't my wayward sister!" He scarfed a cookie. Then he took the bottle and headed into the kitchen. "This is a good start to paying off your debt, but when are you planning to scrub my bathroom tile?" I gave him a fake smile.

He returned with two glasses with ice, set them on the table, and gave me an honest hug.

"You okay, sis?" I had been so strong until that point, but Tony's genuine concern was just too much. I started to cry. Tony has a way of making me feel like a kid again. He always picked me up when I crashed his skateboard. He checked my skinned knees when I fell off my bike. He fed me chocolate and told me dirty jokes when my heart was broken, and here I was again in search of emotional first aid.

He patted me on the back. "Hey, it's okay. I've been to Utah too. It's pretty scary, but you'll eventually get over it."

I laughed through my tears. "What am I going to do, Tony?" And then I told him my secret and how I ended up broke in Provo. He was shocked and curious. I told him about my adventures and tried to explain why I did it. We talked until almost dawn.

I woke up on the couch to the sound of Tony's espresso machine. He kissed me on the top of my messy head and handed me a big foamy cup of coffee.

"I've got to get to work. But your secret is safe with me—at least for now. We need to talk about this again soon. I don't like the idea of you just roaming around the country reck-lessly, but I can see the appeal. I have always envied Vince and his wild adventures on the road."

He looked out the window, lost in his imagination.

"I knew you had spirit, but I never imagined you were such a wild thing! God, Jo! How am I ever going to meet a woman as interesting as my sisters?" He slurped his coffee. "I can tell by the gleam in your eyes that telling you to stop won't do a bit of good. Can I talk you into taking one of the com-pany cell phones next time? I know how much you hate them, but I think it's a good idea. You don't need to tell me where you're going, and you don't need to report in, but you will have help in an emergency and maybe we can avoid another mess like we had last week. Think about it." I promised I would think about it. He grabbed my neck in a wrestling hold and we left together.

It was still early, so I was able to tiptoe around the house without waking Nina. I quietly changed into fresh clothes and made her morning thermos of coffee. I don't think I actually took a breath until I was safely down the street. Confessing to Tony was a cakewalk. Nina might draw blood. It's not nice to keep secrets from your sister.

My family loved me. They cared about my safety and happiness, and I had lied to them for years. I was a horrible, selfish person. I was still berating myself hours later when I looked out the smudged storeroom window and saw Joshua's truck pull up. I felt a flutter of excitement. I hadn't seen or heard from him in a while. I jerked back from the window and took a personal inventory. I looked like hell. Skipping a shower after spending the night on a couch is not much of a beauty treatment. I ducked down so he couldn't see me, but sneaked a look in the hopes of a peek at his jeans.

I got an eyeful, all right. Josh and Nina were standing next to the truck with their arms around each other. I stood up for a better view and saw their eyes sparkling as they shared a sweet kiss. Then Nina gave him a flirty little wave and swept into the restaurant, glowing with happiness.

That sneaky little bitch! I go away for a week, spend some time fussing over an old boyfriend, and she just assumes that Josh is fair game! I kicked a file cabinet, grabbed my handbag, and ran smack into my stunning, stupid little sister instead of storming out of the restaurant unseen, as I had planned. Her eyes were still dreamy and bright.

"Hey, Jo! I didn't know you were here!"

"I'm on my way out. I've had a lousy day. No, I've had a lousy week," I answered as I headed for the door. She didn't get out of my way.

"Yeah, I guess. But *I* had a pretty good afternoon. I ran into Josh downtown. We went to lunch. I gotta tell you, he's really an amazing guy."

Just what I wanted to hear. I forced my face into a blank, bored response.

"Josh? Yeah, he's okay, I guess."

"I think he's fabulous! He's smart, he's funny, and he's rich as Rockefeller." She wouldn't stop.

"Yeah, well, whatever turns you on. I think I've gotten everything finished up. I'm getting out of here. See ya." I dodged past her and sped home.

I didn't kick the cat, but I did throw a cheap table lamp across the room. As it smashed to bits, I remembered how much I hated smug little Nina Cerbone. She never put the cap on the toothpaste. She always got more chocolate syrup on her ice cream. Now she had stolen my new boyfriend! Well, technically Bob was kind of my boyfriend. Josh and I had had one official date and a charming trip to pick up livestock that ended in separate beds. I didn't count the night of margaritas as a date, since I kind of attacked him. But I thought there was something going on there! He let me drive his car! Damn Nina and her big boobs and her clean, fashionable clothes! Damn Joshua for his beautiful skin and thick, wavy hair. Damn the both of them!

I felt a little better after a long shower. I used the fancy soap. Clean hair and a pretty smell can do wonders for an attitude. I picked up the lamp pieces and went to see Bob. He loved me. He might have bolts in his head right now, but as a rule he was an attractive, successful man, and he loved me. I probably loved him too.

That was my frame of mind when I got to Bob's house. So when he handed me the velvet box with a huge friggin' diamond ring in it, I naturally said, "Yes, Bob, of course I will marry you." I mean, why the hell not? It was perfectly obvious that all of the intriguing men in the world were going to fall in love with my sister. Clearly I should count my blessings to have found a nice guy whom I could spend the rest of my days with. Even if he did eat fat-free cheese.

We managed a clumsy embrace around his rigging and agreed that it was about time. Well, actually, I believe he used the romantic words, "There comes a time in a man's life when he has to decide whether to shit or get off the pot." He had a bottle of good champagne in the cooler but he couldn't drink it with his medication, so we decided to save it for another day. I helped him take a bath; we watched some TV and went to bed. I spent most of the night watching my left hand. I would lie on my back, wiggle my fingers, and marvel at how a diamond could catch even the smallest amount of light to sparkle and show off. And this was definitely a diamond that wanted to perform. It was huge. I wondered what the ring would look like with pasta sauce in the crevices. I don't think I slept at all.

Chapter Twenty-two

The next morning it occurred to me that I had forgotten all about calling my family in breathless excitement about the wedding. It was a step I had always imagined would accompany my engagement. I tried a few conversations in my head.

"Hi, Mom, how are your scrambled eggs? Bob asked me to marry him last night and I said yes." It just didn't have the momentum I was hoping for, so I decided to let the ring speak for itself, but when I went to work, I found myself tucking my hand in my pocket whenever I saw a family member. A couple of times I was tempted to take the thing off because it was so damn flashy. This wasn't right. I grabbed my handbag, told Rocco I'd be back later, and went to Bob's.

He didn't look surprised to see me. He told Wendy, today's massage therapist, to take the morning off and led me to the sofa.

"Bob, I think this is a mistake. You're feeling helpless and desperate right now, and I might be playing the role of sexy nurse to avoid my own problems. We don't really want to get married, do we?"

He flashed his beautiful smile and tried to cock his head in a debonair style but couldn't. "There's the Josie I know and love. You were just too easy last night. I never thought you would agree on the first proposal." He continued, "I've had a lot of time to think lately. And you know me. When I don't want to deal with something, I get physical. I put whatever it is that is bothering me out of my mind and run a dozen miles or so. But this time I couldn't do that. I couldn't do *anything*. I couldn't feed myself or even take a piss without someone helping me. It's been rough! I've been having a lot of night-mares. And then you showed up and I started getting better. I finally get it. I can't stop thinking of all the great things in my life that I've never appreciated, and Josie, you're the best thing of all.

"I love you. I've always loved you. So for the past week or so, I've been figuring out how to get you to marry me. When you said yes without a fight, I was shocked. I was pleasantly stunned."

I just sat there in amazement.

"So go ahead and tell me why this is such a lousy idea. I'm ready for anything."

I was disarmed. I meekly explained my hesitations. We were just so comfortable together. There was no magic. Yes, I would agree that we loved each other in a tame, friendly way, but was that really any reason to get married? We prized our independence and we clearly liked to date other people now and then, and there was the issue of the ring—it would look just horrible with meatball mix in the crevices.

Bob listened attentively and then came back with a strong rebuttal. "Listen to yourself, Pussycat. You just listed all of the reasons why we *should* get married. We've been dating on and off for ten years now. We love our independence, have seen plenty of other people, and yet we still end up back to-gether. We love each other. Maybe we don't see fireworks when we kiss anymore, but doesn't that just prove that we can be together even when things go a little flat? That our relationship isn't just based on sex and chemistry? We're partners, and I want you to be my partner for real now. I want to marry you." I was speechless. "And as for that ring, I just asked my buddy to bring me the biggest rock he could find. We can go back to the jeweler's right now and exchange it for some old, ugly thing you truly love."

He was very convincing.

"I just don't know, Bob."

"I know you don't, sweetie. That's why I love you. You think things out for yourself. The fact that you said yes last night just blew me away. But I know in my heart that this is the right thing, and I will keep asking you until you say yes and mean it."

I crawled into his lap, and we held each other as best we could. I waved my hand around again and looked at the diamond.

"You want to go shopping?" he asked.

"Naw, let me wear this one for a while longer. Maybe I'll get used to it. Besides, Nina will wet her pants when she sees it!" We laughed and kissed, and then I called my mother to tell her the news. She whooped with glee, and immediately asked if I was pregnant. When I told her I wasn't, she teased me and suggested that Bob and I had better get busy. She laughed and cried and said all the right things; then she passed the phone to my father. We talked a bit and he asked to speak to Bob. I could tell by Bob's short, serious answers that Dad was drilling him, reminding him of how important and special I was and that marriage wasn't something you just jumped into. I guess Dad had written a script for when this moment arrived and he wasn't about to skip it because he knew the groom as well as he knew his own boys. When he was finally convinced that Bob had only good intentions and had promised to make an honest woman out of me, he gave us his blessing. It was almost like what I had dreamed it would be.

I went back to the restaurant grinning.

"Hello, everyone. Please don't ask me to do any cooking today, because I don't want to get my hands dirty!" I waved my ring around and reveled in the attention. Rocco walked in from outside and everyone made way so he could hear the news.

"You're going to marry Bob? That's great, Jo. Congratulations! It's about time someone else in this family straightened out and took the plunge. Bob's a good man, too." He pretended to be blinded by my ring and asked all of the pertinent questions. Then he said, "Let's go show Vince." He put his arm around me and admired the ring and led me to the back alley. "He's out back playing handball with Josh."

I dug in my heels. Whoa.

"Josh?"

"Yeah, I don't know how it got started, but Vince and Josh found out that they both wasted a lot of their youth batting around a handball. Today they had some free time, so they're having quite a game out back behind the old school." I stopped for a minute to get myself together. I put things in perspective pretty quickly. Rocco seemed genuinely pleased about the wedding announcement, and so what if Josh knew I was getting married? I didn't need to explain anything. I loved Bob. I set my jaw, tossed back my hair, and strode out to the neighbor's parking lot.

Vince and Josh were totally into their game. Vince had stripped off his shirt and was taunting Josh. "You think that was a good serve? You ain't seen nothing."

"Give me what you've got, my friend. I'll try to stay awake."

Vince slapped the ball. Josh moved like lightning and smashed the ball into a shallow bounce. Vince stooped and ran and blasted it back against the wall. Josh missed it.

"You awake now? Or do you need a little more?"

They continued to talk trash and posture in healthy competition. When Vince saw us he stopped for a moment. Josh turned to see what caught his eye. When he saw me his white teeth flashed in a wide grin, and his eyes sparkled with copper. He ran his fingers through his long hair to push it off his face. He was actually glistening from the exercise. I kicked myself for noticing and kept repeating in my head, *He kissed my sister. I love Bob. He kissed my sister. I love Bob.*

Rocco held up my arm and said, "You won't believe this! Jo's getting married!"

Josh's face crumpled. I swear, his smile just dripped down his chin and dropped right off onto the concrete. I looked away, embarrassed. I wasn't exactly sure why.

Josh and Vince both spoke at the same time. "Jo's getting married?" Then Vince added, "Who the hell to?"

Rocco jumped in. "To Bob, of course! Isn't that great?" Then, to Josh, Rocco explained, "Bob's a great guy! We used to play ball together. I think he's always wanted to be a part of our family. I was always trying to keep the two of them apart, but I guess there's no stopping true love. Or maybe he just realized that Jo wasn't going to wait around forever. I guess he's ready to stop his bird-doggin' and finally get serious. It must have been that blow to his head that smartened him up, hey, Jo?"

"Yeah, I guess so." I forced out a lame chuckle.

Josh composed himself and managed some words. "You're getting married? Well, how about that? I hope you two will be very happy together. Congratulations!"

My skin started itching all over and I couldn't stop fidgeting. Something in Josh's sad eyes made me wonder if I had made the right decision.

Rocco turned to Vince. He was bouncing the ball, obviously eager to get back into the game. "Vince! Have some manners for once, will ya? Give your sister a hug! This is a big deal!"

Vince wiped his forehead, laughed, then threw a sweaty arm around my neck. "Congrats on the jewelry, sis, but I

think I'll wait until you're actually walking down the aisle before I bother giving you and Bob my blessing."

I jerked out from under his arm and glared at Vince.
"What do you mean by that?"

"I mean, I'll believe it when I see it. You two have been
fucking since you were teenagers. Why all of a sudden do
you need to make it legal? Is your clock ticking loud these days,
or is Bob just worried that with all that metal on his head he
might not be quite such a hot ticket?"

"Bob loves me, you son of a bitch!" I slapped him on the
side of his head. "Show some respect for the betrothed!"

He rubbed his head. "All right, all right. I wish you a lifetime of happiness." He said it sarcastically. "But it won't surprise me if I was married and leading the Cub Scouts before
you and Bob even settle on a wedding date." I slapped him
again. "At least he'll make pretty children, I'll give him that."
I flipped him a double bird and stormed back inside.

I had wasted enough of the day. I needed get some work
done. But I couldn't concentrate. I found myself daydreaming about Josh's obvious discontent at the announcement of
my wedding. We had shared some good times. Incredible, in
fact. But I wasn't about to fall for another player. Josh clearly
had plenty of women in his life. I was just another name in his
black book, penciled in next to my own sister.

I was lost in a sea of numbers when Vince came in about
an hour later.

"Hey, Jo, you know I was just kidding out there, right? I
mean, if this is really what you want, then I think it's great." He
gave me a squeeze. "I shouldn't have rained on your parade."

"Thanks, Vince."

"I've been thinking a bit about the whole marriage thing
myself these days."

"What?" I gasped.

He almost blushed and tried to shrug it off.

"Well, yeah, I mean, Anna's the most amazing woman I've ever met, so why shouldn't we get married?"

"Vince! That's so great!"

"Well, it's nothing official or anything. I just like being around her. She's different. I swear, the more time I spend with her, the better she gets. The better *we* get."

I sighed a romantic sigh and could feel my face going all sappy and sweet.

"But don't go blabbing to the family or anything. She's not the kind of girl that I can just kneel down and propose to. We're going to have to talk this thing out. God, she'll probably want to get married skydiving naked or something."

I grabbed his face and plastered his cheeks with big sisterly kisses.

"See? That's how I should have reacted when you told me about you and Bob. Sorry, Jo. I guess I blew it."

"Don't kick yourself around too much, Vince. I kind of reacted the same way myself at first. Who would have guessed that Bob and I would eventually get married? But it seems like the right thing to do. I forgive you," I said. "Phew! But the customers won't! Man, you reek!" I scrunched up my nose.

Vince sniffed at himself and started walking away.

"Yeah, I'd better wash up. That Josh can really play. I mean, I thought he was good when we first started batting the ball around, but he really turned it on the second half of our game. I thought he might send the handball straight through the bricks! He killed me!"

My skin started prickling again.

Chapter Twenty-three

I was doing my best to ignore my inner romantic turmoil and concentrate on a spreadsheet when a high, disturbing voice whispered in my ear.

"Did you enjoy Las Vegas, Giovanna?"

I jumped from my seat, spun around, and landed on my feet like a cat. Dolfe. He was standing too close and he knew my secret. I tried to compose myself.

"Uh, hello, Mr. Dolfe. I didn't see you there." I sounded calm, but I am sure my eyes betrayed me. They always do.

"You didn't answer my question, Giovanna. Did you enjoy your stay in Las Vegas?"

"I can't imagine what you mean." How could he know?

"You look concerned, Giovanna. It is a simple enough question. I heard from a friend that you went on a trip. Well, I guess he is more of an associate. In fact I've been paying him to keep an eye on you. Unfortunately, he lost you when you checked out of your hotel so abruptly. Where did you go?"

My mind was flashing colors and scenes behind my eyes. Adrenaline coursed through my veins. I tried to concentrate. Dolfe just smiled. He stepped even closer.

"Do I make you uncomfortable, Giovanna?"

This horrible little man gave me the creeps from clear across town, and now he was breathing on my cleavage. You could say I was a little uncomfortable. I decided to try Bella's technique for dealing with confrontation. I would hear him out, nod with understanding while he said his piece, then ice the cake by thanking him for his enlightening view of the situation. I needed to do something or there was the distinct possibility that I was going to start screaming uncontrollably.

I forced a smile.

"Not at all, Mr. Dolfe. Actually, I am glad you stopped by. Now that our lawsuits are all straightened out we can talk and get to know each other better. It never hurts business to have a few familiar faces amongst the crowd, and I think everyone has seen Mr. Hagstrom in your television ads." I should have gone into public relations.

The words I was so proud of clearly irritated him. "Are we going to be friends now, Giovanna? Will we take long walks in the park and go to the movies?" His face contorted into mock joy and his mustache twitched. "Do you really think I'm that stupid, Giovanna? That naïve?"

There was no way to respond, so I just stood there.

"You think that everything in the world can be smoothed over by a pretty face and nice manners, don't you? And yet my very existence proves you wrong. I'm not so pretty, am I? And I don't waste my breath on shallow praise and lies. I will never pretend that I like you or your family. Beauty and kindness are crutches for you people. You will never know the power and depth of someone who has been dismissed because of appearances.

"I repulse you, don't I, Giovanna? Don't be afraid to admit it. Don't be afraid to let it show. All my life I have seen disgust, pity, embarrassment, mockery, horror. Even my mother couldn't stand to look at me. But I learned at an early age that the strong and powerful can always be toppled by the small

and cunning. When the handsome and strong become pleading, desperate fools, begging me to save their empires, to give
them pity, they no longer see me as a small and unattractive
man. They see a titan who, through patience, determination,
and very legal manipulation of the American judicial system,
has been their ruin.

"You see, Giovanna, you once found me offensive because
of my looks, but now you are afraid of who I really am—a
strong and powerful man. You see now that I can destroy you
and your precious family. Do you finally understand why you
should have settled with Mindy when I gave you the chance?
If you had played my game, you would have been rewarded.
Now, by treating me like a freak, like the enemy, you will
probably lose everything. You will never know where the
threat will be. Perhaps your loyal customers will get sick
from your food. Maybe someone will slip and fall on a stray
ice cube. A restaurant is a very dangerous place. You never
know what might happen.

"I've been watching you, Giovanna. I know everything
about you and your precious family. I know Rocco's darling
twin girls like to go for ice cream at Bright's after their dance
class. The one that wears blue likes peppermint. The curly-
haired one prefers rainbow sherbet."

He hit home on that one. I officially could no longer
breathe. He went on.

"Vince and big Anna haven't been going to their meet-
ings lately. Vince hasn't started drinking again, has he? Is the
stress getting to him? And let's not forget about the pretty
boys that Tony sneaks into his condo late at night." That one
caught me off balance. I wasn't sure what he meant. "Oh, you
look surprised. You mean you didn't know that your beloved
brother is gay? How unfortunate that I had to be the one to
break it to you." I opened my mouth to object. Tony's not gay!
But he continued spewing more and more alarming informa-

tion. I couldn't respond quickly enough, before he had yet another terrifying tidbit to taunt me with.

"Ever since that day we met again in the conference room—the day that you and your precious family ruined my life . . . again—I have made quite a hobby of watching the Cerbones. I know everything about your family, and I don't like any of it. I don't like your looks, I don't like how you laugh, and I despise your incestuous devotion to one another.

"At first I thought it was your father who needed to be taught a lesson in humility. He swaggers and boasts and talks a lot about fair play. He has a similar look to another man I hated. Remember Coach Beckett? Remember what happened to him? He was involved in a tragic car accident. It was a shame, really. Somehow his brake cable snapped. Tsk, tsk." Dolfe lost himself in a moment of memory, and I looked around for some kind of weapon. Damn the computer age! A mouse and keyboard just don't have the menace or heft of a crystal inkpot or bronze paperweight. This guy had clearly gone crazy. You could see it in his eyes.

"But never mind all that. It's ancient history. What concerns me these days is you. It's you, Giovanna, who is the Achilles' heel of this operation. *You* are the puppet master of this family. They all look to you for strength and guidance. If you fall, you will all fall. Someday, somewhere, I am going to cut your strings."

I couldn't stand it any longer. I had to say my piece.

"Are you still fighting playground battles, Dolfe? Is that what this is about? You were stuck with a rotten mother and never got picked for the kickball team, so now you have to hurt everyone who is happy—anyone who was born with good bones and a loving family?"

He was surprised to hear me respond. So I kept talking.

"You are not a strong and powerful man, Dolfe. You are a small, rat-faced egomaniac with a small penis and a big fucking chip on your shoulder. You may follow us, and sue us, and even burn down our restaurant. Yes, I know you burned Louie's down—Mindy told me how you got the keys. She told me everything.

"But if you have, in fact, been watching us, then you must have seen us stand in the smoking ashes of the restaurant my grandfather built and get even stronger. The more you antagonize us with threats and petty lawsuits, the more you will see us respond with dignity, respect, and, yes, good manners, because that is how decent people act." Once I started I couldn't stop. I was a flood of rage and emotion. "Go ahead and believe that fantasy that I am somehow the strength of this family. Give me whatever you've got and I'll send it right back, all wrapped up in ribbon. Your pathetic attempt at flattery won't fool me, Dolfe. If you have picked me to torment, it only proves once again how weak you are. I'm no fool. But I'll play your little game, because you are no threat at all, Tiny Dick, even for the weakest Cerbone girl. Bring it on!"

Dolfe's black eyes, which had been shooting around my body, my desk, finally homed in on my face. His teeth were clenched. I could feel his breath on my neck and the hate radiating from his body.

Just then it occurred to me that he didn't belong here. He was in the private storeroom/office of our family restaurant and I was well within my rights to insist that he leave. I was just gathering my courage to kick him out when he grinned like a reptile. He lunged toward me and shouted, "Boo!"

I couldn't help myself. I screamed and covered my face. Dick just started laughing. It was the laugh of the institutionalized, an evil, uncontrolled sound. Then the room exploded. Dolfe was thrown into the air and slammed against the file cabinet. Rocco had him pinned and Vince was looking over at me to gauge how much damage to do. They had heard me scream and came running. Two other cooks were at the door, armed with ladles and a rolling pin. A waiter had the phone in hand, ready to call 911.

Luckily I gathered my wits quickly.

"Stop, Rocco! Don't, Vince!" I barely got through to them in time.

"He's a goddamn personal-injury attorney! You can't beat the shit out of him in our own restaurant. It's giving him what he wants! It's okay. I was just startled. Whatever you do, don't hurt him!" It took a minute for this to sink in. Dolfe was still pinned against the cabinet, barely recovered from experiencing the brothers' poisonous vengeance. Vince's fists were still ready. Rocco's eyes were furious. They were still dangerous.

"Just hold him a minute, Rocco." I took a few deep breaths and stepped from my corner. I arranged myself in front of the helpless, horrible man. I shook out my hair and smiled like Miss America on crack. Then I stepped up close to him. My lips brushed against his ear and I murmured to him in a slow, sultry voice.

"Thank you for stopping by, Tiny Dick. Have a nice day."

Rocco dropped him, and he and Vince just started laughing. Dolfe scampered away. When he was finally gone, I fell into a chair and had to put my head between my legs to stop the room from spinning. I talked tough, but in reality Richard Dolfe scared me to death.

My brothers fussed a lot in their loud, accusing manner. But I refused to answer any of their questions. I didn't want to call the police, because I didn't quite know what to say. Dolfe made me uncomfortable; he claimed to be watching my family and he had indeed been very threatening, but I wasn't sure if he had actually done anything illegal. I mean, they couldn't exactly arrest him for shouting "boo" in the back office of a public restaurant, could they? Rocco and Vince were wired. They wanted to fight, and I knew that if I stayed, we would end up screaming at each other for no reason.

I gathered up my stuff to go. I was a wreck. I needed to walk, to get some air, but I wouldn't risk it now that I knew about the surveillance. I wanted to be held. I wanted strong arms to wrap me up and protect me, and I thought first of Josh and the sanctity of his farm. Damn! Finally I dashed out to my car and drove to Bob's. I burst through the door on the brink of tears. Bob instantly knew what I needed. He struggled up out of his chair, took a few stiff steps, and held out his arms. By the time he managed to arrange his shoulder and neck frame in a safe manner for embracing, my moment of need was long gone. It's pretty impossible to ask someone in a body cast to feel sorry for you. We spent a while holding hands and watching baseball highlights. We talked a bit about the wedding. At about ten, I realized that I hadn't spent a night in my own house, in my own bed, for ages. I made sure Bob had everything he needed for the night, gave him a kiss on the cheek, and went home.

Nina was out, so I stole the horrible cat off her bed. I smothered him with affection and gave him a long description of the evening. He purred in response. Then he wrapped himself around my neck and we slept comfortably until morning.

Chapter Twenty-four

At the crack of dawn I smelled fresh coffee. I pulled on my robe and cautiously headed down the stairs. Nina was sitting on the living room sofa, glaring at me.

"You're up early! Do I smell coffee?" I asked.

"Do you for one second think I would be upright at five-thirty in the fucking morning if coffee wasn't involved?"

I looked at the clock and said, "It's six."

Nina mimicked me like a child and followed me into the kitchen. I wasn't amused.

"Go back to bed, Nina. I have no interest in starting my day by being yelled at by my cranky little sister."

She didn't let up. "Oh, you mean I really am still your sister? I was beginning to wonder." I poured myself a cup, took a sip, and then faced her squarely.

"What is your problem?" I demanded.

"My problem is that you have been avoiding me. I know, I agreed to take some time off, but I didn't expect that meant losing all contact with you. We live together! We work together! And now I have to wake up at some godforsaken hour of the morning to even talk to you? I have been sitting here for an hour now waiting to talk to you instead of curled up in my bed having sexy dreams of navy men. What the hell is going on, Jo? Are you really going to marry Bob? What on earth for? And why would you disappear for a week and then lie to your family, to me?"

I closed my eyes and hoped that this was just a bad dream. Maybe she would go away. Nope. She was still there.

"I mean, if you have decided to disown me as your sister, that's fine, but you could at least be kind enough to fill me in as, say, maybe a coworker? No one bothered to tell me that Mindy's case was closed, so I sounded like a total idiot talking to Vince about it the other day, and then last night I was told by a busboy how you actually allowed yourself to be cornered by that little nasty lawyer. I swear, it's like you're sixteen again! What the hell has happened to the world when I am the responsible sister?"

I have a bit of a temper, and most people know to just get out the way when I am mad, but not Nina. She blows on the fire. She always has. Mom never allowed us to kick and scratch each other like we wanted. She wouldn't tolerate her precious little girls getting into physical disputes. So we learned to throw our punches verbally. If I couldn't find a way to deflect her fury, this was going to be a doozy.

"I'm sorry if you've been feeling left out, Nina. I guess I have been staying away from the house quite a bit lately, but can you really blame me? I mean, the restaurant *did* burn down and Bob *was* paralyzed. I'm sorry we haven't spent more time giving each other manicures, but I've been a little busy." Oops, maybe sarcasm wasn't the best way to start this. Judging by the face she made, I had connected with the first hit. She quickly gained her composure and responded with a low blow: guilt.

"Fine. I guess you don't want to talk about it. How selfish of me to want to spend a few minutes talking to my only sister and *best friend* about what has been going on lately. Clearly you're just too busy. How I feel about the state of the family business, then thinking you were dead, and then finding out you're getting married is my own business. I guess I'm just being a pest. I'll go back to bed."

She did her pathetic little-sister thing. I hate that. I blew out a long sigh.

"Okay, you're right. I should have been more concerned about how you're dealing with all of this. I'm sorry."

She saw my soft underbelly and reached in with claws bared.

"You damn well better be sorry! You have been a total bitch lately, and I want to know why! You lied about going to that bed-and-breakfast. It was cloudy that week and you came back with a suntan. Where the hell were you? Why would you need to lie to us? Why would you need to lie to me? And I can tell something is going on with Mom and Dad. They're totally freaked out and trying to act normal. I think you know why." She threw herself into the chair.

"And my God, Jo, why would you even consider marrying boring Bob when a rich, sexy farmer is so crazy about you? Have you embezzled a bunch of money? Are we going to have to shut the restaurants down? Do you have cancer?"

"What?" She had lost me.

"Well, I keep trying to make sense of all of this, and all I can figure out is that you must have a secret addiction or somehow wrecked the accounting and lost all of Mom and Dad's money. Did you burn down Louie's for the insurance? That night you said you'd be right home. I bought ice cream and you never came home. Did Mindy give you the idea?"

I stared at her in disbelief. I had no idea where to start— she was just so wrong.

"And then I figured that you must have cancer and you had to go see a specialist somewhere and that you decided to marry Bob because he probably has great health insurance."

Her voice started rising. She twisted her hair in her fingers. She started crying for real now. "Now I don't know what to think!" She buried her face in her knees and sobbed.

"Oh, honey!" I sat down next to her and started to cry too. I was a regular waterworks these days.

I told her everything. Well, almost everything. I left out the part about seeing her kiss Josh. What was the point? Nina was totally pissed off, but it's way better to have someone pissed off at you for the truth than have to defend a bunch of lies. She reinforced my belief that lying about it was the only way I would have been able to do my "bird-watching" in peace. She was horrified that I had needed to run off alone each year. She was even more enraged when I told her about Dolfe and his threats.

"He is such a freak show!" she exclaimed. "That man needs some serious therapy. I would feel sorry for him if he just weren't such a weasel. How are we going to get rid of him?"

"I have no idea. It's like he gets worse every time he loses, so the only way to get him off our backs is for him to win, and *that's* not going to happen," I said. "I am so glad I can finally talk to you about this. I've been going crazy thinking about all of the ways he can get to us. It's like we have a big-ass bull's-eye painted on our restaurant, and I've been trying to deflect the bullets single-handedly. Now at least I can have an extra set of eyes and ears."

She agreed and pointed out a few vulnerable places I hadn't thought to look, like booby traps in the parking lot and front sidewalk. And she was going to have someone come out and check the front patio supports before summer diners came to enjoy the view alfresco.

I started looking at my watch and reluctantly admitted that I had better get ready for work. Then I flashed Nina a conspiratorial look and let go with a top-quality slapstick sneeze.

"Ohhhh, that sounds bad!" said Nina. Then she made some goofy hacking sounds.

"Goodness, this might be pneumonia! It would be down-right irresponsible for us to be near food today!" I called Rocco and told him that we were contagious and needed the day off.

I could practically hear him shaking his head over the phone.

"Yeah, sure, I'm surprised you even crawled out of bed to call. Good thing your disease came when we have so much extra help, or I might wonder if you were faking it."

Nina made some background noises for effect. She was clearly dying from tuberculosis. I sniffled and said, "Oh, just listen to that poor girl! But don't you worry; it's probably just one of those nasty twenty-four-hour things. We'll be good as new tomorrow." We both had a giggling fit. Rocco guffawed and fired us both for the hundredth time. I hung up and Nina reached for the phone. She called Mom to share the news of our illness.

We flipped on the TV and poked through the fridge for possible signs of cheesecake. No luck. We had divided up the last few tablespoons of yogurt and some cornflake crumbs and settled in to watch the Teletubbies when Mom arrived.

I leaped up and met her at the door.

"Are those apple fritters? How did you know?"

"Oh, please. If I hadn't arrived with something sweet and fatty you wouldn't have opened the door." She threw half a dozen bridal magazines onto the coffee table, and then asked, "Is this a disease that can be cured with coffee? Or is this a Bloody Mary kind of sickness?"

Nina and I looked at each other and threw our hands up. Thank God, Mom was here. We had forgotten about the med-icine! Mom conjured most of a bottle of vodka, a bottle of mixer, and some lemons from her handbag. Nina dashed into the kitchen and set up glasses. I killed the TV and loaded the CD player with Aretha Franklin. We ate our fritters and were licking the sugar glaze off our fingers by the time the next course was ready. (Working in the food business gives you the right to eat and drink whatever, whenever you choose, no matter how gross it sounds; tuna melts and fine port, champagne and Cheetos. It's true! Ask any chef.)

Mom makes awesome Bloody Marys. She's generous with the Tabasco and horseradish. Nina got the garnish plate ready. Rather than deciding on a single garnish, we decided long ago that it's best to load a plate with celery sticks, pickled asparagus, spicy beans, and olives and then use your drink like a party dip.

After one sip of Mom's magic medicine we were feeling better. Nina grabbed a pad of paper and a pen from the kitchen drawer. "All right. Let's get to work! I may not be thrilled with your choice of grooms, but that doesn't mean I won't be involved in every last detail of this wedding."

Mom raised her glass in agreement. "Hear, hear! It's about time we had another wedding in this family. I want more grandchildren. Get to it, girls!" She snapped her fingers. "One thing about Bob; he will no doubt produce pretty kids. We just have to get him free from that jungle gym he's wearing these days." She sipped her drink and we settled into the living room to devour the drinks and magazines.

"What about you, Nina? Is the navy coming home anytime soon? Has Byron dropped any hints about getting hitched and making babies?"

"Yeah, Nina! What about you?" I jumped at the chance to redirect the conversation to her love life. I had a few questions of my own.

"Oooh! Byron will be back on dry land pretty soon and ready to be with a woman." She hugged herself. "We aren't ready to actually have the kids yet, but in just a few weeks, I promise you that we'll start practicing how they're made."

Bella recoiled in mock horror. Nina continued, "I love

that part of our relationship. He spends months cooped up with a bunch of stinky guys, and for release he only has a picture of me and a few X-rated letters via e-mail. He works off his steam by throwing around weights, so when he gets into town he's carved and horny and swears I am the most wonderful, sexiest woman who ever walked this planet." For a moment she was lost in her thoughts and wearing a dreamy little smile.

"Mom! I think Nina's actually in love!" I said. Nina beamed.

Mom smiled. "Oh, dear! Maybe we should get to work on these magazines. It may be a busy summer."

That got me thinking of something Dolfe had said last night. "So we all seem to be lucky in love these days, except for Tony. Has he said anything to either of you about dating? Do you know if he's seeing anyone?"

Nina said, "I think I heard him say something about having a date the other day, but I didn't catch her name. Tony's always going out. He probably has a dozen girls sitting by the phone every weekend."

Mom agreed. "I don't think we have to worry about Tony. And believe me, if he does ever go through a dry spell, I have probably a dozen mothers who have asked me to set him up with their daughters." Nina and I tried to get names from her, but she clammed up.

We each grabbed a couple of magazines and started comparing gowns, bouquets, and decorating ideas. Of course, Mom got all weepy over the fluffy white dresses that looked like her confirmation gown, but she knew she would never get me into something that was covered in scratchy lace and sequins. Nina kept pointing out sleek satin gowns. My guess is that in the real world, only supermodels, and maybe my sister, could ever pull one of those off with confidence. I would feel like I was walking down the aisle in lingerie. We admired and tagged the pretty pictures, but I couldn't quite get my mind around the idea that this wedding was for Bob and me. It was ridiculous. I was going to marry Malibu Ken!

I looked over at my mother. "Mom, you were so beautiful. I'm sure you had a dozen boyfriends. Why did you decide to marry Dad?" She set down her magazine and smiled.

"I married your father because he was strong enough to handle me." Then she stopped and thought about it for a minute. "And because we were best friends. I know it sounds corny, but it's true." We questioned her. "I had plenty of boyfriends. Actually, that's why your grandfather sent me here! He didn't like all of the attention I was getting back home, so he sent me to stay with your great-uncle Victor and aunt Sally. He always said it was because they needed a hand running the drapery business, but I found out he couldn't stand it when I started turning heads back in Brooklyn. When he saw the guys at the garage and the old men that smoked in front of the newsstand checking out my hemline, he packed up my suitcase himself. He didn't want to watch his precious Isabella being admired by his own filthy-minded friends." We laughed together.

"Ooh, I was pretty hot stuff back then. A real Gina Lollobrigida. I don't know how Aunt Sally stood it! I walked around with these big-city airs. I talked about the shopping at Macy's and Bloomingdale's like I spent every day there. Then I would go on and on about how I was meant to be sipping martinis with movie stars at the 21 Club, not chopping wood and slurping canned beer out west.

"The truth was that I was desperately homesick. I talked quite a game, but I had only been out of the neighborhood a few times. I went to Manhattan on school trips, but that was about it.

"Of course, we went to Louie's Restaurant. Uncle Victor

and Aunt Sally were old friends with Big Louie and had been going for years. Your father was a waiter back then. Oh, he was handsome! Tall and strong, with thick black hair he combed through with Butch Wax to keep it all in place. I would watch him, but I never let him catch me glancing his way. He was completely full of himself, strutting around the restaurant, flirting with the old ladies.

"He and his buddies ran through this town like a pack of wild dogs. I acted like I was above it and did my best to remind everyone that I wasn't from around here. There was this little coffee shop I went to all of the time that I pretended was a European café. I would smoke cigarettes and read books that I didn't understand. Sometimes my cousins would join me, and we would drink tiny cups of espresso or sweet vermouth on ice. Your dad and his friends would cruise by in Jack Miller's old Buick. Louie would hang out the window and ask us to come to a party or go for a drive. Of course, I ignored him. Oh, I was such a snob! It was as if I were waiting for Tony Bennett himself.

"Eventually, I couldn't stand the idea of all of these parties going on without me. We were young, and pretty, and bored to death with the tweedy poets at the coffee shop. I went on about a hundred dates that year. A very nice medical student even asked me to marry him."

Nina and I were stunned. "What? You were engaged to somebody other than Dad?"

"Don't look so shocked! Actually, two other men asked for my hand. Of course, I never accepted their proposals. I could have dragged them around like they had rings in their noses, and, as you both know, that's only fun for a little while. I know I made the right decision. Your dad was all hair and muscles when he was in a crowd, but when no one was looking, he would stop by with flowers or candy, and we would take long walks on the beach and talk. He joked around a lot and did these horrible impressions of John Wayne. He made me laugh.

"He would tell me his ideas for the restaurant. Big Louie wouldn't let him do anything and it drove him crazy! Your dad had the Midas touch even back then. He was eager to give his ideas a try, and he loved to talk about them. We started seeing each other every day, and eventually it was clear that we needed to spend the rest of our lives together. Don't get me wrong now, girls! If Tony Bennett ever showed up to whisk me off to Paris, I would have left your daddy in a heartbeat, but so far, so good."

It was a lovely moment. Then Nina had to open her mouth. "Hey, Jo, that reminds me. I know we worked out everything else this morning, but I still don't really understand why you and Bob decided to get married. What changed? Is it because of the accident?"

"No, it's not because of the accident. He just convinced me that we should do this. I mean, why not? We've been to-gether for years. We're comfortable together. And jeez, it's not like great men have been beating down my door. I love Bob. Isn't that enough?" I flashed the rock, but she didn't seem too impressed. I was disappointed.

"Yeah, I guess it's all very practical, but you know I have never been so good at the practical side of love. And as for available good men, what was wrong with Josh? He's crazy about you, and you dumped him like old oatmeal. I thought you two were perfect for each other."

I sent her an evil look. "Yeah, I know all about how much you like Josh. I saw you. If you like him so much, why don't *you* go ahead and marry him?"

She screwed up her face. "What are you talking about?"

"That day you met for lunch, you were all hugs and kisses and giggles. When you came into the restaurant you couldn't stop talking about how great he was. Why should I waste my time with a guy who kisses me and the next day dates my sister? I can deal with Bob's infidelity—I mean, his past affairs—but that's all over. I'm no longer interested in being just another woman to a good-looking player. Josh is obviously just another sweet-talking playboy."

Nina just stared at me for a minute. Then she exploded. "You are such an idiot, I can't even believe it! If you had bothered to spend two seconds talking to me that day instead of running out the front door, I would have had a chance to explain. Josh and I saw each other downtown. He asked me out to lunch so we could talk about *you!* He's completely crazy about you, you dumbass. Mostly he wanted to know if you were for real. He thinks you're some kind of a smart-mouthed angel. Personally, I can't see it, but being the devoted and thoughtful sister I am, I talked you up pretty good. Yeah, I might have given him a hug and a kiss when I left, but jeez, I've been known to kiss Mr. Dunkleman after he polishes off a plate of 'double the anchovy, triple the garlic' puttanesca. That's just the way I am! Mainly I was excited that something good might actually work out for you, but I was dead wrong. You are obviously way too stupid for someone as cool as Josh. I guess you'd better marry Bob."

I was stunned into silence. Nina grabbed our empty glasses and stormed into the kitchen. Mom said nothing and followed Nina. I sat for a while and pondered what I had just learned. Josh really liked me! I was thinking of giving him a call when my diamond ring lit up the room again. God, my life was such a mess! I was lusting after Josh while officially engaged to Bob. I sucked on the ice cubes in my drink and rested my head heavily in my hands.

It was time to change out of my bathrobe. I looked out the front window to check on the weather and gasped. Dolfe's silver Lincoln was slowly driving by. I froze. He knew where

I lived. It was bad enough that he could stroll into our restaurant anytime, but now he was in my front yard. For the first time in my life I actually understood what compelled city people to own guns. My murderous thoughts were interrupted by my mother's cheerful voice. "Okay, lazybones—go get dressed. We're going shopping!"

"Mom says I can pretend I'm getting married too!" hollered Nina. She grabbed the arm of my robe and dragged me up the stairs. By the time I was ready to go I had convinced myself that it wasn't Dolfe's car at all. I was addled and just being paranoid. Surely there were hundreds of silver Lincoln Continentals in town. That was probably a couple of old farts who couldn't read the street numbers. We piled into Mom's sedan and headed out for a day of pure girl fun.

Once I stopped looking over my shoulder, I had a great time. Actually, I don't think I had had such a good time in years. We tasted cake at all of the pastry shops in town. I merely flashed my ring and free samples appeared like magic. At a fancy wedding boutique two charming sales associates sat Mom in a comfy chair and brought her tea as Nina and I tried on perhaps a hundred dresses. Nina found four that made her look like a movie star. I didn't find anything I loved, but I did have a great time trashing the things I hated. One of the employees got us started making catty comments about past weddings we had been to. We snorted like naughty schoolgirls as we recalled miles of celery-green chiffon and one ceremony that included hand-loomed hemp tunics and the ceremonial waving of a twig. We made little or no progress on my wedding plans, but it was a great bonding day. I didn't have to hide from my sister or console my mom anymore. It felt great.

After all the cake we ate, it seemed impossible that we might find ourselves hungry. As with a pride of lionesses, gathering and consuming food is an inherent need of Cerbone women. We drove by a few diners and talked virtuously of salads but ended up at the Longhorn craving red meat. I was still wearing a silver plastic tiara Nina had purchased at a toy store when I swirled in the front door and ran smack into Josh.

"Oh, hi!"

"Hi," he replied. Then we both looked away.

Mom and Nina jumped in to rescue me. "Josh, how wonderful to see you! Are you coming or going?"

"I'm just leaving. I stopped by for a burger fix. Jo introduced me to the place a few weeks ago, and I can't seem to get enough." Another awkward silence; then Nina piped in.

"You must be busy this time of year. We hardly see you anymore." They made small talk about vegetables and the weather. He swore that Murakame must have planted magic seeds, because things were growing like in the fairy tales. He had hired three new crew members just to keep up.

I looked carefully at him, trying to get a read. Was there still some chemistry there? Poor guy, he was working so hard and I had trampled on his heart. How would he ever manage?

Just then a beautiful, elegant woman with sleek dark hair came out of the rest room and slipped her arm through his. Josh introduced us all to Maria. She smiled confidently. I instantly hated her and her designer clothes.

Josh put his arm around her and said, "You must be making plans for the big wedding. Pretty exciting, huh? I'm just so happy for you, Jo. I hope you and Bob have a great life together. If there is anything I can do—flowers, produce—you just let me know."

So much for Joshua Tran's undying love for me. He gave us all one of his killer sideways smiles and then said good-bye.

I sneered at Nina. "He's crazy about me, huh? He didn't look too broken up about my wedding, did he?"

"What does it matter? You're getting married to Bob," said Mom.

Nina was perplexed. "Something's not right. Maybe Maria's his cousin or something."

I blew out a sarcastic sigh.

"He offered to sell me produce for my wedding. He knows I sign the checks at the restaurant, and he's a savvy businessman. That's all. End of story."

We ate in relative silence. After dinner I begged out of a movie so I could go home. It had been a long day.

Chapter Twenty-five

The phone rang at 3:30 A.M. and I leaped out of bed. After the news of the fire, I was on high alert. It was Rocco. He sounded tired and pissed off.

"Sorry to bother you, but the alarm at the restaurant keeps going off. The cops have called me three times now. They keep driving by and nothing looks wrong. I just went down there myself and did a quick walk-through. The money and booze are still there, so the system must be acting up. I thought I'd call and let you know that I'm gonna shut the damn thing off and try to get a few hours of sleep."

My heart was racing. Nina stumbled into the hallway and asked if everything was all right. I told her it was a false alarm and to go back to bed. She did a zombie walk back to her room. I took a few deep breaths to relax and thanked Rocco for calling. We agreed to meet earlier than usual to make some adjustments on the security system.

I spent the next few hours in one of those hallucinatory states of half sleep. I could have sworn I was really awake and thinking coherently and had figured out a practical way to make a wedding dress out of Parmesan cheese. When I did wake up, I felt like the Wicked Witch of the West. I just knew if I stepped into the shower I would melt into a sticky, steaming glob. So I dusted liberally with powder and called it good. I cheered up a bit fantasizing about the damage I could do with my own troop of flying monkeys.

I got to the restaurant first but waited in the parking lot for Rocco. Everything looked fine from the outside, but I had a bad case of the heebie-jeebies. I made Rocco go in ahead of me. He unlocked the kitchen door and we flipped on all of the lights. I checked the register. The small amount of cash we kept on hand was safe. The credit-card machine was undisturbed. Rocco looked over the kitchen equipment and coolers. I inspected the dining room. The stereo was intact, no booze was missing, and there were two whole beef tenderloins in the walk-in. We had not been robbed or vandalized. Obviously the alarm system had gone haywire. We both sighed with relief.

"How about some breakfast? I'll make us some eggs," said Rocco. It sounded good to me. I went to the coffee machine and ground some fresh beans. I made double cappuccinos while Rocco clanked around in the kitchen. I looked around the dining room again. The front door and windows were unmolested, but I couldn't shake my uneasy feeling. I had become too accustomed to disaster these past few weeks.

Rocco brought out two plates of scrambled eggs and toast. We sat at the table near the window and chatted about normal restaurant stuff. We discussed inventory and labor costs. It was nice. Then he took the dishes to the back and I headed back to the office to grab some files.

I opened the storeroom door and screamed. The room was alive with rats. I slammed the door closed, only to have it bounce off a scampering river of vermin. I kicked at them as they ran over my feet and under my shoes. Rocco had come running at my shouts and was spinning, searching the hallway in astonishment, and trying to figure out what was happening. I was frantic.

"The storeroom is full of them. Help me close this door! Rocco, they're everywhere!" More rats escaped as I struggled with the door. Rocco slammed into it and the crash was accompanied by squeals. The rats in the hallway and dining room scattered.

"Holy shit!" was all Rocco could say, over and over. I couldn't speak. I just quivered with revulsion. Then I went into the bathroom and threw up breakfast. I could hear them now. There were so many that it had been just another white noise—thousands of scratchy toenails, chatters, and gnawing teeth blending into the refrigerator hum and ice-machine clatter. Opening the door had been another sensory attack— the smell. I shuddered again as Rocco pounded on the bathroom door.

"You okay in there, Jo? You okay?" I scrubbed my face and hands in the sink and caught sight of a mottled black-and-white rat scampering behind the toilet. I ran into my brother's arms. The way he clung to me made me realize that he wasn't worried about me being sick in the bathroom as much as he was freaked out about being left alone. We stumbled down the hall together and into the middle of the dining room. There was motion in the dark corners and on the counters, but we felt a little safer in the open space.

"Now what?" Rocco asked.

"I don't know about you, but I'm thinking we torch this place and get out of the restaurant business altogether! I'm sick of this shit!"

A few of the braver rodents had gotten onto the countertop and started nibbling on the sugar packets. Rocco threw a saltshaker at them and they scattered.

"You go to the kitchen phone and call everyone," I said. "Tell them to stay away. We don't need anyone else here right now. I'm going to call the health department."

"The health department? No way. I thought you were

kidding when you said you wanted to get out of the restaurant business! They'll shut us down for good!"

"No. They'll shut us down if we don't call them. We need them now."

I used the phone at the reservation desk so I didn't have to go through any corridors. Maneuvering through the government's voice-mail system and surly office assistants was truly a test of endurance. The entire time I was on hold my skin crawled. I jumped at every little sound. But I wasn't about to explain our predicament to a computerized phone system or underling. Miraculously, it took only a matter of minutes for the inspector to arrive once I explained that I needed help with a serious rodent problem. She arrived at the front door with her standard-issue clipboard, sensible shoes, and a tolerant smile.

"I understand you have a little rat problem?" I pulled her into the dining room and slammed the door. The noise was accompanied by a few scurrying forms. Her eyes widened and she looked at me in alarm.

"No, what we have here is a fucking horror movie." I told her about our morning and immediately knew that I had made the right call. She got straight to work with professionalism and efficiency. After a quick look around and a split second of pressing her ear against the storeroom door, she started making calls. Rocco came back into the dining room and we sat together at a center table, picking at our fingernails in nervousness.

The inspector's name was Lorraine Sheridan. She sat down across from us with a very serious look on her face.

"I called in my supervisor. He's gathering a team of officials for complete documentation and some specialists to clean this mess up."

Rocco stammered a minute. I could tell he wanted to explain that this was a freakish event. We didn't keep a dirty restaurant, but he couldn't find the words.

She seemed to understand. "I checked your inspection records before I came down here. You run a clean shop." We nodded in agreement.

"Rats will just appear at times. I remember it happening in Pioneer Square one summer. They were doing some work underground, and the streets and alleys were overrun." I shuddered. "That's not the case here. From what I've seen of your furry friends, they are not your everyday sewer rats. These are lab animals. They're bred in cages and sold wholesale to scientists and snake fanatics. Obviously someone bought them and dumped them here. Is there a window in the storeroom?"

We nodded.

"Someone must have loaded them in through the window and then taped it up or something. Now we just need to find out who and why. The police are on their way."

Just then the first of many official vehicles arrived. We met the inspectors at the door. Rocco and I spent the rest of the day answering questions, gobbling aspirin, and listening to rats die.

It was a relief to leave this disgusting work to the professionals—not just the exterminating, but the whole nasty ordeal. I carefully spelled out every incident involving Dolfe, starting with his colorful childhood. I told a very patient police detective about the ill-fated meeting in Hagstrom's law office, subsequent offers of reconciliation, and carefully worded threats. I explained about the veal protest and my gradual understanding of the insurance scam through conversations with the appliance king and Manny Gonzales. Then I walked the cop through the night of the spilled soup, the fire, and how I learned about Mindy's keys disappearing. Rocco sat in astonishment while I talked, then sputtered when I explained that Dolfe was watching me, watching our whole family. That he seemed to think hurting our family would somehow make his life better. I realized then how much I had kept secret. I should have spoken up sooner. I looked over at Rocco and apologized, then told him something I should never have kept to myself. "He watches the girls."

Rocco officially freaked out. "Why didn't you say anything? I can't believe you didn't tell me! I thought he was just being a pest, hanging around the restaurants and trying to get me to hit him or something, just like in school. This guy has to be stopped."

That pissed me off. What did he think I had been working on the past few weeks? "And how are you going to do that? Huh, Rocco? Are you going to march right over to his office and beat him up?"

"Yeah! I mean, no! I don't know! We could have called the cops. We could have gotten the kids and you some protection. Maybe a restraining order or something."

"I should have told you earlier. I'm sorry. But I never once thought he would really harm your kids. It's our generation he's after. And he's been pretty vague about it. He swore he would somehow ruin us. He wants to prove that he's the better man, but he's never really threatened to physically hurt anyone. He threatened to sue us, and what are the police supposed to do about that? The guy is a freak, and I get the creeps just thinking about him, but that isn't exactly a crime."

I looked over to the detectives. "I was hoping something would turn up connecting him with the fire. Lucky me, it turns out they have more incriminating evidence against yours truly than anyone else. This thing with the rats may be the first real mistake he has made."

"Yeah, as if he'll be carrying a receipt for a couple hundred rats around in his wallet," said Rocco.

The detective agreed that there wasn't much the police could do. In fact, this rat thing was not even much of a crime. It was vandalism or malicious mischief, according to the law.

If we wanted compensation, it was once again in the hands of the courts and insurers.

I had just about given up all hope when an officer interrupted our meeting. He whispered to the detective at our table and they both got up to have a hushed conversation with a new team. A plainclothes officer came and asked us some additional questions.

"Is it correct that a Miss Mindy Louise Monahan worked here?"

I answered, "She worked at the original Louie's downtown. The one that recently burned down. Actually I think she might have had some connection to the fire."

The officer nodded and flipped open his notebook. "Well, it looks like you're right about that. She admitted setting fire to Louie's in her suicide note. She even left the key."

Nothing about that sentence made sense to me. I tried to comprehend what I had just heard. It was all wrong.

The cop continued, "I'm sorry, but Miss Monahan was just rushed to the hospital in very serious condition. She may not make it. It looks like she's taken a drug overdose. Her body and the suicide note were discovered when the fire department was alerted to an apartment blaze."

"No!" I replied. "No! No! That can't be right! I spoke to Mindy just the other day. She was her dumb, happy self. She was talking about getting a new job." I thought about it a minute more. "Mindy would never kill herself. I can see her *threatening* suicide for attention. I can even see her maybe taking too many drugs, but a note? There's just no way. And besides, she couldn't have set the fire at Louie's because she lost her keys that night. She told me everything!"

The words haunted me. I had spoken those exact words to Dolfe just two nights ago in the back room of this restaurant. *I know you burned Louie's down. . . . Mindy told me everything.*

Now Mindy might be dead. I felt dizzy. I closed my eyes and held my head in my hands. Someone brought me some water.

When I had gathered my composure, I methodically explained again how everything pointed to Richard Dolfe. Dolfe had met with Mindy the night of the fire. He had hot-wired her car because she lost her keys. Finally I remembered that I had documented everything on the computer. I forced myself to go back into the storeroom, face the filth and the stench, and make a copy of the file. The police agreed that Dolfe was worth questioning. While they were at it, they would ask Hagstrom a few questions as well.

Before they left, every single officer took a minute to personally offer his or her support. They recounted old memories and family celebrations at the original Louie's. One officer proposed there just last year. The cops in this town were active in sports and they liked Italian food. Dad always gave generously to their community programs and charitable events. I knew they were the good guys, but I wasn't prepared for the wave of emotion that came with their loyalty and heartfelt concern for our family business. I understood now how important the Louie's restaurants were, not just to the Cerbone family, but to the entire town. I was overwhelmed. Another rat trap snapped shut with a loud squeal and clatter, and I started to shake uncontrollably. Rocco threw his coat over my shoulders and held me tight.

"Too much coffee, that's all," I said. "Give me just a second. I'll pull myself together. I need to call the staff, purveyors, people with reservations, the insurance company. . . ."

Rocco's voice was oddly tender. "I don't think so. You've done more than your share already." He rubbed my back. "Why don't you go home, Jo? I can handle it from here. Dad probably called everyone important by now." I just sat there. "The worst is over. Now I'm going to work with the exterminators and try to figure out how fast we can get this place up and running again. It'll take at least a couple of days, maybe a week. I'll get Vince and Nina to get their butts in gear once the rats are gone. I want you to give yourself a break. Take the rest of the week off. Do something pleasant. Why don't you go to Bob's and start working on that wedding?"

It felt as if a cartoon lightbulb blinked on over my head. Bob! My fiancé! What a wonderful idea. I would go to Bob's house, where life was simple, and slow, and boring. I would have tomato soup and crackers and watch TV under a blanket.

Rocco called Tony and told him I needed a ride. He didn't want me driving. I thought it was a bit condescending, as if I were too delicate a flower to drive myself. I objected but I didn't really have the energy to start a fight over a kind gesture. I must have *really* been exhausted.

Chapter Twenty-six

I hadn't had a breath of fresh air in hours, so I went outside to wait for Tony. It had started to drizzle. I stepped from the protection of the eaves and let the cool drops cover me. It was like medicine. I watched the water collect and drip off my fingers. I raised my face to the cleansing rain and sucked in the wet breeze through my nose and mouth. I closed my eyes and listened to the patter on the street and the tinny ring off the cars.

Tony pulled up and swung the passenger door open. "You turning into some kind of a frog? Absorbing water through your skin?"

I got into his car, turned to him, and asked, "Why didn't you tell me you're gay?" It was the day of reckoning. I wanted no more secrets and dark shadows.

He was clearly shocked. Eventually he composed himself, reminded me to buckle up, and started driving toward Bob's. "Well, there are lots of reasons I didn't tell you. The main one being: I'm not gay."

I snorted with disbelief. "Oh, please. You don't have to hide it anymore. I found out." After the morning I had just had, I wasn't about to hold back. "What pisses me off the most is that you thought you had to keep it a secret. I can't believe you didn't tell me."

He dramatically slapped his forehead and gasped, "How exactly did you find out?"

"That's not important. When I start thinking about it, I can't believe I didn't figure it out before. You *never* introduce us to any of your girlfriends. You're compulsively neat. You're way more emotionally accessible than any other Cerbone male. And let's not forget that you played with my Barbies tons more than I ever did."

He couldn't concentrate on the road anymore, so he pulled over and looked at me with incredulity. "Are you serious? You really think I'm gay?"

"Dolfe told me. He said you had all these pretty young men that you entertained overnight in your condo."

Now it was his turn to be angry. "You're going to trust Tiny Dick after all this shit? Jesus, Jo!" He hammered on the steering wheel. "Okay! Yes! I do have young men staying with me from time to time. They're brothers. And they are young and handsome. *Really* young! Fifteen and seventeen, to be exact. I met the oldest one at a job site. They have a totally fucked-up family life, and now and then I buy them some dinner and let them crash on the couch when things get too ugly or too dangerous at home. Does that make me gay? Or does that just mean I'm a softhearted sucker who's gonna get his DVD player stolen soon?"

"But Dolfe said—"

"And as for why I never introduce you to my girlfriends, I have been dating Jessica Monroe now for almost a year." I made a face of horror. "See? That's why I didn't tell you. You looked happier when you thought I was gay!"

"But Jessica Monroe is so—"

"She's great, Jo! Sure, she was a little uptight in school,

but she's different now. She's smart, and funny, and beautiful, and I really like her."

Jessica Monroe was the kind of child who never once got dirty. She had good posture, neat hair, and corrected everyone's grammar. She always asked for extra-credit projects. She played dreamy pop ballads on the clarinet at school talent shows.

"She's a dermatologist. She has a condo in my building. We kept running into each other at the mailbox and just kind of hit it off."

"Why didn't you say anything?"

"Because I knew you would make that face! And things have been really good. I've asked her to come to do some casual family stuff but she always has an excuse. I don't think she's quite ready to take on the entire Cerbone clan yet. She's still scared to death of you and Nina."

"Scared of us?"

"Of course! Any woman in her right mind would be scared of you two. Add Mom to the mix, and it's amazing that I can find anyone in this state who will go out with me."

I had always bemoaned my brothers and how they interfered with my love life, and yet I had never considered how a pair of strong-willed sisters might affect my brothers' romantic aspirations. In truth, I had never given up the illusion that Tony was mine. I wasn't exactly jealous of girls that he dated, but when I think back, I might have treated them like amusing pets instead of relationship material. I *had* actually been less disturbed when I thought he was gay. Another man I could make room for; another woman was another thing entirely.

"I never actually *hated* Jessica. She was just so perfect all the time."

"Believe me, she's not perfect. In fact, she's really been letting herself go. She hardly ever shaves her legs, she snorts when she laughs, and you should see the stuff growing in her fridge!"

I laughed for the first time all day. He pulled the car back onto the road and talked nonstop about how wonderfully flawed Jessica Monroe was.

Rocco must have demanded door-to-door service, because Tony insisted on coming inside with me. He said he wanted to see how Bob was doing. I used my key. The music was on, and there were sandwich makings on the counter. I ate a slice of tomato and grabbed two bottles of seltzer from the fridge. I handed one to Tony.

"He must be in the bathroom." I kicked off my shoes and wandered toward the living room. We both heard the agonized moan. Bob must have fallen. He had hurt himself again. We ran into the bedroom to rescue him and my breath left me in a shriek: "Bob!"

Bob's massage therapist, Wendy, jumped up onto her feet, pushed back her hair, and wiped at her mouth with the back of her hand. Bob reached for his pants but he couldn't quite manage alone. His legs flailed and he teetered on the edge of the bed with his pajamas coiled around his ankles. "Josie! Honey! This isn't what it looks like!"

"What?"

"It isn't anything! Really! Wendy here was giving me a massage, and . . . well, things just started happening and . . ."

Wendy straightened her clothes and messy hair. She was mortified.

I looked from her to Bob. "You call that a massage?"

"She was just trying to make me feel a little better." His eyes were panicked. "I don't know how it happened. I'm really not even attracted to her. It must be all of these drugs. I'm just not thinking clearly. It will never happen again. I promise."

Wendy didn't exactly find his words complimentary. She grabbed her bag and ran out the front door. Tony left the room to give us some privacy. Bob continued to struggle with his pajama bottoms. The cage around his head and plastic body cast made it difficult for him to reach his ankles. His penis had shriveled into a limp cocktail pickle. I just let him grunt and flounder while I processed what I had seen. Then I let out yet another heavy sigh, sat down next to him, and helped him get his pants up.

He grabbed at me in desperation. "Honey, it will never happen again. I love you. Things just got out of hand, that's all."

I patted his thigh and looked carefully into his face. Then I stood up, put his big diamond ring on top of the dresser, and left.

Tony drove me home without speaking, but I could tell he was steamed. When we got inside I slumped onto the couch. Tony paced and snorted for a few minutes, but thankfully he knew not to speak. He drew me a hot bath and set out my comfiest sweats. He handed me a tumbler full of Mom's leftover vodka and unplugged the phone. He thumbed through the CDs but couldn't find whatever it was he was looking for, so he just walked around in circles for a while. Finally he kissed me on my cold cheek and left. He understood that what I needed the most was to be left alone.

I just sat and stared into space for a while. A stronger woman would reach deep into herself and find a kernel of inner power. She would transfer this negative energy surrounding her into a creative, giving force (it happens on *Oprah* all the time), but my kernels of inner power were all gone. They had popped while I wasn't watching, and now all I had was a used and burned vessel with exploded bits of my life scattered all around me.

I took one sip of the vodka, gagged, and dumped it out. I pulled on the sweats, fell onto my bed, and pulled the covers over my head. Then I cried myself to sleep.

Chapter Twenty-seven

I stayed in my dark bedroom for over thirty-six hours. I slept a lot. When I couldn't sleep, I listened to the rain and the birds outside my window. I stared at the ceiling and inspected the glass light fixture and the two dead moths inside. I absently rubbed my hand across the gentle texture of the walls and watched the shadows in the corners of the room change as the hours passed. The bedroom door creaked open a couple of times and a head would peek in and meekly ask if I needed anything. If I buried myself deeper into the bed they would go away and I would go back to sleep.

Eventually my skull felt like it would explode from caffeine withdrawal, so I had to get up. My mouth had manufactured some kind of industrial adhesive. My tongue was stuck to the roof of my mouth, and my lips seemed glued together. I took a long shower, put on some clothes, and went downstairs in search of orange juice and coffee.

Mom was sitting in the big chair doing a crossword puzzle. She put it down and looked over the top of her glasses at me.

"You get stuck baby-sitting?" I asked. She ignored my snide comment.

"Get me some more coffee while you're in there, will

you?" She held out an empty mug. I took it from her. There was no juice, so I drank about a gallon of water and gnawed on a stale bagel. I filled our cups and shuffled back into the living room. We sipped our brew in quiet for a few minutes, and then Mom spoke. "It looks like Mindy's going to make it." I sighed a breath of relief. Who would have guessed I would one day care so much about Mindy Monahan's health?

"I guess Tiny Dick was a bit of a firebug in his youth. He spent some time in juvie for blowing up a neighbor's garage with homemade fireworks. I can't believe the school gossips missed something as juicy as that.

"There isn't enough concrete evidence to connect him to the fire and the rats quite yet, but the police interrogated him for a good long time and have asked him to stay in town. He's considered a person of interest.

"Pretty boy Dane Hagstrom, apparently, has some friends who are known drug dealers, but he should be more concerned about the state insurance investigators. Your documentation of his strong-arm scams has piqued their interest."

I raised my eyebrows but said nothing.

"Things are looking pretty grim for both of them. Mindy's friends are swarming like mad bees. They all know this suicide thing is a setup. Her whole life had been a series of hard knocks, and she always bounced back. She was never suicidal. They have even gone so far as to explain that the drugs in her system were all wrong. Mindy liked uppers, not downers. When she got high she wanted to party all night, not lie around in a stupor.

"The doctors say she might be off the respirator in a couple more days. She's a pretty sick girl. The smoke did a number on her lungs."

Mom and I locked eyes and shrugged in disbelief.

"The restaurant key was lying beside her 'suicide note,' but it was wiped free of fingerprints. And the letter itself was all wrong. It was written on a computer instead of in her trademark smiley-face handwriting, and it was grammatically correct. Mindy could never have spelled *depressed* correctly, and I think we all know she didn't know the meaning of the word *remorse.*

"Our insurance agents have been falling all over themselves apologizing for wrongly accusing you. Mindy's letter, fake or real, was proof of foul play. They finally believe you weren't involved in the fire, and they hand-delivered a big fat check yesterday. They have also agreed to take care of the recent problems at Twelfth Street. Rocco has already turned that place inside out. It'll be like a brand-new restaurant."

I cradled my mug and tucked my feet in the couch cushions. Mom stopped talking and looked out the window for a few minutes. She took a sip of her coffee and filled in another few squares of her puzzle before she told me the rest.

"I'm not here as a baby-sitter. I'm on Bob patrol." That got my attention. "We've been taking turns. He's a real mess. He's desperate to see and talk to you, but once Rocco and your father heard what happened they set up a front line. I guess it's against their sense of honor to pummel a man with a broken neck, so they are punishing him by keeping him away from you. When you give the all-clear sign, we'll turn the phone back on. Until you get yourself together, we thought it would be best to just leave you alone."

I started to cry again. What a stupid, brutish, wonderful family. Mom came over and curled up next to me. She rocked my head on her chest like when I was a little girl.

"I'll sit here for a year if that's what it takes, honey." I knew she would.

We shared a nice moment, but I knew Mom. She wasn't a big fan of whiny or helpless women. If my pity party lasted another day, she would have dumped a bucket of ice water in my bed. In truth, my day and a half of complete inertia just about killed me. It felt good to be upright. We polished off the coffee and most of the puzzle; then we went to the restaurant.

I figured I should check in and let everyone know I was okay, and I needed to pick up my car. Mom drove me to the restaurant and let my brothers and sister pat and squeeze me. They told slimy-lawyer jokes and cursed the wretched Bob. Once they were content that I was doing okay, they hustled back to work.

The restaurant was a jumble. There was fresh paint in the kitchen and bathrooms. A team was ripping up the carpets to be replaced. Everything in the storeroom had been tossed. Rocco had replaced the old wooden shelves with stainless-steel racks and hard plastic bins. There was even a rough framework in place to make a proper office space.

Nina was seated at the new desk surrounded by files, binders, and panels of Sheetrock. She grinned and showed me her plans for the grand reopening. It was going to be a big soiree, with invitations to all of the regulars as well as the local press. There would be mountains of meatballs and an assortment of Vince's new delicacies to try out on the public. I took a few minutes to look through the stack of cards, photos, and notes sent by our devoted clientele. I was touched by all of the offers of labor, materials, and money to help us rebuild.

Rocco insisted that I take more time off, and I was glad to leave. I said my good-byes and then just sat in my car for a few minutes trying to figure out what I wanted to do. As always, I felt like walking. My muscles and bones were complaining from their days of inactivity. I didn't feel up to a full mountain attack, so I drove to a nearby state park. I still felt like I needed to think things through, and nothing nurtures clarity like a Northwest beach.

When I got to the shore, I pulled on a windproof jacket and wandered down to the water. I was relieved that it was another gray, drizzly day. Hollywood has tried to convince us that we can only be happy in sunshine; that a beach should always have white sand and blue skies, but anyone who lives on a northern coastline knows better. Rainy days are the perfect time to wander the Puget Sound. The shores are empty of people and full of activity. Noisy seagulls fight for clams, crabs skitter under rocks, and anemones are in full flower in shallow tide pools. I will not deny that the sky, the water, and the muddy sand have only minor differences in color, aroma, and texture, but that's fine with me. The beach instantly envelops me in fresh, briny wetness, and something deep in my soul settles down. I felt as safe and protected as I had at home, buried in covers.

I wandered awhile and tried to make sense of the emotions I had been battling. I was exhausted. That was a lot of the problem. What I needed was a routine—more exercise, more fruits and vegetables, maybe a multivitamin. I sped up my stride and did a few lunges. I would get a workbook and keep track of what I ate, and then next year I would run a 10K race or maybe do a triathlon. All I needed was a little focus. I needed to be a stronger, more disciplined person. I would take a few days off and then get back to work and dig into my job like never before.

The gloom returned. I parked my butt on a beach log and tried to stop fooling myself. At first I had assumed that the ache in my chest and constant flow of tears were heartbreak. The symptoms and timing were all right, but then it occurred to me: It was *Bob!* We'd broken up half a dozen times over the years, usually in very similar circumstances. Why was I so wrecked about it this time? Did his accident stir my emotions too? Did I finally love him? No. In fact, I was secretly relieved to call off this charade of a marriage. I explored a little deeper to try to find what was eating up my soul.

It was Mindy's near death. And the rats. I shuddered. It was the restaurant. The excitement of the past few weeks had been so difficult, but it had also sparked something in me. I had felt alive and clever and useful. Right now what disturbed me the most was the idea that everything would soon be back to normal. I would take my place in the new storeroom office. I would pay the bills and print out checks. I would roll meatballs now and then. Gradually everything would be just as it was. Chances were good that I would eventually forgive Bob and let him back into my bed. When the routine got to me, I would run away again, but in search of what? A life?

Arrgh! It was the same circular argument I'd had with myself for years. The same perpetual debate in my head. I have a life! I have a *great* life! I have everything; I'm healthy, attractive, and young! I have a wonderful family that loves and supports me and a good, solid career. I have hobbies and a gorgeous, successful man who wants to marry me. Why can't I just get on with it? Why do I have to be such a whiny, selfish, miserable person?

Because it's not enough, said my internal voice.

I fought it. *That's ridiculous! Of course it's enough; it's more than enough! What more could I want?* But inside, I knew that I desperately wanted more. I wanted to live my own life. Then it finally hit me. I wanted to be an adult.

I was a grown woman whose daddy still called her "young lady" and ruffled her hair. My big brothers still beat up the bad guys. I shared clothes and makeup with my sister in my grandparents' house. It was all so comfortable and perfect, and it was killing me. I was a complicated woman with a creative and adventurous spirit, and what had I done with it? Nothing but throw the occasional temper tantrum and recklessly tempt fate by running away like an adolescent. Internally I had wanted to rip and tear at this effortless existence. Finally someone had done it for me.

So now what? How could I explain such a revelation to my family, to my parents? It's not like returning a pair of shoes. I couldn't very well call them up and say, "Thanks for the great life, but it just doesn't fit quite right. I'm going to exchange it for something new." It would be so disrespectful! I might have been able to throw it all away if I had figured out what I wanted before the recent disasters. But now I was aware of my responsibilities. I finally understood what the Louie's restaurants meant not just to my family, but to this town. How could I walk away from that? I would be a quitter. They would assume that the pressure had been too much, that Tiny Dick had beaten me down. Worse yet, they might assume my weakness was the result of my breakup with Bob.

I looked out across the water to the heavy container ships on their way to distant lands. A seagull sang out and broke my contemplation and I was reminded of exactly where I was. I was sitting on a beach log, looking out at sea in the middle of a workday, and the world was still revolving.

Tiny Dick had changed things. He had freed me from my daily routine of adding machines and spreadsheets, and the restaurants were still functioning. I was still a good daughter, a good sister, and Louie's was on the verge of being better than ever. And the most amazing part was that it was all happening without me.

The beach had once again worked its magic. I ran back to the car, drove to Louie's, and called my own family meeting.

Chapter Twenty-eight

I asked everyone to be at my house at four for an early dinner. Inspired by the beach, I made a big pot of clam chowder. Dad got there a few minutes early, and I asked him if he would make sure everyone got settled. Then I ran out the door to pick up more beer and oyster crackers.

Before I entered the house to make my big announcement, I peeked in the front window to see everyone. But Dad was still alone. He had moved the chair to the most desirable listening spot and was sitting back with his eyes closed, grooving to the LA4.

I opened the door and asked, "Everyone's running a little late, huh?"

He got up, turned down the music, and grabbed a beer from the grocery bag. "Actually, I think I might be it. Your mom had a hair appointment but said she'd get here as soon as she could. Tony couldn't get off work. Anna and Vince went to a meeting. Rocco and your sister called and said they were just too busy trying to get the restaurant back open. So I guess it's just you and me, babe."

"Oh." I was disappointed, so I whined a little. "But I said it was important."

"Of course it's important, sugarplum. That's why I'm here!" He handed me the beer and opened another for himself. I went to the kitchen and filled two huge bowls with soup and crackers. Then I sat down at the table with my dad and quit my job.

I started carefully and explained myself in Dad-friendly words. I told him that it was time I stopped taking the easy path. That if I were to live up to my potential, I needed a break from the security of the restaurant. I needed to challenge myself. Instead of storming around the room, calling me an ungrateful waste of DNA, he just nodded and listened attentively, so I told him a little more. I told him about my revelations at the beach, and my yearning for freedom and adventure, and then I let it all out. I told him about my fake bird-watching trips. I showed him my fairy drawings. He listened to it all without protest until I had talked it all out. Then I looked carefully at his warm eyes and overworked body, and I realized what a horrible mistake I had made. "I'm so sorry, Dad." I felt my eyes going glassy.

"Sorry? For what?"

"For everything. You've worked so hard all your life. You've given me everything, and here I am telling you how much I hate it all." I wiped away a tear.

He sat back in his chair. "Is that what you're doing? I guess I misunderstood. I thought I was sitting here getting to know my oldest daughter again. I thought I was listening to an intelligent, motivated young woman talking about her dreams."

I sniffled and said nothing, so he continued. "I might have put you to work early, to keep you out of trouble, but I always said that once you were old enough to get a real job, you were free to do whatever you wanted. How many times did I say that? I supported your interests, made sure you each had a chance to try new things, to get involved in school clubs and activities. I sent you to college! Five kids within seven years of each other, and I made sure each and every one of you could go to college."

"I know, Dad. That's what I mean. I let you down."

He made a face and slammed his hands down on the table in frustration. "Argh! Maybe your mother's right. I can't seem to say what I really mean." He rubbed the back of his neck and started again. "I never wanted you kids to feel like I did. Like you had no choices. That damn restaurant was my father's dream, not mine. I wanted to be a cop."

"You what?"

"Yeah, I wanted to be a police officer. Don't look so shocked; I would have been damn good at it."

"You would have been the best! I just had no idea. Why didn't you just do it?"

"How? I had to work at the restaurant. It's not like they could have hired someone to do what I did. They couldn't afford to. I swear, when I took over the books, Big Louie seemed to forget everything he ever learned about running a business. He would have gone broke in six months, the way he started giving the food away." He let out a low chuckle as he reminisced. "And then there was your grandmother. The waitresses would come to me in tears, complaining about how she chased them around the dining room, redoing their work and questioning their parentage. No wonder your aunties ran off and got married. I swear, that woman was so stubborn, she would have worked herself to death, twenty-four hours a day, to avoid paying someone to do what she considered to be a lesser job.

"No, I knew early on that Louie's was going to be my life." He reached over and held my hand. "And while it would have been nice to have some options, I can't really complain. The restaurant business has been good to me, and you kids would never have had the life you did on a cop's salary. I never wanted any of you to feel like my restaurant depended on you. I always hoped you would want something more for yourselves.

"By getting out of the business you aren't letting me down. You are actually doing what I always wished you would do. You're living up to my dreams, and I'm damn proud of you."

He pondered things a moment longer. "If I worry about anyone these days it's Rocco. I swear, he can't make a simple decision without checking with you or me first. I'm not sure what's going on with him. He's got the smarts; he just doesn't have the confidence anymore. Maybe it's because of Vince. I don't know, but you'll be doing him a favor by leaving him on his own." I raised my eyebrows, and he kept on talking.

"You know, Vince was on my list for a good long time. I used to think he was some kind of weak link in the Cerbone chain, but he's finally pulled himself together. I always knew he had it in him. I guess he just needed a little extra time to grow up. He never liked doing anything that was hard. He was always looking for the easy way out. Your mother always said he was searching for something. Maybe he finally found it, 'cause he sure isn't afraid of hard work these days. He looks almost happy. I mean, happy in his own angry Vince sort of way. And he's doing some things in the kitchen that would make your grandfather proud. That boy is one hell of a cook.

"Tony and little Nina, well, you can't help but love them, can you?" He smiled, "You've all had your moments. I've lost sleep over all of you at one time or another. Those boys you used to bring home, Jo! What were you thinking?" I threw my hands up in surrender. "But I don't think there's a runt or a weakling among the lot. I'm proud of each and every one of you."

He wrapped me up in his big arms and I started to cry again. Mom arrived as Dad was wiping away my tears. She dropped her things and ran to console me. She petted my hair and said, "Jo, honey, it's going to be all right. Don't cry; it's going to be just fine. I promise." It made me start crying all over again. Pretty soon she was crying too. I had cried so much recently, my eyes were going to dry up. When I had finally run out of tears, she wiped away her own and asked, "Not that it really matters, but what exactly are we crying about?"

I snorfled. "I quit. I'm not going back to the restaurant."

Mom gasped. Then she jerked away from me and smacked Dad a couple of times on his beefy arm. "Damn you, Louie Cerbone! After all those years of talk, all those promises! You go and make your daughter cry because she doesn't want to spend her life in a restaurant? Don't you think she's been through enough lately? What are you thinking? Jo has so much talent, so much potential. If she wants to move on, you will let her! No, you won't just let her; you will offer your total support!" She whacked him again, then turned to me.

"Jo, you don't ever have to step foot in that place again if you don't want to. Don't listen to this dinosaur over here. He always said he never wanted you kids to feel trapped. He just doesn't know how to say it, that's all." She grabbed me and squeezed the air from my lungs. My laughs turned into hacking coughs.

"Jeez, Bella! Don't kill the poor girl! Give her some air!" Dad pulled me a step away from my rabid she-bear of a mother. He and I wore matching grins.

"What?" Bella looked at us with confusion.

"I was giving our daughter my blessing when you walked in, supporting her decision, not busting her chops. I don't exactly know why she was crying, but we were doing okay, weren't we, Jo?" I nodded and we started to laugh. "And then you started acting like some kind of crazy woman, beating on me and telling me what's what. I'll probably be covered in bruises!"

Mom tried to recover. She opened and closed her mouth a few times before finding any words, then rubbed her husband's battered arm. "But I thought—"

"You made it perfectly clear what you thought. Good grief!" Mom started to laugh a little now too. "If you're done beating on me, might I suggest that you go into the kitchen and get a bowl of Giovanna's delicious soup? Then maybe we'll fill you in on what you missed." She did as he suggested. Dad and I ended up filling our bowls again too. Then we sat around the table and updated Mom on my decisions.

I explained that I had called my friend at the ad agency. I told her I was ready to get serious about illustrating and she sounded genuinely thrilled. She promised to hook me up with an agent and help me put together some samples for a professional portfolio.

"I don't know much about the drawing business," said Dad. "I never understood how artists made their money, but I do know that if anyone can do it, it'll be you. You have a real knack with numbers. We're going to miss you at Louie's."

"Louie! Don't make her feel guilty!" snapped Mom.

"What? By saying we'll miss her? What am I supposed to say? Good riddance? My girl has a good head for business! She'll be hard to replace, and I'll miss having her around all the time. She knows what I mean." I did. But it was nice to hear it. "I must say that your little sister is really turning out to be some kind of dynamo. She was always good out front, but I never really knew how clever she was. She's got some damn good ideas. I think that deli plan is a winner." We agreed and discussed some of Vince's authentic creations.

"Yep, I think they've got something there. That's why I've decided to let them have the old Louie's space." I was stunned. I guess I wasn't the only one with big news today.

"Your mom and I have been talking about it since the fire. We've decided it would be best to just let the old place go.

The old Louie's was all about nostalgia and tradition. It can't be rebuilt."

Mom added, "It would cost a fortune to replace all that awful red wallpaper and those thick velvet drapes. That's if we could find a source for them. And what would Louie's be without the classic décor and years of tradition? Nothing but a spaghetti house, that's what."

"Maybe the kids won't be interested," said Dad. "They might have plans of their own, or a different location in mind. But if they want it, the property is theirs to do whatever they want with. I'm retiring."

"And we're going on another cruise!" added Mom.

Chapter Twenty-nine

My inactivity became action. I spent the next day twittering with excitement and focused my energy in the studio. My fairies were getting feisty. The naked, wild-haired nymphs went nuts. They danced with lusty abandon in gnarled fall leaves, pulled the wings off gnats, and bashed seedpod drums with pine-needle sticks. I loaded the CD player with loud and proud female singers and cranked it up. The windows only rattled when the subwoofer kicked in. I was howling along with Carrie Smith when I saw movement in the backyard. A man was waving his arms, desperately trying to get my attention. It was Josh.

My heart leaped with joy until my mind alerted me to potential trouble. I turned the sound down, cracked open the back door, and asked, "What are you doing here?"

"I need to talk to you." His eyes were intense and determined.

I didn't need another crazy man in my life right now. "No, I don't think that's a good idea. You should go."

"No! I need to say something!" He pushed through the door and grabbed my shoulder. I flinched and tore myself away. I took a few steps back and looked at him with alarm. He immediately let go.

"See why I need to talk to you? I don't grab at people like that! You're making me crazy!" He stepped away and rubbed his face with both hands. "The last time I saw you I sounded like a complete idiot. I told you how happy I was that you were getting married. I even offered you produce! Jeez! But it was all a lie. I just can't stand it anymore. I don't want you to get married; I can't even quite get my mind around the fact that there's another man in your life. I just assumed you were obsessed with me, the way I'm crazy about you."

Okay, maybe I would let him keep talking.

"I can't stop thinking about you, Jo. You're the most amazing woman I have ever met, and it's killing me that I never bothered to tell you. From that first day, I knew. You stepped onto my farm and looked around at those trees and mountains and you did the impossible: You made that valley even more beautiful. You took my breath away.

"I just assumed that you felt the same way. I'm so used to getting things my way, it never occurred to me that you might fall for someone else. I thought we could take it slow. I've been living in this freakin' fantasy where I would work the land and live a simple life, but while I've been spreading shit on a bunch of vegetables, some jerk named Bob stole my fairy-tale princess." He continued pacing around my studio. "What's it going to take? What can I do to convince you to rethink this wedding? Vince made it sound like . . . I don't know, like maybe I had chance. I'm in love with you, Jo. My dog even adores you, and she hates everyone! If this guy doesn't do absolutely everything possible to make you happy, give me a chance."

I looked carefully at his sweet face and remembered the marvelous times we had had together, how warm and genuine he was. Then I remembered the women.

"Maybe," I said. I gave him an impish look.

His eyes questioned me.

"I'm serious, Jo! Don't toy with me. I've never done anything like this before. I've never had to. I'm out on a limb here." He was on the verge of losing his diplomatic composure. If he were a sibling, I surely would have tortured him some more, but he didn't look up to the drill. I decided to give him a break.

"Turns out that Vince was right. I'm not going to marry Bob after all." I wiggled my fingers in the air. "See? No ring. I don't approve of his definition of physical therapy."

Josh stared blankly for a few seconds, then picked me up and spun me around like a doll. Then he kissed me.

I laughed and kissed him back, but when things heated up I pulled away. "Not so fast, buddy! I'm still a jilted bride, and I have a lot of things to work out. I'm damaged goods."

He nibbled on my neck. "You taste fine to me."

"Yeah, I'm quite a dish. But I'm more concerned about all the other women you've been snacking on. I don't want to be just an hors d'oeuvre or sweet treat. You choose me and I've got be the whole friggin' FDA food pyramid. I'm a ten-course meal plus wine and tips. You get me?"

He looked at me like I was crazy. "What are you talking about, exactly?"

"For once, I need to be with someone I can trust. If we're together, I need it to be exclusive. No more dating other women."

"Not a problem. I don't think I've even looked at another woman since I met you."

I shook out of his arms. "See? Right there! That's what I'm talking about." I turned away and mumbled to myself, "What was I thinking? This will never work."

"What is it? I'm serious, Jo!" Josh was pleading.

I looked incredulously at him, then listed his flagrant indiscretions. "First, Inez, the bartender at my favorite Mexican restaurant, clearly wanted to use you as her own private bath toy. Then, when I called you the next day, some barefooted, tou-

sled young woman answered your phone in a *very* familiar
manner. Then I see you kissing my own sister. Well, that doesn't
really count. I'll let that one slide, since she told me about your
lunch date and she does kiss a lot of people. But what about that
hottie Maria you introduced me to the other night. Huh?"

Josh's apprehension transformed into affection and amusement. He threw up his hands in surrender. "Was Inez hitting
on me? I didn't notice. I know her brother; he works at the
feed store." I scowled.

Josh laughed a bit, then stroked my hair and said, "I guess
you're right. There are a lot of pretty women in my life. There
always have been. I like to think it's my debonair personality,
or the boyish charm of having dirt under my fingernails. And
the fact that my grandparents are loaded and I went to a
swank European boarding school doesn't hurt my chances either. But let me assure you, those women mean nothing to me."

I slanted my eyes at him and asked pointedly, "So the
woman I spoke to on the phone was nothing? Just a quick
romp? And don't make up some excuse about her being your
cleaning lady. Your house is a mess. I'm not that stupid."

He bowed his head. "You spoke to Gretchen. And, quite
honestly, I'm embarrassed as hell that you found out about
her. I'm totally ashamed of our arrangement."

I knew it!

He continued. "Gretchen lives on a nearby farm, but
they're not doing too well. It's kind of a New Age, hippie com-
mune thing, and quite honestly, they like the lifestyle more
than the work. You're right: She's not my housekeeper. I've
had people cleaning up after me all my life, and it's high time I
learned to take care of myself.

"My parents and my grandparents worked hard. They
didn't want me to grow up a spoiled and helpless snob, and
for the most part I think they did a pretty good job.

"But I still had privileges, one of which was a never-ending supply of ready-to-wear clothing. My closets and drawers were always filled with perfectly pressed or folded clothes that smelled like a summer day. And as clever as I am, I can't seem to make that happen. I totally suck when it comes to doing the laundry. Everything ends up this gray-blue color, or I leave it for too long in one machine or the other. I swear, irons must have been invented by the devil himself. So I pay Gretchen to do my laundry twice a week. She makes some extra money and gets caught up on her soap operas without breaking the 'no TV' rule of her co-op, and I get clean underwear and pressed shirts.

"I'll call her right now and cancel our arrangement. I don't blame you for being mad. It's pretty pathetic when a grown man can't manage to do his own laundry."

He seemed genuinely ashamed of himself. I couldn't stay mad at him.

"So Gretchen isn't a concubine?"

"God, no! Gretchen is a sweet enough kid, but she lives with goats—right in the house! And between you and me, all that healthy food gives her some really rank gas. I have to air out the house for an hour after she leaves."

I laughed with him and let myself be pulled back into his arms. But there was one last beautiful woman he needed to explain. "So I guess that leaves Maria. What is she, your cousin?"

He idly dismissed my concern. "Forget about Maria. She's nothing. Don't worry about her."

I had heard that line too many times from Bob. "She didn't look like 'nothing.' She's a very beautiful woman, and she took your arm with a very possessive and familiar attitude." I looked at him with suspicious eyes. He looked back with such innocence and adoration that I couldn't help but believe him.

"You noticed that, huh?" I shrugged my shoulders and he kissed my neck. "You're right, Maria is a very beautiful woman, and I'm pretty sure she wouldn't mind having babies named Tran."

"Uh-huh?" I stiffened a bit.

"Her uncle thinks we would make a beautiful couple."

"I agree. You did look very good together. She has excellent taste in clothes."

"Maria has excellent taste in everything. That's part of the problem. I've known her for ages, and she never fails to remind me of how cultured and sophisticated she is. Since you were getting married I finally gave in to her persistent phone calls and agreed to go out with her. She actually flew in from California for our date. Can you believe that?"

He wasn't exactly convincing me that this relationship was nothing. I prodded him to continue.

"I took her to the Longhorn because I had such a good time there with you, but I think she was expecting oysters and champagne. God, she just hated the place! She sent back her chardonnay and picked out every last bit of iceberg lettuce in her salad as though it wasn't worthy of her chewing."

"She sounds like a very elegant person."

"Oh, yeah, there's no question. Maria is elegance personified. In fact, I had just managed to resign myself to the fact that I would be stuck forever with sophisticated, well-bred women like Maria when you came swirling into the restaurant door with that stupid plastic tiara on your head."

I slapped my forehead. "I must have looked like a complete idiot!"

"You looked like an angel. A bright-eyed, messy-haired, laughing angel, and I realized right then that I couldn't live without you."

We collapsed onto the window seat pillows, our bodies seamlessly intertwined.

"So do you plan on seeing Maria again soon?" I teased.

"I might invite her to our wedding, but only if you say it's okay."

"Wedding? Are you kidding? We hardly know each

other!" I sat up. "I just got out of a serious long-term relation-ship. I'm in a very delicate state right now!" I shushed him when he tried to object. "I quit my job. I'm trying to establish a new relationship with my family. I'm a mess! I can't just marry the first guy I fall in love with!"

He looked like a scolded puppy, but then a sly smile spread over his face. "You love me?"

"Of course not! I didn't say that, did I?"

"Yeah, I think you did."

"Well, I take it back. I can't be in love with you. It doesn't fit into my schedule."

He kissed me again and pulled me back into his strong arms and said, "Okay, if you want to take it slow, we can take it slow. I'm fine with that, but I'm gonna have to hold on to you like this for at least a few hours. Maybe a week."

I snuggled into him again. It felt so right. "I don't know. Sweet talk and cuddling like this are red flags for me. In the past they have signified commitment, a relationship, and then heartbreak, and while it feels good at the moment, I'm not sure I can handle it right now." I rested my head against his chest until I came up with a brilliant solution. "How about if we just have thoughtless and passionate sex like complete strangers for a while?"

His eyes lit up and did their adorable scrunchy thing. His smile gleamed. "Well, if that's what you need to heal, I guess I'd be willing to offer my assistance. Um, what was your name again?"

We untangled ourselves and raced upstairs.

It was what sex is always supposed to be like. It wasn't just another workout or physical task. It was heat and lust and pas-sion. It was lips and legs, fingers and tongues. My skin was no longer just a protective covering for flesh and blood but a wet layer of electric clay that could be stretched and blended seam-lessly with his. The sex was loud. It was fun. It was perfect.

Chapter Thirty

I never would have believed it, but there does indeed come a point when the sex has just got to stop. Early the next morning we stumbled from the bedroom with rubber bands for bones and big messy hair. We were starving.

I poked through the kitchen cupboards but things were bleak. Even I couldn't come up with a delicious breakfast with a half jar of peanut butter, two cans of tuna, and a lot of cold clam chowder.

"Looks pretty grim," I said.

He shrugged. "We could go out."

I shook my head. "Naw. Why don't you take a shower, and I'll run to the store. I feel like cooking this morning."

I threw on some clothes.

"You want me to go along?" Josh asked.

"Nope. I know exactly what I want, and you'll only get in my way." I kissed him good-bye and shut the door behind me. I had gone only a few steps when I turned back around. He knew exactly what I had forgotten. He tossed me the keys to his car before I even had a chance to ask.

Half an hour later, Josh met me at the door and helped me with the groceries. He was wearing a sneaky grin.

"What?" I asked.

"Bob stopped by while you were gone. At least, I assume it was Bob. Sandy hair, tan, rebar bolted to his head?"

I grimaced. "That sounds about right. Crap. Oh, well. I guess I'm going to have to face him sooner or later." I started unpacking the bags.

"He pounded on the door pretty hard for a guy with a broken neck. I thought you might have locked yourself out."

"Mmm."

"So I jumped out of the shower and answered the door in that short little robe of yours."

I stopped and stared at him a moment. "The pale blue one with the roses?"

"Yep."

"Bob gave that to me last Christmas."

"It kind of looked like he recognized it. It's very nice. I imagine it brings out your eyes." I used my eyes to marvel at him.

"I told him you'd be back shortly and suggested that he call." Josh radiated smug pleasure. He was a devil!

I put him to work scrubbing red potatoes while I chopped up the onions, fresh morel mushrooms, and asparagus. I was craving a fancy spring hash with smoked salmon and poached eggs. I heated my grandmother's old cast-iron skillet, my favorite pan of all time, and started frying up the ingredients. Josh lit a fire in the fireplace; then he scrunched a piece of paper into a ball and had Nina's fat, lazy feline jumping around like a kitten.

I brought the steaming skillet into the living room and set it in front of the fire. We sat on the floor and ate our breakfast straight from the pan like a couple of starving refugees.

"So what are we going to do today?" I asked when we were finished.

"I don't know about you, but I need to get back to work. Murakame takes care of a lot, but it's still my farm."

"What? I thought you were a gentleman farmer! Can't you pay the help, harvest the profits, and play with me the rest of the time? What happened to all that money you're supposed to have?"

I had found out at some break in our love fest that Josh's grandparents, the bakers, were actually the Litzens—as in Litzens' coffee cake. I've known the jingle since I was a child. Everyone has.

"I hate to disappoint you, my love, but my trust fund's just a bunch of dirt these days. I spent it on the farm. I'll inherit more someday, but my grandparents aren't planning on dying anytime soon. And I'm a big supporter of that plan. I've gone to visit them a couple of times lately, and I can hardly keep up with them. They're keeping fit by spending their hard-earned money at the great golf courses of the world and giving huge lumps away to charity.

"It looks like I'm going to have to stick to growing vegetables. Lucky thing I'm pretty good at it."

"Well, if you can grow 'em, I can cook 'em. At least we won't go hungry."

Chapter Thirty-one

We walked arm in arm to his car and managed to tear ourselves apart after one last kiss and a promise that I would meet him at his place that evening.

I drifted inside. In my warm, fuzzy bliss, I decided to make Josh an apple tart. (Forget expensive perfumes. If you want a man to desire you madly, dab your pulse points with fresh baked goods.) Mom called just as I got started. I tucked the phone under my ear and floated around the kitchen, gathering tools and ingredients as she spoke.

"I hope I'm not interrupting anything. I just wanted to give you an update on how Mindy's doing. She's off the respirator, and she's been able to talk to the investigators. We heard a few more details about her ordeal." Mom told me what she had learned, and I could hardly believe it.

Since she was no longer supposed to use scented candles, Mindy had started simmering potpourri in a special electric pot. But because she was Mindy and not a rocket scientist, she had dangerously combined scented wax pellets with dried flowers and wood shavings. The overheated mixture eventually ignited, setting fire to a dead plant and then her curtains. The fire department and aid unit had arrived just minutes before she would have died from a "suicidal" drug overdose. Her last clear memory was of driving to a party.

Mom and I marveled at Mindy's invincibility for a while. Then Mom got a little more personal. "I also wanted to check and make sure everything's okay. Bob's still trying to contact you. He may stop by. I wanted to give you a heads up."

I giggled, thinking of Bob and Josh's earlier meeting. "Bob stopped by this morning. I think he understands the situation now. Don't worry about me. Everything is fabulous, wonderful!"

"Yeah, about that. Nina mentioned something about a cute red car parked in your driveway last night. She felt especially charitable after all you've been through lately and decided to spend the night here. Your feeling fabulous and wonderful doesn't have anything to do with Josh, does it?"

"Perhaps." I was being coy.

"I don't want to preach, darling, but you be careful. You don't need to be rushing into anything right now. Your plate is pretty full."

"Oh, Mom, I'm just fine. Don't worry so much!"

I heard Nina come in the front door and I used her entrance as a chance to avoid this conversation. "I'm in the middle of baking something, Mom. And I just heard Nina come in. I haven't seen her in ages. Let me call you back."

I hung up the phone and shouted to my sister, "Where have you been? So much has happened, you won't believe it! Josh came over and we talked things through. He really *does* love me! You were right! And you know, I think I might love him too! He's amazing!"

"Well, isn't that just precious." It wasn't Nina's voice. It was Richard Dolfe's. He stepped into my kitchen.

I spun in terror and started throwing whatever I could grab at him. "Get out! Get out of here!" I threw the measuring cups, a cube of butter, an apple. He managed to dodge out the kitchen door, injury free. I chased him into the living room waving my French rolling pin. (It's a twenty-inch length of solid boxwood and a very convincing weapon.) He ran for the protection of the big couch and we ducked and bobbed as if playing a twisted game of tag or musical chairs.

Dolfe was in horrible condition and must have realized he would lose any type of physical confrontation. He started shouting, "I'm leaving, Giovanna! I'm leaving town for good."

I stopped lunging at him once I comprehended his words. "You're leaving?"

He tried to catch his breath. "I'm done here. I've carried Hagstrom long enough. There have been some unpleasant visitors at the office lately, and I don't feel the need to get involved or to tarnish my good name with his misdeeds. It's time for me to move on. I merely came for one last, important conversation."

"You can't just leave. You've ruined our restaurants! You poisoned Mindy. You've terrorized my family. You think you can just walk away from all that?"

"Don't be ridiculous, Giovanna. Of course I can walk away. Do you see handcuffs? Do you see a police guard? I was merely an innocent employee following the instructions of an unethical and tyrannical boss."

"Innocent, my ass!"

"Giovanna, I have the law on my side. Why would the police believe anything your family has to say? You're a bunch of has-beens who have been plagued by some hard times. You're looking for someone to blame, and my involvement in a recent lawsuit against your family has made me a convenient target. In reality, all the police have are some pitiful accusations from a desperate family."

He puffed out his hollow chest and lifted his nose a bit to stand tall. "I won. Don't you see, Giovanna? I won. And rather than stay and flaunt my success, I'll graciously walk away.

But first I need for you to acknowledge my victory. I need to hear you speak the words."

Instead of being impressed by his grandeur, I was stricken by his delusions. I spoke quietly. "You're sick, Richard. You need help."

My pity pissed him off. "Say it, Giovanna! Tell me I won. Use those good manners of yours. You know the rules of the game—a good loser will shake the victor's hand and congratulate him. I'm here for my handshake, Giovanna. I'm ready for your acknowledgment of a match well played."

I was horrified. "What exactly do you think you won? Was this just a game to you?"

"Don't be stupid, Giovanna! Everything in life is a contest, a battle. You know that. And now I can say that I defeated the mighty Cerbones. Your restaurants are rubble. Your family is in tatters. I see the way Rocco walks in circles, barking at everyone. I see the desperate look in Vince's and Nina's faces as they work around the clock. They're trying so hard to piece it all back together—to resurrect the past.

"But *you* know it's over, Giovanna. You and your father and your mother, you're the clever ones. You all stopped playing after the health department discovered that horrible infestation. You knew enough to quit when my victory was obvious. And now all I ask is that you admit it. Tell me I won, Giovanna. Say it." He posed again, proudly waiting for his fantasy to play out.

I considered it. I knew, deep down, that if I said those very simple words—"You win, Dick, congratulations"—he might have pranced away, feeling like a superstar. But this pathetic, egomaniacal sociopath had stretched my good manners to the breaking point. My words hissed from tightly clenched teeth. "You. Won. Nothing."

The last word took a minute to sink in. Dick looked concerned, as if I had misunderstood his request, so I shouted it again. "Nothing!"

. I waved my rolling pin like a madwoman, jumped over the couch, and cornered him behind the front door. My eyes were blazing and rage radiated from my very core. We stood that way for a few silent, tense minutes. Finally I composed myself. I took some deep breaths and backed a step away. I knew words would hurt him more than any blow.

"In fact, Tiny Little Dick, your evil pranks and petty vendettas might have been just the challenge we Cerbones needed." I smiled a false, perky newscaster smile. "We've all been in a bit of a rut these past few years. You gave us a nudge, an opportunity to reinvent and improve our business and ourselves. Thanks to you, I have a new appreciation of how resilient my family really is. Each of us has grown from the experience. We've reached new levels of understanding and communication. We are, in fact, stronger than ever before."

Dick shook his head in denial. "Don't lie to me, Giovanna. I saw the fire. I know about the rats. Louie's restaurants are closed. It's over. You're a sad and beaten team. Just admit it!"

He would never comprehend what I had just said. Finally I felt genuinely sorry for him. I mumbled mostly to myself, "I never once thought about how things must look from the outside." I snorted a bit. "We must look like a disaster!"

Dick jumped at what he thought was an admission of weakness. "So you admit it! It's over. I won. Just say it, Jo." He was almost pleading.

My pity evaporated and my rage returned. "Jo? You've never called me Jo before." I stopped and thought about it for a moment. "No, I don't think I like it. My family calls me that. My friends call me Jo, and you most definitely are not a friend. You're not allowed such intimacy." I set my feet, bent my knees slightly, and went into a battle-ready posture, my rolling pin still a genuine threat.

My voice was even and my words precise. "Say good night, Dick. It's over. You didn't win. The moment you step out of this house I will be on the phone calling the police. They will find you and arrest you for attempted murder. Mindy Monahan has found her voice again. And we both know how she loves to tell stories."

His eyes opened wide. "But . . ."

I chirped out another forced laugh and twirled the wooden club like a baton. "Did you think you really killed her? How did you get her to take the drugs? They must have been something she didn't recognize; although that's hard to imagine. Mindy's hobby was pharmaceuticals. You must have mixed them in a drink.

"What you didn't remember was that people like Mindy don't just crumple and die like delicate flowers. Mindy and her kind are the hearty weeds of the world, like horsetail or blackberry vines. You can drench them in poison, thrash them to bits, and dig at their roots and they'll be back, thriving, the following spring."

I could practically hear the rusty gears of his deranged mind trying to figure all of this out. I decided to share some of the details.

"How wonderful that I get to be the one to tell you that she survived. It's just so ironic. She was well on her way to dying from the drugs you loaded her up with when her apartment miraculously caught on fire. She's in the hospital with severe lung damage and still more dead brain cells. But I guess God isn't done with her yet. For some oddly divine reason, Mindy's here to stay."

Dick Dolfe began edging toward the front door, as if ready to run.

"Are you leaving now, Dicky? I guess I'd better make that phone call. Bye-bye, *loser!*"

Looking back, I regret the "loser" comment the most. He reacted with an earsplitting shriek and then lunged at me, leading with his sharp little teeth and fingernails. Instead of cleverly defending myself with my trusty rolling pin, I stupidly dropped it and turned to run away.

It was a catfight. Dick was shrieking, clawing at my face, and pulling my hair. I grabbed at his flailing limbs and tried to keep away from his snapping teeth. I had the advantages of superior strength and a lifetime of sibling wrestling experience, but it still took a few painful minutes before I managed to pin him to the floor.

He had been in that helpless position so many times as a child, his reaction was second nature. He couldn't help himself—he spit right into my face. Oooh, I wanted to hurt him right then. Instead I wiped the spittle off on his shirt and twisted his left arm around so he was forced to roll onto his stomach. Then I sat on him and tried to cool down.

He was breathing hard, but wouldn't stop writhing until I tightened the half nelson. I took a moment to inspect the bite marks on my hand and dabbed at the worst of my facial scratches. I had a fat lip and it felt like a few clumps of my hair had been pulled out.

I thought long and hard about my next move. But I knew in my heart what I had to say. I leaned over and spoke close to his ear. He needed to hear my words clearly the first time, because I would never repeat them.

"Dick. This is life. It's not a game or a contest. My family hurt you. I understand that and I'm sorry. You didn't deserve it. You want us to pay for the pain we caused you. We have. Can we just call it even now and get on with things?" Dick stopped struggling for a moment.

"We tied," he said.

I sighed in resignation. "Yeah, okay. We tied."

I sat on him a few minutes more until he asked, "Will you get off me now? I can't breathe very well, and my arm hurts."

I stood up and looked down at him. He sat up and rubbed his arm and shoulder. He was wearing a baggy jacket that looked to be army surplus, a pair of tattered khakis, and oversize athletic shoes. If it weren't for that silly mustache, he might have been mistaken for a twelve-year-old.

"Are you okay, Richard?" I asked.

"Yeah. I guess so."

I turned away from him, took two steps toward the phone, and felt a solid crack at the back of my knees. I fell face-first in front of the fireplace. That son of a bitch had hit me with my own rolling pin!

He hit me again. I felt my ribs crack and my left side go numb. I curled up in a ball and used my right arm to blindly feel around for a defensive weapon. Miraculously my fingers wrapped around the handle of the most perfect object ever made, my grandmother's orange-enameled cast-iron skillet. I had forgotten about it after this morning's breakfast with Josh. As Dolfe raised the club for another blow, I rolled and shielded myself with the skillet. The kitchen tools crashed together ferociously. (Both were chosen for their high quality.) I scrambled painfully to my feet and swung the skillet with all my might. Dolfe dodged the hit and whacked me again with the rolling pin. I shouted and he cursed. His fury gave him new strength. My cracked ribs and newly bruised shoulder kept me bowed and cautious, but I battled through my pain. We were mad culinary gladiators, lunging, blocking, and parrying until finally the police arrived and pulled us apart.

Mom had alerted the police. After talking to me that morning, she called the restaurant to tell them about Mindy, and Nina answered. My mother found it odd that someone other than my sister had just let themself into our house. She paced for a few minutes, trying to figure out who it could be. She didn't want to be an overprotective or hysterical parent, but she felt in her bones that something was wrong and knew better than to doubt her maternal radar. While she dialed 911 she silently vowed to make the officers lasagna if they arrived to find me safe and sound.

I wasn't safe. A mother just knows, I guess. The cops arrested Tiny Dick and took me to the emergency room to be patched up. Two days later, my ribs bound and my arm in a sling, I helped Mom make lasagna for the entire squad.

Epilogue
Six Months Later

Tiny Dick and Dane Hagstrom are in jail. Well, Hagstrom finagled a short sentence for insurance fraud in a white-collar, minimum-security prison. He's not exactly suffering, with his satellite TV and regular tai chi instruction. I comfort myself by knowing he will never again practice law. And sometimes I enjoy picturing him in a jumpsuit that is scratchy and binding, his silk hosiery and alligator shoes replaced with white athletic socks and flip-flops. I imagine he's not trying to look quite so pretty these days.

No way was Dolfe going to get off easy. If he hadn't stopped by my house, he might have been able to get out of town and disappear, like he had planned. It was his obsession to win that ruined him in the end.

The jury slapped Tiny Dick with everything they had. In addition to insurance fraud and arson, he was found guilty of attempted murder, breaking and entering, and assault with a deadly rolling pin. I guess they took pity on me with my broken ribs and Mindy with her obvious health problems. When it was her time to testify, Mindy left nothing out. She named names, pointed fingers, and was, quite honestly, a force to reckon with. She's clean and sober for the first time in two decades and she's finally in what looks like a healthy relationship. Her new nurse boyfriend sat with her through the whole ordeal.

You won't believe what I just found out. It's the icing on the cake. Remember Anderson, the linebacker Dick got thrown off the high school football team? I guess he got a good job as a prison guard at the Walla Walla state pen—Dick's new address. Imagine that!

My family is doing great. It's just like I tried to explain to Dolfe that day: The challenges made us all stronger. We may not be as physically close as we once were, but emotionally we've come a long way.

Nina is my biggest fan. She has told the story of the rolling pin–skillet battle to a million people. If fact, for someone who wasn't there, she tells it a lot better than I do. Byron returned shortly after the incident and insisted that Nina move into his place. She called in sick every day for an entire week once he hit dry land. She's taken him a couple of times to admire the ring that Bob once gave me. I think he's getting the hint.

Nina and I have both been trying to warm up to Jessica Monroe. We've gone out of our way to include her in family dinners and social events. I'm still not crazy about her; she's oddly formal and doesn't laugh enough. (Maybe she just doesn't get my jokes?) Tony seems smitten, and I guess that's worth something.

Vince's Deli will be opening late next month on the old Louie's Restaurant grounds. It looks great. They already have a waiting list of local stores that want to carry his bread and cured meats. Nina sneaked out samples during construction and then convinced Vince to develop an entire line for wholesale distribution. She's cracking the whip and getting more work out of the team than I could ever manage.

Vince and Anna moved into our house. They're officially engaged, but Vince doesn't like to discuss Anna's bizarre wedding plans. The other day he did admit to talking her out of "taking the plunge" by jumping off the top deck of a Washington State ferry together. He'll humor her for a while, but in the end he may just drag her down to the courthouse and be done with it.

Rocco decided to stay with what he knew. He bought out Dad's share of Louie's on Twelfth, brought Mike Coccio on as executive chef, and is keeping the locals happy by serving all their old favorites. Emily asked to work a few shifts up front. She loves the chance to get dressed up and talk to actual adults a few times a week. Rumor has it that the girls can already roll meatballs like little pros. Imagine that.

I found a cute little cabin in the mountains. It's small, but there's plenty of natural light and just enough room for my computer, the stereo, and Mica's plush new dog bed. My portfolio was a great success. In addition to custom clip art, I have branched out to include technical drawings for manuscripts and flyers and have a pretty impressive list of new customers. I'm even working on a contract to illustrate a local bird guide.

I'm making a comfortable living, and I love working for myself. I like being able to alternate my creative impulses and my love of numbers. Whenever I miss the old times, I spend a day helping Josh or Tony with their paperwork, and I'm quickly over it.

Josh continues to talk about getting married, and I'll agree pretty soon. I've even sketched out the invitations, but to me, the wedding is just a formality.

We're going to Indonesia next month so I can meet his parents. I've talked to his mom on the phone a bunch of times, and I can't wait to meet her. It was she who insisted that Josh change out of his private-school clothes and play soccer and stickball in the street with the local children. She made him leave the protection of the embassy every day and appreciate the world's diversity. She didn't want him settling into the ivory towers of her youth. If not for her, he most certainly would have fallen for one of the many Marias who have vied for his attentions, instead of me.

And then how would he have ever learned how to do his own laundry?

Recipes

Louie's Meatballs

2 pounds of meat scraps, cut into 1-inch pieces
 (Use any combination of beef, pork, veal, pancetta,
 ham, and salami ends)
¼ cup good quality olive oil
2 tablespoons red wine vinegar
1 tablespoon mashed or pressed garlic
4–5 slices bread, crusts removed, soaked in ½ cup milk
3 eggs
2 ounces Parmesan cheese, finely grated
½ cup golden raisins, very finely chopped
2 tablespoons chopped fresh parsley
1 teaspoon dry oregano
1 teaspoon dry basil
½ teaspoon freshly ground fennel seeds
Plenty of salt and freshly ground black pepper

Stir the meat together with the olive oil, vinegar, and garlic. Cover and let marinate for at least an hour. Soak the bread in the milk to soften, then crumble it with your fingers.

Grind the meat in a meat grinder, using the medium-sized attachment. Mix in the crumbled, milk-soaked bread, eggs, cheese, chopped raisins, parsley, oregano, basil, fennel, salt, and pepper. Using your hands, combine the mixture until well blended, then knead until the meatball mix develops a slightly firm, cohesive texture.

Form meatballs by pinching off about an ounce of meat between your thumb and forefingers, then roll in the palms to form a smooth, firm ball, about the size of a walnut. Place the finished meatballs on a baking sheet.

To cook the meatballs, fry in olive oil until brown and cooked through, about 8 minutes. For Louie's spaghetti and meatballs, drop raw meatballs in simmering tomato sauce for 10–12 minutes, then toss with pasta and serve.

Makes about 6 dozen walnut-sized meatballs

Pasta Carbonara

2 tablespoons butter or olive oil
3–4 ounces pancetta, diced
6 cloves fresh garlic, sliced
Pinch of red pepper flakes (optional)
3 eggs
1 cup grated Parmesan cheese (the real stuff)
2 tablespoons chopped fresh parsley
Plenty of salt and freshly ground black pepper
1 pound spaghetti or linguine

Place a large pot of salted water on to boil. Heat a large skillet over medium heat. Melt the butter and fry the pancetta until it is brown, about 4 minutes. Do not drain. Add the garlic and pepper flakes to the pan with the pancetta and sauté until the garlic is tender and sweet, about 2 minutes more. Set the skillet aside.

In a large bowl, whisk together the eggs, cheese, parsley, salt, and pepper.

Cook the pasta in boiling water according to manufacturer's directions until just tender. Drain well and toss the pasta in the skillet with the pancetta and garlic over medium heat for 1 minute. Transfer the hot pasta into the bowl with the eggs and cheese and toss quickly and thoroughly until the pasta is coated and creamy-looking. Turn the pasta in a large, warm bowl and serve immediately.

Serves 4–6

Rosemary Roasted Chicken

2 free-range roasting chickens
1 lemon
8–10 whole cloves garlic
1 small onion, quartered
4–6 stalks fresh rosemary, bruised
½ cup olive oil
Plenty of coarse salt and freshly ground black pepper
1 cup white wine, chicken stock, or water

If you cannot find good-quality free-range chickens, try brining your birds for better flavor and moisture. Dissolve ¼ cup salt and ¼ cup sugar in a large container of water. Submerge the chickens in the brine for at least 15 minutes.

Preheat the oven to 450º.

Pat the chickens dry. Cut the lemon in half and squeeze the juice into the cavities of the chickens. Rub the skin of the chickens with the squeezed lemon half and then place the used rinds in the cavities of the chickens. Divide the garlic, onion, and rosemary equally and place in the cavities of the chickens. Truss, if desired, for a neater appearance.

Place the chickens on a rack in a roasting pan. Drizzle or brush the olive oil evenly over the chickens. Sprinkle very generously with salt and pepper. Add the wine, stock, or water to the bottom of the pan and place the roaster in the oven. Roast the chickens for 30 minutes at high heat, then reduce the temperature to 350° and continue cooking another hour until golden brown, crispy, and tender.

Remove the chickens from the rack, carve into portions, and serve hot.

Serves 4–6

Pasta with Scallops and Mussels

1 pound fresh linguine or fettuccine
2 tablespoons olive oil
2–3 cloves garlic, sliced
2 tablespoons minced fresh onion
Pinch of red chili flakes
4 ounces scallops
12–14 Penn Cove mussels, scrubbed and debearded
½ cup dry white wine
½ cup good-quality fish stock or clam nectar
1½ cups good fresh tomato sauce or marinara sauce
Salt and freshly ground black pepper
1 tablespoon chopped fresh parsley

Bring a large pot of salted water to boil. Cook the pasta according to manufacturer's directions until just tender.

Heat a large skillet over medium-high heat and add the olive oil. Sauté the garlic, onion, and chili flakes until they are aromatic, but not brown. Add the scallops and mussels and sear quickly in the oil. Toss well to evenly distribute the flavorful oil and seafood. Deglaze the pan with the white wine and let reduce until nearly dry. Add the fish stock and tomato sauce and cover for 3–4 minutes, until the mussels open. Check the sauce for seasoning, add salt and pepper as needed.

Toss the pasta with the sauce over gentle heat for about 1 minute, then divide into two large bowls and sprinkle with fresh parsley. Serve immediately.

Serves 2

Minestrone

¼ cup olive oil
1 onion, diced
1 carrot, peeled and diced
1 stalk celery, diced
4–6 cloves garlic, chopped
A good pinch of red pepper flakes
1 cup dry red wine
1 large can (28 oz.) diced tomatoes in juice
8–10 cups good chicken stock
2 cups cooked cannelli, cranberry, or garbanzo beans
Cheese rind, if available
1 bay leaf
1 teaspoon dried oregano
Salt and freshly ground black pepper
2 cups sliced green cabbage (preferably Savoy)
1 cup chopped or shredded fresh kale

Variations: Add spicy Italian sausage, diced ham, or proscuitto to the onions for a meaty variation. Substitute or add any fresh vegetables in season, such as green beans, zucchini, potatoes, cauliflower, or peas.

Heat the olive oil in a large soup pot over medium heat.

Add the onion, carrot, celery, garlic, and red pepper flakes and cook, stirring often, until the vegetables are golden brown and aromatic, about 8 minutes. Add the red wine and simmer to reduce by half. Add the tomatoes and juice, chicken stock, beans, cheese rind, bay leaf, oregano, salt, and pepper and simmer for 15 minutes. Add the cabbage, kale, and any other good seasonal vegetables and cook until vegetables are just tender, 10–15 minutes. This soup can simmer for a long time, but the vegetables will go soft. If not serving immediately, cool the soup completely and heat again before serving.

For a complete meal, garnish each bowl of soup with a thick slice of toasted bread rubbed with a clove of garlic, and plenty of grated Parmesan cheese.

Makes about 3 quarts of soup

Bella's Bloody Marys

**6 cups tomato juice (or 5 cups tomato juice and 1 cup
   clam nectar)**
¼ cup Worcestershire sauce
2 teaspoons grated horseradish
1 teaspoon celery salt
Vodka
Fresh lemon wedges
Lots of Tabasco sauce
A few grinds of fresh black pepper
**Plenty of celery sticks, stuffed olives, pickled beans,
   peppers, and asparagus**

Mix the tomato juice with the Worcestershire sauce, horseradish, and celery salt. Pour the juice into pint glasses filled with ice and a healthy shot of vodka. To each drink add a good squeeze of lemon, a couple of dashes of Tabasco sauce, and a grinding of black pepper. Serve with a selection of garnishes. (In a pinch, just use Stingray Bloody Mary Mix.)

Makes 6 very large, icy drinks

Fancy Spring Hash

2–3 tablespoons butter and/or olive oil
¾ pound red-skinned potatoes, scrubbed and diced
½ cup diced sweet onion
1 teaspoon chopped fresh garlic
4–5 morel mushrooms, quartered
6 thick asparagus spears, sliced
1 teaspoon fresh thyme, chopped (or ¼ teaspoon dried)
½ teaspoon salt
Plenty of freshly ground black pepper
3–4 ounces dry smoked salmon, flaked
2–4 eggs, cooked as preferred

Heat a large, heavy skillet over medium-high heat. Swirl in the oil and butter and heat until butter is bubbly. Add the diced potato and onion. Cook, stirring regularly until the potato begins to soften, about 5–6 minutes. Add the garlic, mushrooms, and asparagus spears and continue to cook until the potatoes are crisp and brown, and the vegetables are tender, 15–20 minutes.

Season the hash with thyme, salt, and pepper. Add the smoked salmon and cook another 2 minutes, stirring gently, until the salmon is evenly distributed and warmed through. Meanwhile fry or poach the eggs. Serve the hash warm, topped with the eggs.

Serves 2